PUNISH MENT

SCOTT J. HOLLIDAY

†THOMAS & MERCER

Text copyright 2018 by Scott J. Holliday
All rights reserved.

Published by Thomas & Mercer, Seattle

www.apub.com

Amazon, the Amazon logo, and Thomas & Mercer are trademarks of Amazon.com, Inc., or its affiliates.

ISBN-13: 9781503949058 (hardcover)
ISBN-10: 1503949052 (hardcover)
ISBN-13: 9781542047449 (paperback)
ISBN-10: 1542047447 (paperback)

Cover design by Damon Freeman

Printed in the United States of America

First Edition

This is where it begins, so this is for Nichole, who will be there at the end.
Zub.

Reality exists in the human mind, and nowhere else.

—*George Orwell*

1

Detroit homicide detective John Barnes sat in an unmarked sedan, squeezing a fifth of bourbon by the neck. He stared through the windshield at the closed gas station where his vehicle was parked. It was dark outside. The food mart was full of shadowy shapes outlined by the glow from the pop coolers and coffee machines. The OPEN sign just inside the plate glass was a formation of dead bulbs. Barnes closed his eyes. He dropped his forehead to the steering wheel and rubbed a hand over his scalp, now bristling with a few days' growth. The cooling engine clicked and hissed. An uninvited vision came to the detective then—a Vitruvian Man test pattern, overlaid with the words *Please Stand By.* The test pattern was reminiscent of an old television station experiencing technical difficulties, but instead of an Indian head, there was da Vinci's ideal form. He heard a female voice from inside his mind: *"Prepare for transmission."*

Barnes chuckled, flipped the door handle, and stumbled out of the car, catching the frame to stop his fall. The bourbon in his guts sloshed in time with what remained in the fifth. He wore a leather jacket over a button-down shirt and tie, a shoulder holster containing a .45-caliber Glock, black pants, and black boots. His badge hung from a chain around his neck. It rested heavily against his chest bone. He took a pull from the bottle, swallowed the burn, and looked up the darkened street. Just beyond the gas station was Calvary Junction—the three-way intersection of Eight Mile Road, a Canadian Pacific railway crossing, and the Rouge River laughing through a culvert beneath the two. The silhouetted hardwoods and evergreens of Whitehall Forest, which lay beyond the junction and spread out for miles, looked like black smog rising from the earth. The station added gasoline to the odors of ozone and red cedar in the air. As a boy, Barnes had loved that gasoline scent. He spread his arms now and breathed it in, expanding his chest and filling his lungs.

The candy-striped barrier arms at the railroad crossing stood straight up. They swayed in the wind like the jousting poles of medieval knights, frozen in near confrontation. A few feet down the tracks, three short white crosses stood in a semicircle, the middle one slightly taller and set back from the other two. Their bases were littered with decaying flowers, their perpendicular arms tattooed with the names of the dead. The roadside crosses memorialized those lost at the junction over the years—some by car, some by train, a few by water. Their formation gave the intersection its de facto name. The junction had once been home to temporary tripod wreaths and crosses in all directions, but the city had removed them and set up these three permanent memorials, declaring them sufficient. People now used Magic Markers to commemorate their loved ones in list format.

Barnes tossed his bottle toward the crosses. It landed with a pop and shattered at their feet. He stood still until he smelled the spilled bourbon wafting back toward him, until the river's laughter was drowned out by a sound like rising wind.

The train.

The asphalt beneath Barnes's feet began to shiver. He pulled a rubber coin purse from his jacket pocket. There was a Batman logo on the purse's outside, six quarters inside. It was the kind of purse you could squeeze and its mouth would open like a gasping fish—the kind preferred by kids and old men. Barnes hefted the purse as though testing its weight. He clenched it inside a fist as the railroad crossing came alive. A bell sounded like someone hammering steel—ding-ding-ding-ding-ding-ding-ding. Red lights blinked. The barrier arms fell to horizontal with mechanical efficiency. The rising-wind sound turned into that of a thousand galloping horses.

Barnes moved toward the tracks. The asphalt went from shivering to quaking as he stepped around the near barrier arm. His soles crunched cinders on his way toward the steel rails gleaming with reflected moonlight. He stopped between the tracks, both feet on a wooden tie, and faced the oncoming train. The cold air made icicles in his nose. It cooled his chest. The crossing's blinkers turned the scene red, then dark, and then red again until the train cleared the bend a quarter mile off and the light from its front lamps washed the blinkers' glow away.

His cell phone buzzed against his leg. The thought of answering it made him laugh out loud. *What message could matter now?* Still, his fist opened and retrieved the phone from his pocket.

He flinched when the train sounded its horn in three blasts. The first two were quick ear-shattering bursts. The third was a sustained scream, long and loud enough to jangle bones. The train's silhouette grew larger behind the lamplight. Shafts of white moved up and spread out over the tracks and the nearby trees. The light intensified from a candle to a flashlight to an interrogation beam until it was splashing Calvary Junction like an atomic-bomb blast. Detective Barnes squinted and shielded his eyes. His breathing had turned erratic. He gritted his teeth and forced his shielding hand away from his eyes, balling it into a fist. The cinders between the ties at his feet began to rattle and hop. He lowered his head and prepared for the damage.

His thumb clicked on the cell phone. In the blinding light, and with his eyes turned down, he could barely make out the words on the screen:

Calavera, again. 1124 Kensington St.

Barnes stepped off the tracks.

The train screamed by, clacking and grinding and sending leaves up into a frenzied wind. The barrier arms rippled as though the jousting knights had just clanged them off each other's shields.

Barnes pocketed his phone and moved outside the barrier. He turned back and watched the train pass. Its wind was strong and cold. It carried the scents of steel and smoke. Bits of emerging morning light blinked between the boxcars like he was watching a spinning zoetrope. He was taken back to a moment, some twenty years before, when he stood in the same spot as a twelve-year-old boy. The back wheel of his BMX bike had spun where he'd thrown it down. He'd peered through the gaps between the passing cars then, just as now, hoping to catch a glimpse of his ten-year-old brother, Ricky, on the other side, one sneaker on a pedal, one on the ground, waiting for the train to pass.

After the last car rolled by, the first sliver of sun peeled up from the horizon beyond the edge of the forest. Airborne leaves spun as they fell back toward the ground in pendulant motions. The blinkers ceased and the clanging bell fell silent. The candy-striped barrier arms moved back up. The train's fading Doppler effect was bullied aside by the river's rush.

A voice cut through the morning. "Whatcha doing out there, pal?"

Barnes turned to find an elderly man standing in the gas-station doorway, a silver key ring in his hand. Blue coveralls. His voice was nasal and full of distrust. No doubt years of stick-up jobs and local kids snatching candy bars had justified the old guy's razor-cut eyes. Without moving from the doorway, he yanked a small chain beyond the glass, and the **OPEN** sign came alive in blue-and-red blinks. He flicked on the interior lights to confirm that the store offered slushies, chips, and little jars of mayonnaise and peanut butter you might take camping. A soda-fountain machine stood where there had once been two arcade cabinets.

Barnes called over to him. "How long to make coffee?"

2

Barnes pulled up to 1124 Kensington Street just as the technicians were walking the machine out the front door. He swished black coffee in his mouth to mask the bourbon. The house was a cookie-cutter ranch. The neighborhood looked like a giant Play-Doh press had been used to squeeze out its houses through a home-shaped template, and then a car-shaped template for the base model sedans in the driveways. The only noticeable differences between the homes were their shutter colors. Barnes imagined a real estate woman with big teeth and too much lipstick telling some sixties-era couple that—with their choice of shutter colors—they could *individualize*.

The shutters at 1124 Kensington were beige.

Barnes surveyed the neighbors' homes. Blue shutters, green shutters, mauve shutters, and more beige. People stood on porches in their robes and slippers, T-shirts and pajama bottoms. Hands cupped mouths or necks, eyes were wide and dazed, some heads slowly shook. How many shocked faces had Barnes seen in his career? Hundreds? Thousands? They never changed. Murder and death were resistant to desensitization, which explained why the evening news always led with blood. Tell us the globe is boiling or the ozone is Swiss cheese, we'll yawn and flip to *The Big Bang Theory*. But tell us someone ax-murdered our neighbor, and we'll press "Pause" to toss a bag of popcorn in the microwave.

Yellow-and-black crime scene tape was stretched between a street lamp at the far edge of the yard and a hedge this side of the one-car garage. Barnes stooped while showing his badge to the uniformed officer holding the tape not quite high enough for him to walk under.

The technicians were now in the driveway, prepping the machine to be loaded into the back of a van. "How much?" Barnes said, lifting his chin toward Warden, the machine's lead tech.

"Maybe three minutes on the girl," Warden said. "Could be pretty good." He had raccoon eyes. His face was hatchet-shaped, his nostrils long against his nose. The way Warden looked and moved reminded Barnes of an ROUS—a rodent of unusual size. He always imagined Warden hiding in some alley when he wasn't at work, snarling and waiting to attack pedestrians from a four-point stance. "Thirty seconds, tops, on the mother, and likely nothing but disjointed dreams on the father. Bad attachment—not much to work with."

Barnes nodded. He'd sipped coffee as he listened, swished it around, swallowed. He watched as Warden and the other tech, an almond-skinned woman who appeared to be of Latin descent, packed up the machine. He'd never met her. She was young and mostly pretty. Her black hair was snatched back in a severe ponytail, her eyes a medium brown when caught by the morning light. Her tightened jaw muscles twitched as her hands moved quickly to their tasks. She was dressed to be taken seriously in a pantsuit that hid more than it revealed. Smart. Cut too close to the curves and they'll throw you behind a desk and ask you to smile and make coffee while the men in leather chairs lean back for a better look at what their wives no longer have.

The machine was situated on a gurney-style cart with retractable legs. The technicians slid it into the van.

The machine. An assortment of dials and switches, tubes and suction cups, and one IV needle. It reminded Barnes of an electroshock device straight from the early days of mental-health therapy, only this machine didn't fry the brain—it pulled from one and pushed into another. Barnes didn't fully understand the science behind it. Something to do with the cerebral cortex, with intercepting impulses traveling inside the hippocampus. Some impulses were memories, and somehow the machine was able to detect whether an impulse had come from memory or imagination. Even more impressive, the machine stitched memories together to represent them chronologically. It retrieved and stored memories from the living, the dying, and even the recently dead. Hook a different person to the machine and reverse the flow, and they'd relive the other person's memories. The machine was invented and designed as a tool for investigative purposes, but announcing the technology had been like announcing fingerprinting. Then, criminals just shrugged their shoulders and pulled on gloves; now, practically all premeditated crimes were committed by men in masks.

All too predictably, criminal-justice applications were only the beginning for the machine. Its existence gave society a new underbelly, a new drug for a new millennium. Machines were stolen—warehouses robbed of their stock and delivery trucks stopped and relieved of their payloads like trains in the Old West. The machine's technology was reverse engineered, the serum's ingredients replicated. Homemade machines were illegally produced and sold. Black markets arose. A new form of crack house appeared on the American landscape—one with a good network connection. Celebrities began to sell their memories. *Be a Kardashian for a day. To hell with Internet sex tapes—be the actor banging the starlet. Be the starlet getting banged.* High-profile athletes soon joined in. *Pummel your opponent. Get pummeled. Pitch a no-hitter. Score a touchdown. Dunk a basketball.* B-level celebrities were right on their heels—porn stars, circus acts, street performers, daredevils—and it wasn't long before everyday people saw the same monetary opportunities as celebrities. *Get a promotion. Smoke crack. Shoot heroin. Get a tattoo. Eat all day and never gain weight. Want to know what it's like to die?*

The options didn't end with recreation. Scientists were investigating ways to medicate patients with other people's memories or even their own taken from a happier time in their lives. A way to distract us from pain while under the knife or undergoing chemo. Militaries were looking at new ways to torture prisoners of war. The rich were conceiving ways to live forever, collecting a lifetime of memories to pump into a host body after death.

And then there was punishment. Hundreds of machines were being used not just by police forces and homicide detectives for investigative purposes but also by prisons and mental-health systems for rehabilitation. At any moment in America, there were dozens of murderers, rapists, and domestic abusers having their crimes pumped into their skulls from their victims' points of view. The feeling of a punch that breaks a nose, the sledgehammer impact and burn of a bullet, the indescribable feeling of one's neck being opened like a zipper. They smelled the blood and cordite, felt the pheromones of fear. They heard the screams, the cries, the unanswered pleas for mercy. *A Clockwork Orange* had nothing on the machine, and Barnes had experienced all varieties of its punishments.

Barnes turned to find his partner, Big Billy Franklin, standing on the sidewalk in front of 1124 Kensington Street. *Big* was an appropriate term for the lieutenant detective. He'd been an offensive tackle at Wayne State, where he had majored in criminal justice. The NFL hadn't come calling, so Big Billy had put his degree to use. He'd started out as a beat cop but soon applied his brain to the situation and made detective. He was in his fifties now and still big—only slightly less muscular. The morning light threw a red hue on Franklin, making him look like a statue of unpainted clay. He nodded at the machine in the back of the van. "You two lovebirds will be together soon enough."

The statement made Barnes's needle-marked elbow pits tingle. His head ached, and his teeth rang with soreness, like they'd been struck by a tuning fork.

"We should have her ready in a few hours," Warden said, his rodent head sticking out from the back of the van. He patted the machine lovingly, then winked and drew back inside, pulling the two doors closed behind him. Two uniforms stepped on the crime scene tape to force it under the tires as the van pulled away.

"What do we got?" Barnes said. He stepped in next to Franklin as they approached the home's front doorway.

"You okay?" Franklin said.

"I'm fine."

"Been drinking?"

No response.

Franklin shook his head, then nodded at the house. "Three dead." He looked down at the small black notepad in his hand, flipped back a page. "The Wilsons. Dale; his wife, Andrea; daughter, Kerri. Father was hit first. In bed, probably still sleeping. Never saw it coming. Seems like the wife made it halfway across the bedroom but was dropped just short of the hallway. Spined. Might have seen something when she first woke up, might have turned over after she went down. After that, it was the back of the head."

"And the girl?"

Franklin flipped forward a page. He drew a breath and sighed. "Found hiding in the closet, dragged into the hallway. Maybe awakened by the noise. She managed a scream. Neighbors say they heard it."

"They dialed?"

"Yep."

"We got 'em?"

"Yep. Flaherty took their statements. Don't ask; they ain't got nothin' more."

Barnes gripped the bridge of his nose. "We don't know that."

"Drink your coffee and investigate your scene," Franklin said. He walked off the porch toward one of the uniforms at the crime scene border. "Wexler, let me know when the coroner boys arrive."

Barnes entered the home. The coppery scent of blood was thick. Shit and piss, too—the final, inescapable indignity of death. There was mildew underneath it all, no doubt from a crawl space beneath the home. The small living room held two paisley-patterned couches set longways and facing each other like pews in a breakneck chapel. The wear patterns on the carpet indicated that the family hadn't been into rearranging the furniture very often. The small room seemed to offer little choice. A flat-screen TV sat on a squat entertainment center against the far wall, bookended by knickknack shelves filled with porcelain owls, turtles, and doves. There was a giraffe with a broken neck superglued back together. Above that, there were dozens of collectible salt-and-pepper shakers—Tom and Jerry, Abbott and Costello, the sigils of Stark and Lannister. The walls were off-white and in need of a fresh coat. The electrical outlets were old two-prongers gone brown from decades of use, some with smoky burns on the drywall above them.

Barnes moved into the kitchen without looking down the home's single hallway. There were voices and movement down there, flashbulbs popping.

The refrigerator was small with rounded edges and steel handles and brackets. Ancient. It was covered with Realtor and dentist magnets likely pulled from inside junk-mail envelopes with the weight and promise of something worth opening. No soap, unless you felt it was thrilling to know that Joe Lymon, your friendly neighborhood Realtor, was *at your service!* The magnets held down shopping lists, Christmas photos of other people's families, and what Barnes assumed were young Kerri's crayon drawings. He moved closer to see a calendar of Mrs. Macintyre's Homework Schedule—Fifth Grade Math. The school year had just begun; only a couple of weeks' worth of days had been X'd out. Near the bottom of the fridge there were colorful letter magnets. Most were in a jumbled mess, but several had been moved to form the phrase TOO LATE. The letters were coated in fingerprint powder.

The stove was electric and greasy. It smelled of fried burgers and pork and beans. Barnes opened a cupboard to find boxes of mac and cheese, bricks of ramen, cans of SpaghettiOs. The kitchen table was

Formica over gold legs speckled with rust, a transplant from the seventies. The chairs around it were cracked-vinyl editions with duct-tape repair jobs. There was a sliding glass door with an old, useless lock that'd been replaced by a dowel rod laid on the tracks. The rod was now shattered. The glass door, wide open, led to a small patio outside—a ten-by-ten square of brick pavers holding up black iron chairs and a mesh-topped iron table missing the umbrella. The door's white frame had already been dusted for prints. Near the base was a familiar dent in the frame from Calavera's pickax. He'd entered a home this way at least once before, applying slow pressure on the door until the dowel rod cracked or, in the case of a metal rod, bent. The Wilsons' dowel rod had been wooden—a hacked-off broom handle—and it had splintered down the middle like a tree struck by lightning.

The useless lock, combined with Calavera's weapon of choice, had once been the biggest lead in these investigations. Former detective Tom Watkins, with Franklin before, and now Barnes and Franklin again, had followed up with a few hardware and home-improvement stores in the area, hoping to catch a break on a recent pickax purchase, but it had proved fruitless.

Barnes stepped outside and looked across the small backyard encircled by a cyclone fence. He imagined a man in a white Day of the Dead sugar-skull mask hopping the fence and creeping toward the home. The imagined man wore all black clothing down to the gloves. He stopped halfway through the yard and waved at Barnes with a tilted head before disappearing like a bad jump cut.

Barnes turned to go back inside but stopped when something on the ground caught his eye—a smear of green against one of the pavers. He bent down to find a leaf from a red cedar tree, some might call it a needle. It'd been smashed beneath a shoe. He scanned the morning skyline for cedars but only found an oak and a few maples. He picked up the leaf and bagged it.

A voice came from inside the house. "We good?"

"Yeah," a second voice replied. "That should do it."

Barnes moved back through the kitchen to the hallway mouth. He found the crime scene photographer packing his gear into a hard-sided suitcase with brushed-steel bindings. These guys weren't paid or respected like they'd been before the machine had rendered them nearly redundant, and it seemed there was always a new guy replacing the one who had just quit. This one was so young Barnes wondered whether his balls had dropped yet. The other man in the hallway was Adrian Flaherty, a freckle-faced officer with a wide, flat forehead and a high-pitched voice. Barnes figured he was picked on as a kid, which seemed to have left handfuls of chips on his shoulders. His thumbs were hooked into his belt loops.

"What's up, Barnes?" Flaherty said.

Barnes nodded.

The photographer moved out of the hallway to reveal the girl's body. She was against the back wall, sitting up against a full-length mirror, eyes open. She was haloed by the fingerprint work on the walls and mirror above her head. Neat two-inch circles had been shaved into her temples where the machine's suction cups had been attached. There was a pinhole in her arm where the needle had been inserted, the serum manually pumped through with an artificial heart. Some of the opaque white liquid dribbled out of the wound, mixing with the little girl's blood as it traveled down her arm, turning the dark-red streaks to soft pink.

You might swear she was just taking a rest if not for the pickax sticking out her front. The weight of it was bending her slightly forward. Its long wooden handle was propped in the pool of blood that had spread out from between her legs. The thinner of the two blades had entered her body above the left clavicle, which was broken. The length of the pickax was buried deep in her organs. Barnes felt a tickle in his stomach where he imagined the ax's end might be. She was holding a small flashlight in her stiff right hand.

"What do you think?" Flaherty said. He was chewing gum. When he spoke, Barnes could smell the flavor. Grape.

"I think you need to leave."

Flaherty harrumphed. He crossed his arms over his chest, smacked at his gum. A sneer came to his face. "What's the magic word?"

A male voice responded from within Barnes's mind. *Tell him to go to hell.*

"*Shhh,*" Barnes thought. Bourbon rose up from his stomach. He closed his eyes and swallowed. His legs felt rubbery. He breathed deeply and tried to steady an internal plumb bob.

"The magic word is *step off before I brain you.*" Franklin had come back into the house and stepped into the hallway behind Barnes.

Flaherty harrumphed again; then he moved slowly toward them, chomping and eyeballing Barnes. He turned sideways to pass between the two detectives and said, "Watch your step, munky."

"You're beggin' for it, son," Franklin said, following Flaherty out the front door. He pulled the door mostly closed after them but stopped and looked back. A new cruiser was pulling up to the scene. Its spinning lights flashed behind Franklin's head. "You sure you're good?"

Barnes nodded.

"We haven't found it yet."

"I'll find it. Hit the lights."

Franklin flicked off the lights and closed the door. Barnes turned off the hallway light, leaving himself in darkness, just as Calavera would have been. He tucked his tie into the breast pocket of his button-down shirt and snapped on latex gloves, produced a voice recorder and a long, black flashlight. He held the flashlight overhand, club-style, clicked it on, and brought the small microphone to his lips. "The mirror isn't cracked, which indicates the girl was placed against it gently. The flashlight may have been placed in her hand, postmortem." He lit up the pictures lining the hallway walls. There were three people in each of them—a small, happy family in a variety of poses. Some of the frames were square, some rectangular, some oval, some metal, some wood. The girl would have grown up pretty. The father was marginally handsome, though balding, and the mother seemed a crumbling beauty. The three-person unit reminded Barnes of the short life he'd lived with just his parents before his little brother, Ricky, came onto the scene. He had only flash memories of those days—a soccer ball, autumn leaves, plaid pants—and there were only two pictures in the hallway of his childhood home with just Mom, Dad, and Johnny. They used to laugh about the story when, a few days after Ricky arrived, Johnny asked, "When are his parents picking him up?"

Barnes tilted each picture frame and looked behind, though he suspected he wouldn't find the poem on the wall; the girl's eyes weren't pointed there. He stepped around the blood patterns on the carpet and shined his light into the house's master bedroom. The father was as Franklin described—lying in bed with his head caved in. Save for his hands and feet and the pajamas he wore, the man was hardly recognizable as human. In some cases the crime scene was worse for Barnes than the real-time punishment the machine doled out. To be inside a person who opens their eyes a split second before the darkness of death is a blessing compared with witnessing the results of the pickax in still life.

Barnes spoke into his recorder. "The father was likely asleep when he got hit, but maybe he caught a glimpse. Don't skip him."

The wife was set up in the bed next to her husband, no doubt placed there postmortem; the pool of blood on the carpet in front of the bed trailed up to her final position. Her eyes were closed, making her look as though she'd fallen asleep sitting up. Her hands were crossed over her waist, and if not for the bald spots on her temples, she could have been patiently waiting at a doctor's office or a tire-repair shop. Her face remained in decent condition, but the gore at the back of her head told the tale. Her pajamas were satin—green and lacy. Lingerie. Barnes felt a tinge of envy to believe that the couple had spent the last night of their lives having sex. A thought like that might once have disturbed him, made him wonder whether he was depraved, but now such thoughts were like wind gusts through a keyhole. Again into the recorder, "The poem won't be in the bedroom; the wife's eyes are closed."

"It's with the girl." A female voice from within.

"Definitely." A crack addict's voice.

"Shhh."

The bedroom had been dusted, and it could be explored later, if necessary. The first thing was to find the poem. Barnes turned back to the hallway. He stepped past the bathroom toward where the girl was sitting and shined his light into her bedroom. For a surreal moment he saw the shared bedroom of his youth—Bruce Lee posters on the walls, stacks of comics piled high in the corners, and a Nintendo connected to the old TV Mom and Dad had let the boys keep. Sometimes you had to blow into the Nintendo cartridge to make the game work. Barnes had the technique down—he'd put it into the slot and press it down just so. Ricky would close his eyes and clasp his hands together like a prayer, squinting hard over the spring and click of the clean connection. Barnes would tap the "Reset" button, smirk, and sock Ricky's shoulder. "Ready for an ass-kicking?"

Barnes blinked and the room was once again Kerri Wilson's. It was a testament to Justin Bieber as well as the difference between young girls and boys; here everything was neatly in its place, whereas the Barnes brothers' bedroom had looked like a resale shop had barfed in it.

Barnes didn't enter the room. He squatted next to the girl's body in the hallway and tilted his head to match her angle. He lined up his flashlight beam to see what she might have been looking at. It struck him that he would soon be doing that very thing—seeing, through Kerri Wilson, the final moments of her life, feeling her pain, knowing her terror. A rattle came up from his chest and into his head. It nearly unmanned him, but he bit it back and refocused.

There.

Just beyond the girl's feet, a tuft of carpet was sticking out from beneath the lacquered brown trim. The molding in that spot had been disturbed.

"Found it!"

3

You cleaned the toilets
And mopped the floors,
You washed the walls
And made everything shine;
With a broom you danced
And watched the girls,
Now you lay flat
Upon you, worms dine;
With a rag in your hand
To dust seven calaveras.

The lights were back on at 1124 Kensington Street. Kerri Wilson's body had been bagged and taken away—the pickax mercifully removed from her chest—and the carpet and corrugated padding had been peeled back. The poem was on the plywood floorboards beneath, the words written in Calavera's now-familiar handwriting style in black Magic Marker. The marker's chemical scent had been trapped under the padding. The blood that had seeped through to the plywood came up just short of the poem's last line.

"Shit barely even rhymes," Flaherty said. He was back in the house, standing over the poem, thumbs returned to his belt loops, teeth gnashing away at his gum.

"Didn't know you could read, Flaherty," Franklin said. He was down on one knee, dusting the area around the poem for prints.

"Bite me."

"It's a calavera," Barnes said.

"A calavera?" Flaherty said. "I thought *Calavera* was our guy?"

Both detectives looked up at Flaherty. Franklin's massive body was almost too big to fit in the hallway. As it was, Flaherty was standing half in the bathroom just to give the detective room. The unforgiving fluorescent light above the officer's head gave him an alien glow. "Come on, Flaherty," Franklin said. "Micks don't celebrate the Day of the Dead?"

Barnes's eyes went back to the poem. "It's an imaginary obituary," he said absently. "Popular in the late nineteenth century in Mexico. Around the Day of the Dead, people would post them in the local papers as satire."

"That's sarcasm to you, shithead," Franklin said.

"*Calavera* is the Spanish word for 'skull,'" Barnes went on. "It can mean an actual skull, a sugar skull used in Day of the Dead celebrations, a sugar-skull mask, or one of these poems. And, of course, it also refers to our guy."

"Gee, Teach," Flaherty said. "Sorry I asked."

Barnes turned to Franklin. "Wilson was a janitor?"

"Worked at the same school his daughter attended."

"What do you think of this?" Barnes said. He showed his partner the bagged cedar leaf.

"What's that?"

"Cedar leaf. Found it on the patio. No cedars back there."

Franklin shrugged. "Cedar's a pretty common tree."

"What about 'Too late'? Think he's mocking us?"

"Doesn't seem like him. No prints on the magnets. Could be coincidental."

Barnes nodded. He held out his cell phone above the poem, snapped a picture, and stood up. "Gimme a few hours."

"You got it."

Barnes headed down the hallway.

Flaherty said, "Gonna get hooked into the machine, eh, Barnes?" He slapped the inside of his elbow joint like a heroin junkie preparing for a hit.

Barnes turned on Flaherty. He gripped the officer's throat and slammed him against the wall.

"I hate this asshole." A delivery driver's voice.

Flaherty's eyes went wide, his cheeks crimson. The officer's voice was froggy when he said, "Do something."

Barnes gripped tighter, felt Flaherty's Adam's apple struggling up and down against his palm. Small red veins appeared at the corners of the officer's eyes.

Franklin's hand came to Barnes's forearm. "Let him go."

Barnes squeezed harder. He could feel the tendons in Flaherty's throat. He imagined the snapping noise they might make.

"John," Franklin said, "let him go."

"Do it." An attorney's voice. *"I'll make self-defense stick."*

"Shhh."

Barnes released Flaherty's throat. Flaherty worked his head and neck around in a circle as he tugged at his collar. His face was splotchy red and white. His voice was still rough when he said, "Pussy."

Barnes left the house. For a moment he stood on the porch, his heart hammering.

He passed beneath the crime scene tape and was on the way to his car when Jeremiah Holston, reporter for the *Motown Flame*, stepped out from behind a hedge. He was disheveled and overweight, wearing a Detroit Tigers hat sporting the Old English–style *D*. His face was covered in stubble. He smelled like fast food.

"Stay away from me, Holston."

"Hold on," Holston said. He reached out and gripped Barnes by the elbow.

Barnes stopped, looked down at the hand.

Holston removed his hand, showed his palm. "It's him again, right? People deserve to know."

Barnes kept walking. "They deserve to hear about it from a reputable source, not a paper that covers Bat Boy and Michael Jackson sightings."

"People love Bat Boy," Holston said.

Barnes stopped, rubbed both hands over his face. As much as he disliked Holston's newspaper, he believed in freedom of the press and would argue against anyone who would vote for censorship. John F. Kennedy's voice, complete with its New England accent and stilted cadence, sounded off in his ears. "The very word *secrecy* is repugnant in a free and open society." The voice had come from a speech they'd played on a tape recorder in his high school mass-media class. It was one of the few things to which he'd actually paid attention. "Yeah, it's him again, Holston. Print what you want." He turned to leave.

"People are still questioning," Holston said.

"Questioning what?"

"The morality of the machine."

Barnes stopped at his car, a hand on the driver-side door handle. "You've got something to say? Say it."

"What about the rights of the dead? More importantly, what about the effect of the machine on those who use it?"

Barnes spread his arms out wide and smiled. "I'm as right as rain."

"They say it works by stimulating the hippocampus," Holston said, "by mixing sensory information from the victim with that of the host."

"So?"

"You read *Scientific American*?"

Barnes deadpanned. "Every day."

"The hippocampus is the only place in the brain where new neurons can be built. Did you know that?"

"Doesn't everyone?"

"So, if *new* neurons are being built to house these new memories"—he raised one eyebrow—"aren't they likely to stick around?"

"You tell me."

"Science says no. But look around you, man. Look at all the munkies walking and talking like they're Tom Cruise or Tiger Woods. It ain't an act. They paid their last dime for those memories, and they got their money's worth—Tom and Tiger are still in there."

"So go interview a munky." Barnes got into his car and sat for a moment while Holston shuffled away. It was midmorning now. The neighbors were no longer on their porches. They had started their daily lives, their thoughts now overrun with the harrowing realization that it could have just as easily been them with a pickax in their chest. Instead they would be the stars of the day, telling their stories, watching the eyes of their audiences, hearing their gasps. They'd dwell on death for a day or two, and then blissfully pile benign thoughts on top of it—*I can't believe those people are dead. Anyway, what's for dinner?* And the next time someone was killed, they'd clutch their throats or mouths in shock all over again.

4

In relative terms, Saint Thomas of Assisi was a young church. There were no old brick towers topped with crosses, no walls of stained glass, no expansive narthex. But it'd been a fixture of Barnes's life since his youth, so to him the building seemed ancient. It was a stocky structure, some parts painted cinder block, some parts vinyl siding. The lot was a spread of asphalt with worn lines and weeds peeking over cracked and crooked parking blocks. Legend held that the building had been a speakeasy during Prohibition, operated by Detroit's infamous Purple Gang. It was eventually raided and boarded up until it was bought by the church in the seventies. Once a bustling hive on Sundays, these days the lot was more densely packed for Thursday-morning Machine Anonymous meetings. The Purple Gang would turn in their collective graves.

Ricky would laugh. The kid never took to religion, never bought into anything he couldn't punch or kick. Mom once said God had given him a mule's soul and a Glasgow Kiss on the day he was born.

"What's a Glasgow Kiss?" Ricky had asked.

"It's when you head-butt someone right in the nose."

Ricky had smiled at that. He'd spent the next week proclaiming he'd *kiss* anyone who got too close. Barnes had opted against testing his kid brother's commitment.

Barnes sat in the church parking lot, watching the cigarette-inhaling, coffee-guzzling MA reformers stagger into the church through the side door, some with their hair freshly shaved for that clean connection. He was certain those squinting in the sun were still suffering from the machine's lingering effects. They held the door open and nodded curtly as one after another entered the church, full of the kind of humility only the morning after can bring.

The radio crackled a dispatch. Barnes turned the volume down. One of the MA attendees passed by Barnes's vehicle, his head hung low. Barnes had nicknamed the man *Pacino*, due to the visible scar on his face and his dark hair. He often wondered how Pacino got his scar, imagining a knife fight in a dark alley. No doubt the real story would be much more mundane.

The machine junkies—munkies—met in the church basement. Barnes had spent many a Sunday morning in that same basement as a boy. Both he and Ricky. He recalled the basement layout, the green plastic chairs, the colored tape on the floor, the scents of watercolor paint and pine from the freshly mopped tiles. One Sunday morning, as Dad had pulled their red Chevy Cavalier into the lot, Ricky had asked, "Why do people come to church every week?"

"To be forgiven for their sins."

"Every *week*?"

Dad had laughed. "Yeah, kid, every week."

"What if they didn't sin that week?"

Dad eyed Ricky in the rearview mirror, Clint Eastwood–style. "Think you can go a week without sinning, punk?"

Ricky waved a dismissive hand. "Pfft. That's easy."

Mom had stopped attending church by the time Barnes was twelve. A new pastor had recently arrived, to much fanfare, but each week's sermon dug deeper into a new set of rules for parishioners to follow, particularly the women. No women should go into movie theaters; they're dens of the devil. No women should smoke, drink, or wear blue jeans. But the straw that broke Mom's back was a short film shown about a girl who listened to too much of the Rolling Stones and ended up overdosing. When Mom got home that Sunday, she'd cranked up the volume on her record player, dropped the needle on "Sympathy for the Devil," and shouted, "To hell with those assholes!"

But Mom and Dad insisted the boys continue Sunday school. Johnny and Ricky would stand on the steps of the church, waving to the red Cavalier as it peeled out of the parking lot—Dad hunched low so as not to be seen—and then the boys would run around to the back and slip beneath a fence into the wooded lot behind the church. They'd found a set of double doors near a thick oak back there—a hatch hidden on the ground with the word *sanctuary* carved into the panels. The doors opened up to a booze-runner tunnel that once led to the church basement. Somewhere in the passing years, a church official had sealed up the doorway on the other end, but the one-hundred-foot concrete tunnel was still intact. Johnny and Ricky had spent many Sundays in the tunnel reading comics by flashlight, playing Go Fish, War, and, when Johnny felt like putting Ricky through hazing rituals, the occasional game of 52 Pick-Up. They drank stashed Faygos and ate from a massive pack of communion wafers they'd stolen. After their hour of fun, they'd dust each other off and head back to the church parking lot to get picked up.

How many of these munkies were former Sunday schoolers, too? How many faces might Barnes recognize from the days of beanbag races, watercolors, and ceramics? How many could still recite John 3:16?

The MA meeting leader appeared in the church's side doorway. He scanned the parking lot. Barnes checked his watch: 9:01 a.m.

The leader backed into the church and closed the door.

Barnes jumped at a knock on the passenger window. A man was standing there, bent at the waist and smiling. Barnes recognized him as one of the MA regulars, a munky he'd tagged *James Dean* due to his coiffed hair, perpetual cigarette, and a too-cool-for-school attitude. Barnes imagined him as one of those brooding, dangerous types women threw their panties at. A couple of months and a half-emptied bank account later, those same women would throw a coffee mug, a frying pan, or a hot iron at him. Barnes pressed the button to roll down the window.

James Dean tipped an imaginary hat as the glass descended down across his face. "Sorry for scarin' ya."

Barnes shook his head, pursed his lips.

James Dean lipped his smoke and thrust his hand through the open window, offered it to shake. "Damon Beckett."

Barnes accepted. "John Barnes."

"You coming in or what?" Beckett said, gesturing his head toward the church.

Barnes looked down, smirked.

"Seen you out here plenty of times," Beckett said. "Thought I might check in on ya, see if you needed a guide mutt to find the door." He stuck out his tongue and panted like a dog.

"I know where it is."

Beckett nodded. He looked through the windshield toward the church, eyelids down to slits. "Look, Mr. Barnes, I don't mean to be sticking my nose in other people's business, but I know a man with a problem when I see one. Pains me to watch him suffer. I like to help people out when I can, receive help when it's offered."

"I appreciate your concern," Barnes said. "I'm good."

"Fair enough," Beckett said. He double-tapped the car's roof and stood up. He yawned, and his body bent backward like a longbow, both hands against his lower back. His T-shirt came up just enough to expose the nickel-plated .38 Special tucked into his waist.

Barnes sighed. "Hey."

Beckett came back down, peered through the open window.

"You got a permit for that?"

"Permit for what?"

"The pistol on your waist," Barnes said.

Beckett's face turned sour. "What's it to ya?"

Barnes flashed the badge from beneath his jacket.

Beckett dropped his head. His body began to shiver.

Barnes had seen the process before, had seen it in his own damn mirror. A short circuit of the mind. Beckett shook for a moment before his head came back up. He blinked repeatedly. And then, as suddenly as it began, it stopped. Beckett settled into a bashful grin, and James Dean became George Clooney.

Barnes thought, *I swear I know that face.*

"Well, of course I've got a permit for it, Officer," Beckett said.

"Detective."

"Even better."

"Have a nice day," Barnes said.

After again tipping an imaginary hat, Damon Beckett waltzed off toward the church, flicking away his cigarette butt as he neared the door. It sparked as it bounced on the asphalt.

Barnes left the church parking lot and drove to his small ranch home. His carbon-copy house could have been catapulted across town from Kensington Street, or vice versa. His shutters were red. He made his way to the side door and let himself into the kitchen. He passed the stacks of unopened mail, take-out boxes on the table, and the murky science experiment in the sink. He entered the living room and plopped down on the couch. There was a bottle of ibuprofen on the coffee table. He shook out three pills, popped them dry, and fell to his side to try for sleep, but the gears in his mind turned, whirred. A series of memories flooded in, most of them not his own.

First he was Edith MacKenzie, an East Side hairdresser two years divorced from an abusive addict. Calavera had used rubber tie-downs to bind her to a chair in her own living room. Her mouth was gagged, her lips stuck together with duct tape. She saw the man in the sugar-skull mask and thought maybe it was her ex, stoned and crazy from some masquerade party. She grew confused when the man waved to her and said, "Hello, Detectives."

She screamed against the duct tape when she saw the pickax.

As her body died, Edith MacKenzie wondered why this was happening to her and what would become of her quadriplegic daughter in the next room. She imagined Jesus's face in stained glass with sunlight pouring through, praying that God would take her daughter as well, if only to save her from the hell of a life with a man who didn't have the capacity to care for his own child.

Next Barnes was Edith's daughter, Kendra. She thought she must be dreaming, seeing the strange mask hovering above her in the darkness. *Did Mom put the wrong drugs in my drip?* Her eyes shifted toward the window past her IV stand as she tried to determine the time of day. She felt an impact as the bed shook. She never saw the pickax until it was in her chest. She wondered why the floating mask in her dream said to her, "Hello again."

Now Barnes was Chunk Philips. *That's Raymond to you, sir. Only my friends call me Chunk. Whatcha wearing a mask for?*

Barnes got up and went to the kitchen. He poured three fingers of bourbon into a glass tumbler and downed it all, squinting and gritting his teeth. He went back to the couch and lay out, straightened his legs, kicked off his shoes. For distraction from other people's memories, he whistled the theme to Super Mario Bros. He imagined the sprite, Mario, running across the side-scroller while punching question-mark bricks and hopping mushroom-shaped assailants. He and Ricky had loved the game, loved the Nintendo that had replaced the Atari 2600 in their home. Barnes had caddied all summer to make enough money to buy the system; Ricky had saved his allowance to buy games. Dad had been proud that the boys had done it on their own. "It's good for them," he'd told Mom. "They'll appreciate it more." They'd played that system until it hurt. It'd gotten to the point where Dad, who never once touched a handle, had been humming the repetitive tune to Ring King as he headed off to work, and Mom would say things like, "What does being a plumber have to do with any of this?"

Handles. That's what they'd called the rectangular gaming paddles that came with the system. Barnes envisioned the red buttons, A and B, the black wire that fed out to the console. He felt the calluses in his palms and on his thumbs from long days of Metal Gear and Kid Niki. You couldn't save games back then, only continue, like it or lump it . . .

He awoke two hours later. His neck was kinked, his right arm a shaft of pins and needles from having slept on it wrong. He sat up and struggled to open a fist robbed of blood. Eventually it came around. The drunken sleep hadn't done much, but it was enough. He stretched to the point of trembling with the echoes of eight-bit Nintendo songs still in his head. His chest—rather, Kendra MacKenzie's chest—ached where the pickax had done its damage. The phantom bruise was tender to the touch. Kendra had never felt the pain, but Barnes's mind had made the psychosomatic leap.

> You lay slovenly
> Sucking at love's teat,
> You do nothing
> Make no impact;
> Your broken back
> Is no excuse,
> With a glorious mind
> Still very much intact;
> Burdened with the eyes
> To better see calaveras.

Calavera had written the poem beneath a painting Edith had attached to the ceiling for her immobile eighteen-year-old daughter to view. The painting was a palette-knife oil rendering of a city at dusk, freshly wet from rain. There were two lovers strolling along the city streets. As Kendra died, she imagined the sensations the woman in the painting certainly knew—a man's erection inside her, his body above her, his sweat dripping down onto her skin. Walking. Arm in arm with her man in a rain-soaked city, her legs a little shaky as they sought an all-night diner to kill french-fry cravings. Kendra felt renewed hate toward her mother for putting up the painting, for reminding her of the life she could never have. She died with the scents of mud and grass in her nose, residuals from that day, five years ago, when her treasured and trusted horse, Paddie, had bucked her off and ended her movement.

Barnes's cell phone buzzed with a text from Warden.

She's ready.

She.

The machine.

Barnes got up and went to the bathroom. He liberally coated his head with Barbasol, gagging all the while at the shaving cream's scent. The gag reflex was Pavlovian, he knew; the scent was supposed to be pleasant. He dragged a cheap Bic razor from his forehead straight back as far as he could reach, and then rinsed the blade in the sink.

Once he was fully shaven, Barnes tore off pieces of toilet paper to blot a few cuts on his head. He offered a smile to the man in the mirror, but it came out deformed, like he was smiling at himself from beneath a cheap Halloween mask.

5

Barnes walked across the police station parking lot. The wind blew cold against his shaven scalp. A few cruisers dotted the scene, sporting the signature white paint job and cursive script, DETROIT POLICE. The precinct itself was a brown brick building, late nineteenth-century architecture. Three stories and a basement. The outside was riddled with chipped bricks, unidentifiable stains, and a score of bullet holes that'd been patched but not painted. It looked as tired and as beat-up as the city it was sworn to protect.

Barnes pushed through the station doors, moved quickly down the hall, and entered the technical lab to find Franklin, Warden, and the female tech from the Wilson home inside. Franklin and Warden were standing over a woman in a hospital bed on the near side of the room. She had an IV drip and tubes running to the oxygen mask on her face, suction cups against her bald temples. To one side sat a life-support machine, to the other side, *the* machine. The phantom bruise on Barnes's chest ached at the sight of it.

Franklin read the woman's chart while Warden said, "The family wants the plug pulled by noon or they sue. Doesn't matter. She's not gonna break the record, anyway."

Barnes took off his jacket and shoulder holster, laid them both over the back of a nearby chair. He sat down on the available hospital bed, started rolling up his right sleeve. "Not gonna break what record?"

"For longest memory pull," Warden said. He checked his watch. "She's given nothing for the last few minutes, so she'd have fallen short even if we could keep at it. Still, a five-day pull is impressive. She's only been hooked in for a half hour or so." He popped the suction cups from the woman's temples and slid the needle out of her arm.

"Five days isn't a record?" Franklin said. He tossed the woman's chart onto her covered shins.

"It's six now," Warden said. "Some guy in Kansas. Took a bullet in the stomach, lived for a while until the infection got him." He detached the needle and its clear, plastic tubing from the front of the machine, wound it all together, and stuffed the package into the hazmat box hung on the machine's cart. He wheeled it away from the woman's bedside, into the corner, and started disinfecting the suction cups with a wet wipe. His cell phone rang. "Warden." There was a short pause, and then, "Sure, come and get her."

"What happened to her?" Barnes said.

"Domestic," Franklin said. He came over and leaned against the wall near Barnes's hospital bed. "Broken neck."

"Poor woman." A husband's voice.

"Shhh."

Barnes nodded. The wife-abusing husband would no doubt pick the machine's punishment combined with a lesser sentence. The arrogant ones always did, figuring they're so badass they can handle it. Most were trained chimps once they were done. Docile as babies.

Franklin reached over and ripped a blood-blotted inch of toilet paper from the back of Barnes's head. "Get yourself a better razor."

"Get yourself a better tailor," Barnes said.

Franklin opened his suit jacket, which was lined with silk. He spun his large frame as if modeling his get-up at the end of a runway. The suit had been custom made for his large body, and it was sharp. His button-down shirt was Brooks Brothers, his tie a Lardini, his shoes Allen Edmonds. "You're just jealous, mofo."

Barnes smirked. He wasn't jealous. In a way, he felt sorry for Franklin and his impeccable clothes. Once, on a stakeout, Franklin had confided that in the black community, style was more important than a white boy like Barnes could imagine. "If I roll up in a choice ride, step out of the car in the best suit money can buy, and flash some gold, I'm a well-respected guy, even if my bank account is all zeros. On the other hand, if I pull up in a Honda and some blue jeans and a T-shirt, it won't matter if I got a million bucks in savings, dig?"

Growing up white trash, Barnes had only three T-shirts and one pair of jeans, duct tape on his sneakers, and he and Ricky got their haircuts on a back patio that was more weeds than brick. He couldn't imagine what Franklin's custom-fit clothes must feel like, or what it would mean to walk into a tailor's and start pointing at things on racks.

"Ready?" Warden said. He was holding up the suction cups on the second machine parked near Barnes's bed, the one that'd been out at the Wilson home that morning. After some time in the field, machines took their bumps and scratches, somehow found stickers or bits of paint or nail polish, and gained personalities. Barnes had nicknamed this one Eddie. It had an Iron Maiden bumper sticker on it, plus a long scratch down the side where a cokehead had once tried to shank it, believing it was a robot attacking him from out of the future. The new female tech was attaching fresh tubing and a new needle.

"Who's this?" Barnes said.

She looked up. Her cheeks turned a hard red.

"That's Martinez, Sheila M.," Warden said. He pressed his two suction cups against Barnes's temples. "New kid, setting her own records. First in the state getting certified for machine administration. They got college courses for it now. Can you believe that?"

"So, what's this, then, an internship?"

"Paid, even."

Martinez nodded at Barnes but said nothing. She loaded a bottle of serum into the machine and threw a latch to secure it.

"Who's up?" Barnes said.

"The wife," Warden answered.

"No. The husband first."

"He ain't gonna have shit."

"Load him," Barnes said.

Warden shrugged. He typed on a keyboard and turned one of Eddie's dials. "A'ight, then."

"Shee-it," Franklin said, shaking his head at Warden.

"What, I can't say *a'ight* because I'm white?"

"That's exactly right."

Barnes put out a fist for Franklin to pound. Franklin obliged. Warden rolled his eyes. He handed Barnes the bit—a wooden dowel rod, maybe four inches long, an inch in diameter, wrapped in leather, and riddled with Barnes's teeth marks. He put in the bit and lay back on the hospital bed as Warden approached with the needle. He started it toward Barnes's right arm, where the tracks were less fresh than those in his left—those still recovering from Calavera's last strike just three days before.

The prick of the needle brought back the vision of Officer Flaherty slapping his arm like a heroin junkie.

"I really hate that bastard." Chunk Philips's voice.

"Shhh."

Barnes crunched new dents into his bit.

Though the serum went into his veins at room temperature, room temperature was still more than twenty degrees colder than Barnes's blood. His arm grew numb as the liquid traveled toward his heart. The organs inside his chest suddenly felt artificial. It brought to mind his post–high school days when he lived in a shoe-box apartment and used to donate plasma for beer money. To make up for the lost plasma, they'd pumped a saline solution back into the body, again at room temperature. You could feel the coldness spreading across you, tracking the veins, frosting the machinery. Now the serum moved up through his neck toward his brain, where it provided the conductive material to allow another's memories to enter his brain and become part of his own consciousness.

The lab door opened. Jeremiah Holston appeared in the doorway.

Franklin said, "What's he doing here?"

"Captain's orders," Warden said. "He's covering the effect of the machine on police detectives. Here to observe."

Barnes spat out his bit. "No way. I won't do it with him in the room."

"You will."

It was Captain Darrow. He'd come into the room behind Holston. Early sixties, chiseled skin, short gray hair. A junkyard dog in its waning years.

"Cap," Barnes said, "this guy's going to run a hard-line morality story to shut down the machine. That's what you want?"

"Maybe that's precisely what should happen," Holston cut in. "Look at you, Barnes. Tell me the machine isn't affecting you negatively."

"Tell me cheeseburgers aren't affecting *you* negatively," Franklin said.

Warden snickered.

"You're one to talk," Holston said, slapping his notebook playfully against Franklin's belly. Franklin adjusted his shoulders and buttoned his custom-cut jacket, unamused.

"Look, Barnes," Captain Darrow said, "just do your thing and let the chips fall. You've got no choice."

"Like hell I don't."

"Like hell you do. You walk from this, you grab a uniform and start walking a beat, understand?"

Barnes glared at Holston. The reporter shrugged and turned up his palms.

"Write the truth," Barnes said.

"Always."

Barnes lay back on the hospital bed and closed his eyes. He replaced his bit. The machine clicked and hissed, beginning to transmit. His nervous system reacted to the flow. Visually, the effect was not unlike that of a defibrillator—his body arched, head to heels. A silent, electric scream. For a moment he saw nothing, heard only the hum of the power coursing through him, and then the Vitruvian Man test pattern, overlaid with the words *Please Stand By*, appeared in his mind. Then came Eddie's generic, female voice. "Prepare for transmission."

6

Darkness.

Barnes smelled soap, heard grunting. Dale Wilson's final dream state was like a television tuned to a bad channel—white noise and blurry lines. The distorted memories came in flashes. In the first flash, Wilson was having sex with a young woman who wasn't his wife. Cute. Great figure. The source of the soap scent. Their hands were interlocked, up by their shoulders, gripping tightly with each of Wilson's thrusts. Barnes became dimly aware of his own growing erection. Wilson and the woman were working toward a collective climax, her enthusiastic calls forcing him to the brink, but the dream broke apart too early. The scene shifted.

Now Wilson was mopping a bathroom floor. Barnes reeled from the ammonia scent, heard the squeak of the bucket's wheels moving across the tiles. Wilson pushed open a stall door. Barnes gagged at a shit-clogged toilet. The scene shifted again.

Back in darkness. There was a wet scent, like mold. Wilson blinked his eyes. A white ceramic sink came into focus. Its drain was rimmed in rust and a buildup of green lime. Colorful drops fell down to the ceramic and slid toward the drain. Wilson gripped the sides of the sink. Cold. He lifted his head to see a clown in the mirror across from him, its face demented, its makeup smeared and dripping. It opened its mouth to speak but was interrupted by the sound of splintering wood.

Dale Wilson came out of his dream state, out of sleep. He rose up on an elbow in bed and listened. Barnes felt the arthritis in the janitor's hands, the bursitis in his right elbow. He drew in the musky scent of sex in the room, detergent from the bedsheets. Wilson looked at his wife. Still asleep. The man felt the shame of his sex dream with the newly hired fourth-grade teacher who had smiled at him in the hallway that afternoon. It was her face he'd imagined with his wife earlier that night, her body that he'd consumed with so much pleasure, more than he and Andrea had shared in years. When he came, he'd held tight to the teacher's image, forced his ears to hear her imagined cries of ecstasy. He'd held and held until the dam broke and his body shuddered. He collapsed next to his wife, hoping she wouldn't speak.

When Dale Wilson looked back toward the bedroom door, Calavera was already coming through it. Barnes seized up. Wilson felt fear and confusion at the white sugar skull racing toward him in the darkness. He threw a hand up to shield his face. Barnes's head banked to the side when the pickax impacted Wilson, driving through his temple and clipping him at the atlas. Bolts of pain shot down through his neck and shoulders, down to his fingertips, to his groin. His heart walloped. Blood whooshed like ultrasound in his ears.

The memory went black, and for a moment there was silence. Finally, the machine's voice said, "End of transmission." The Vitruvian Man test pattern reappeared on the insides of Barnes's eyelids. *Please Stand By.*

Through the fog of Dale Wilson's receding memories, Barnes heard Warden. "I'm loading the wife. Just relax."

Barnes lay still, the bit in his mouth, saliva dripping down his cheeks. His head ached where the pickax had impacted Wilson's temple. He tried to recall what Wilson had intended to say to the clown in the mirror. The words in Wilson's head were no better than garbled phonetics. An illogical dream, but what other details had there been? The clown's face was a variety of colors, unlike Calavera's mask. The nose was red, the hair blue, the painted smile in fact a frown, rough over the clown's unshaven cheeks. The clown's outfit was not colorful, but dark coveralls like those of a janitor. There was a rectangle stitched above the left breast: DALE.

Barnes made a mental note to go to the school where Dale Wilson had worked and speak to the principal and the staff. He also noted the wet, moldy smell. He'd sniff out the school for that, too.

"Here she comes," Warden said.

Barnes's body tensed with the flow, drew up into the arch. The Vitruvian Man test pattern blinked in and out. "Prepare for transmission."

Barnes felt more at ease as Andrea Wilson than as her husband. The pickax's physical damage had broken Dale's memories and made them hard for Barnes's mind to accept, like pouring unmixed gas into a two-cycle engine. Andrea's damage had been equally as severe but inflicted upon less vital sites. Her engine was humming, her gas mixture spot-on. She was dreaming of a garden, was down in the thick of it, in the mud, on her hands and knees. Barnes smelled flowers, soil, cut grass. He felt the wet earth squelching between her fingers. She dug a trowel into the dirt and popped a weed from its stronghold, smiled at the satisfaction of plucking the roots out. She tossed the weed into a wicker basket with a twisted wooden handle arching over the top. Beyond the basket was the gingham blanket Andrea had laid out; beside it, a small cooler. Lemonade in there. Tito's Handmade Vodka, too. Barnes savored the taste of her future drink, a reward for a job well done.

Andrea looked at her house. In her dream it was a mansion on the estate she owned. She had let the staff off for the day, declaring that she would do today's gardening herself. Her benevolence gave her a sense of superiority, and with it came calmness. Her striving for something better was over. Their lives were now full.

She flinched at a cracking sound, turned to see a tree branch falling. It flopped against the manicured grass just this side of the koi pond where her husband, Dale, the same man she'd married but with a strength she hadn't seen in him in years, had been cleaning the pond with a pool skimmer. He was looking curiously at the fallen branch. It seemed to be moving, like a snipped worm. The massive pecan tree that had dropped the branch suddenly came alive. It turned and bent toward them. It opened its previously unseen eyes over a previously unseen mouth and said, "You don't belong here."

Andrea Wilson drew back. Barnes pressed back hard against the hospital bed, threw a hand to his chest. The audacity of the tree to accuse her of, of . . . She looked down to find she was in maid's clothing, and she certainly hadn't been given the day off.

The tree uprooted itself. It let loose a primal scream and stalked toward her. The ground shook with its deranged and powerful steps.

She awoke from the dream. The bed was moving, squeaking. Blood in the air. Her skin was cold and wet. She rolled off her side of the bed and stood, shivering and blinking in her lingerie. There was a white mask above Dale, a body clad in all black. A man. He was yanking at something attached to her husband's head. Dale's body jerked like a hooked fish. His legs and arms flailed like tentacles. The masked man pulled out the fishhook and showed it to her. It dripped.

Kerri.

Barnes's subconscious knowledge slipped into the memory. A flash of Kerri Wilson in the hallway, the weight of the pickax tilting her forward, the pink drizzle on her arm.

Andrea ran. Barnes's legs moved like a dreaming dog's. She rounded the bed and started for the door, but her body went limp. Barnes felt a pop as the pickax entered his back. She fell. His legs tingled. She pushed herself up with both hands and tried to bring up a knee, but the damn thing wouldn't come. Her legs were deadweights. She clawed forward, dragging her body along, until a voice stopped her.

"It's over now."

A strange calm came over Andrea then. A restfulness she wouldn't have expected in such a moment. Her eyes focused on her left hand, her wedding ring and the engagement ring above it, glinting in the darkness. Dale had gone all out for the diamond, a round solitaire that'd cost him dozens of Friday nights with the boys. *He tried. He wanted more for us.* She recalled the smile on her husband's face when he rubbed his rough-hewn hands together in their small kitchen and said, "I'm cooking up something to get us out of this shithole."

She turned toward the masked man now standing above her. His face was a skull with ornate patterns carved into the cheeks, forehead, and jawline. The teeth were fully exposed, the eyes black holes. He was again removing his fishhook, only this time from Andrea's own back. Barnes felt the pressure release as Calavera retrieved his weapon.

"Hey, buddy," Calavera said.

Buddy? Andrea Wilson thought.

"See you in a minute," Calavera said. He flipped the pickax over and showed her the wider, flatter blade before he reared it back.

Andrea turned away from the blow. Her mind raced back to her wedding day, to a moment just before the ceremony. Her father hadn't come to get her yet. She'd stood on the back porch of the small chapel they'd chosen on a whim. It overlooked a pond. There was a single swan in the water, its neck formed into one half of a heart. She'd wondered whether the swan had been placed there for the ceremony. She wondered whether, somewhere under the water, one of the swan's legs was shackled to an anchor.

Barnes yelped and then saw darkness. He felt carpet against his cheek.

A moment passed.

Andrea Wilson opened her eyes. She saw her bedroom's carpet fibers up close. First out of focus, then in. She heard feet shuffling around in the dark, could see their shapes, the legs above them. She blinked and felt tired, just really sleepy. *God, if only I could get a bit of rest, I'd feel so much better. Let me just close my eyes for a moment, just a moment, and then I'll get up and figure out what the heck is going on.*

Where's Kerri? She should be at school by now. She better not have missed the bus. I need a drink. I nee—

Darkness and silence.

"End of transmission."

The Vitruvian Man test pattern.

Please Stand By.

A voice cut through the fog. "You all right there, buddy?"

Buddy?

Barnes jolted straight up in the hospital bed. Calavera was standing before him. Barnes went for the Glock in his armpit, but it wasn't there. He found himself being tackled down. He rabbit-punched his assailant, who stank of Warden's aftershave.

"You idiot!" Warden yelled at Holston. He kept all his weight on Barnes while the detective socked his back and sides.

"Sorry," Holston said.

Barnes emerged from the fog of Andrea Wilson's memories. He stopped punching, released Warden, spat out his bit.

Warden did a push-up to remove his body weight. He watched Barnes's eyes. "You there?"

"I'm here."

Warden stood up and straightened his shirt. "You okay?"

"I'm okay."

"Jesus, man," Warden said. He stretched and put a hand against his back where he'd taken Barnes's punches. He turned to Holston. "You don't speak to him until he's fully out of the memory, understand?"

Holston rolled his eyes. "I got it. My bad."

Franklin chimed in. "My bad?"

"I said I was sorry."

"You're a reporter," Franklin said. "So report. Otherwise, shut the hell up."

Warden turned to Barnes. "Still wanna do the daughter?"

"Just give me a second," Barnes said. He steadied his breathing and closed his eyes. He felt Warden checking the IV in his arm. He mentally noted Andrea Wilson's memory of her husband's plan to *get them out of this shithole*. He poked around inside her memories, searching for clues like a kid searching for Waldo. Had she seen Calavera's shoes? Yes, but the brand name was lost to the darkness. What about the mask? She'd gotten a good look at it. He'd have another sketch artist draw it up from the memory in case it differed from the others.

What else, what else?

Warden said, "Martinez. Set him up."

Barnes heard feet moving in the lab, heard typing on a keyboard. He heard the clicks of Eddie's dials as they turned. Martinez said, "Are you ready, sir?"

It was the first time Barnes had heard the young technician speak. Her tone was sweeter than he had expected, and there was the hint of a Mexican accent, likely gained inside her household as opposed to growing up south of the border. He nodded and put in his bit.

His body arched. The Vitruvian Man test pattern appeared, then faded.

"Prepare for transmission."

Kerri Wilson wasn't dreaming, wasn't asleep. She was staring up at the ceiling in her bedroom and biting at the edge of her comforter. An image of Dale Wilson's fury flashed through his daughter's mind. His face was reddened, his eyes wide and angry. Spittle shot from his mouth. Barnes cringed and shrank into himself on the hospital bed. Earlier that evening, Kerri had knocked into the entertainment center while doing a pirouette. The TV had rocked back and then fallen forward, almost crushing her. A porcelain giraffe from the nearby shelving unit had fallen and broken at the neck.

Mom rushed for the superglue.

"I didn't mean it," the girl said, crying. Her tears fell hot and wet on Barnes's cheeks.

Dad stopped screaming and held her close. He told her he was sorry for yelling, but that she needed to be more careful. She clutched her arms around his neck, gripping her own elbows. On the hospital bed, Barnes hugged a circle of air.

The girl's mind flashed to a new scene. She was walking down the sidewalk, holding hands with another young girl. Barnes felt the other girl's hand in his own, warm and sweaty. He could smell fallen leaves, scratch-and-sniff chocolate, and diesel exhaust. An engine revved. Kerri looked back to see the yellow school bus pull away from the curb. A few kids sporting backpacks were skipping away from it in the opposite direction, laughing and smiling. As Kerri watched, a dark-blue sedan sped around the bus and cut it off, forced the bus driver to jerk to a halt. The bus driver shook a fist. As the sedan flew past the girls, the driver honked his horn and waved.

"He's a maniac," the other girl said lightly, waving at the receding sedan. She shook her head. "I can't believe I did that." She smiled devilishly and hunched her shoulders. "Don't tell your mom. I'll get in trouble."

"Cross my heart," Kerri said.

Barnes drew an *X* on his chest.

Kerri Wilson sat up in bed. She checked the wind-up alarm clock on the nightstand. The glow-in-the-dark minute-and-hour hands told her it was 4:03 a.m. She picked up a flashlight and went to the window in her bare feet. She set her chin on the cold windowsill and looked out, tugging at the carpet pile by scrunching her toes. Her eyes found the blank back window of a house on the street behind her own, kitty-corner to her backyard. *Come on, Carla. Be awake.* She placed the flashlight on the sill and pointed at the other window. She began clicking the light on and off. Three times on, a pause, and then three times on again.

Come on, come on.

Three times on, a pause, three times on again. Her breath was fogging up the glass. A cracking sound turned Kerri's head. She tuned an ear for the noise, imagining a big green monster with fangs and claws stalking through the house. She thought she heard movement. She tiptoed back to bed and hopped in, threw the covers over her head, clicked on her flashlight. In her mind the monster was coming down the hall, dragging slime and staggering. She'd read a short story by Stephen King once, where at the end of the story the boogeyman revealed himself and said, "So nice, so nice," in a putrid voice. She heard that horrible voice in her head now, saying, *So nice, so nice* as the monster approached. She heard a whump and the bedsprings squeaking in her parents' room. It was similar to the squeaking she'd heard earlier, only there was less rhythm this time, just a shuddering of metal like kids jumping down off a cyclone fence.

Now footsteps.

Now another whump.

The boogeyman is killing Mom and Dad.

Kerri threw back her covers and ran to the closet. Barnes's legs churned. She dropped to her knees inside, closed the door behind, and put a palm over the flashlight, turning her fingers red.

The boogeyman came into her room. Through the horizontal slats in her closet door, and with help from her seashell nightlight, she could see its outline. It wasn't a slimy monster, but a tall thing in all black, with a skeleton's head. The PA Man. Detroit's real-life version of the Slender Man. His leather-handed grip sounded off against the wooden object he held—*squi-squi-squick*. Dark drops fell from the object's heavy end, fell mutely against the carpet. The PA Man turned toward the closet and stared.

The room strobed with three flashes of light. Carla signaling back.

Kerri screamed when she saw the reflection of his eyes deep inside the skull's dark holes.

The killer took two steps across the room and yanked open the closet door.

Kerri Wilson closed her eyes. She pushed her mind to a different place. A place of fields and flowers, of pastures and barns. A place where the boogeyman doesn't exist—her grandparents' dairy farm in the Upper Peninsula. They visited every summer, had been there only a month before. There were cows, of course, but also horses, goats with oddly shaped horns, and pecking chickens. She especially liked the sheep, the way their lips reached out from behind the split-rail fence to take a piece of carrot.

Barnes screamed through his bit when the pickax broke Kerri's clavicle. He saw stars on the inside of her closed eyelids, felt the tickle of the ax's thin blade embedded near his right kidney. The weight of it leaned her forward like a discarded doll.

"Little piggies shouldn't scream," Calavera said.

Kerri Wilson opened her eyes to the sound of his voice. She looked up. She had dropped her flashlight. Its ambient light cast upward and lit the skull from beneath like a camp counselor telling a ghost story.

Again, the room strobed with three flashes of light.

Kerri smelled pee and poop, wondered whether it was her own. The killer gripped his tool and dragged her body behind him, across the bedroom floor and into the hallway. Barnes felt the tug of the ax inside his chest, felt the carpet sliding beneath him, burning at his skin. They stopped in the hallway. From her new vantage point Kerri could see into her parents' room. Mom was lying on the carpet. The back of her head had been chopped away like a scoop from a carton of ice cream. Kerri tried to scream again, but with two punctured lungs she only managed a painful gurgle.

"So sorry, Barnes," Calavera said.

Barnes?

"The girl upped my timetable with her screaming. I wanted to say you have all the clues now. Just one more thing for me to do." He leaned in close to the girl's eyes. Her vision was fading, darkness at the edges. "Enjoy the altar." He picked her up by the underarms.

Barnes felt the sensation of being lifted. Kerri thought, *Light as a feather, stiff as a board.* She'd kissed Jimmy Dykes on the night she and her friends had played that game. Later, in bed, she'd formed her hand into his lips and kissed him over and over again.

Calavera placed Kerri against the wall, against the mirror. She felt the flashlight being placed back into her hand. One ankle was grabbed, her leg moved. The other ankle was grabbed, the leg moved until her legs were wide open. She heard her mother's voice in her mind: *"Close your legs and act like a lady."* Sirens wailed in the distance. Kerri watched the PA Man peel back the carpet. He started writing on the plywood beneath the padding. Barnes smelled the harsh scent of Magic Marker. After he was done, the killer replaced the carpet, tucking it under the trim against the wall.

The sirens grew louder.

The PA Man turned to Kerri. He moved in close and said, "Don't be sad. Be joyful. Ten-three, good buddy."

Isn't it supposed to be ten-four?

Darkness and silence.

"End of transmission."

The Vitruvian Man test pattern.

Please Stand By.

7

Barnes sat on the edge of the hospital bed. There was a cotton ball and a Band-Aid in his right elbow pit. He flexed his arm, felt the sting where the needle had been inserted. He rolled his sleeve down over the wound. His collarbone throbbed where Calavera's pickax had struck Kerri Wilson. He struggled to breathe with her punctured lungs. His body shuddered like that of a person trying not to cry. His head felt numb from the blows her parents had received. The center of his back tingled, felt out of alignment. He recalled Kerri Wilson's memory of the bus pulling away. On the back emergency door there had been some numbers: 334 in the middle, and what appeared to be a phone number across the bottom. Barnes half-heartedly wrote the numbers in his notebook.

"Get anything good?" Warden said. He was busy wrapping up the machine's tubes and needles.

Barnes looked up at Jeremiah Holston, who was sitting on a stool at the far edge of the room. Barnes said, "We're done here."

"How do you feel?" Holston said.

"I feel fine."

"You don't look fine."

"Bye-bye, Holston," Franklin said.

Holston sighed, wrote in his notebook, and closed it. He stood, tipped his baseball hat to everyone in the room, flipped off Franklin, and left.

Barnes waited a beat after the door closed. He turned to Franklin. "He said we have all the clues now, that he has one more thing to do. He also said, 'Enjoy the altar.' I'm assuming he meant a Day of the Dead altar."

Franklin shrugged. "Sounds about right. 'Ten-three' again?"

"Yep."

"I thought it was ten-four?" Martinez said. She was sweeping the technical lab floor with a broom in one hand, a long-handled dustpan in the other.

"Better hit the books, kid," Barnes said. "Ten-four means acknowledge." He went over and picked up his shoulder holster, cringed from psychosomatic pain as he put it on. He picked up his jacket. "Ten-three means stop transmitting. It's Calavera's sign-off. He's showing us he knows a thing or two about the machine, about our methods."

"Go back to school and learn something, squirt," Franklin said.

"Ten-four," Martinez said. She cracked a smile.

Franklin laughed. The sound filled up the lab wall to wall. His delight cheered Barnes, like a kitchen light scattering cockroaches in his mind.

"You're all right," Franklin said, pointing a big finger at Martinez, whose smile was already fading back to a stern countenance. Franklin nodded toward Warden. "Make sure this punk don't keep you down."

"Everyone starts out sweeping the floors," Warden said.

Barnes put on his jacket and headed toward the door. He noted that the woman who had been on life support was gone now, taken away while he was a Wilson.

"Where we going?" Franklin said.

"To talk to Carla," Barnes said. But his voice was off-timbre to his own ears. Too high-pitched. Not his own. Kerri Wilson's.

Franklin cocked his head. "Talk to who?"

Barnes stopped. He closed his eyes. He fought against the blinks and managed to hold off a shiver as he pushed Kerri Wilson back.

"Shhh."

He said, "To talk to the girl's friend."

The Montgomery house shutters were black, though years of weathering had cracked the paint to show that they were once green. Franklin knocked on the door. Barnes did a scan of the nearby trees. He noted a cedar behind another house, half a block down on the other side. A woman answered the door in a pink terry-cloth robe, pajamas, and slippers.

"Can I help you?" the woman said.

Barnes could barely hear her over the TV blasting in the living room. On the set some trendy-looking couple was being shown their home after it'd been renovated. They were gushing about how beautiful everything looked. Hands slapped cheeks beneath bugged-out eyes. There were long, startled intakes of breath.

"Hello, ma'am." Franklin used his booming voice, typically meant to put God's fear into fleeing suspects. He showed her his badge. Barnes did, too. "Detroit Homicide."

She nodded and pushed the storm door open. Franklin had to move down the steps to give the door room to swing.

"Can you turn that TV off, please?"

She nodded again and went for the remote. While her back was turned, Barnes checked his watch: 1:00 p.m.

The TV stopped.

"Thank you," Franklin said. "I'm Lieutenant Detective Franklin, and this is Detective Barnes."

"Ma'am," Barnes said.

"Beatrice Montgomery."

They sat down in the living room, a pure replica of the Wilsons', save that the couches here were faux leather and plenty beat-up. Barnes could smell pasta, Parmesan cheese, and olive oil, as well as the scent of things left to blacken, crisp, and eventually flake off an electric stovetop. There was a ceramic bowl balancing on one of the couch pillows, pale spaghetti noodles inside, a fork sticking out.

"Can I get you anything?" Beatrice said. She took one step toward the kitchen, stood there like a crosswalk sign. "Some coffee or tea?"

Barnes had smelled the woman's breath at the door. Vodka. Cheap. There was a coffee cup on the end table next to the couch. He wondered how many fingers she had poured, felt a pang of thirst for it. He shook his head no.

Franklin said, "We're fine."

Beatrice moved her half-eaten meal to the end table and picked up her drink. She gathered up her robe and sat on the couch opposite the two detectives. She took a sip from her cup. Her eyes were glassy. Barnes knew the look, knew her afternoon of drinking was just getting started. To worsen matters, the sides of her head were shaved. It'd been no more than a day since she'd hooked in, judging by the stubble.

"You're Carla Montgomery's mother?" Franklin said. His pen was poised above his notepad.

"Yes."

"Who have you been?" Barnes said.

Beatrice turned to Barnes. "Excuse me?"

Barnes tapped his bald temple.

"What does that have to do with—"

"Who?" Barnes said.

Beatrice held his gaze for several seconds. Eventually she turned away. "Someone who's got it better than me."

Franklin said, "Your daughter was friends with Kerri Wilson?"

"Best friends."

The voice had come from the hallway. Barnes and Franklin looked to see Carla Montgomery standing at the corner. One of her hands was gripping the wall, her fingertips as white as the paint beneath. Barnes felt a rush of affection for the girl, the same affection Kerri Wilson had felt for her friend. He was suddenly aware that the two girls had once kissed each other, each closing her eyes and promising to pretend the other was a boy. Kerri had pretended Carla was Jimmy Dykes, a fifth-grade boy with blue eyes and brown hair. Through Kerri's residual memories, Barnes saw the boy in a cool-kid stance—back against the bricks of the school, tips of his fingers tucked into crisp, clean jeans.

"No school today?" Franklin said.

Carla shook her head. "Because of what happened."

"Would you like to talk with us?"

Carla nodded. She moved across the living room and sat near her mother, maintaining a distance from the woman. She put her hands on her knees. Beatrice Montgomery reached out and placed a hand over one of Carla's, patted it. The girl looked away from her mother, rolled her eyes so only the detectives could see. It was apparent she'd been crying.

Barnes saw Carla not just in the reality in front of him but also through Kerri Wilson's mind. The two girls were sitting on benches at the edge of a school playground. Barnes heard the squeal of rusty swings, chattering birds, laughing children. He smelled tar from the hot blacktop beneath their feet, and he heard Carla say, "She shaved her head after Dad left. All she does is drink. She's such a loser."

Franklin checked his notes, where he'd written down everything Barnes told him about the Wilson family on the ride over. He said, "Mrs. Montgomery, we're—"

"Ms. Montgomery," she corrected.

"Excuse me. Ms. Montgomery, we're going to ask Carla some questions of a personal nature. Would it be okay if we spoke to her alone for a moment?"

"She can stay," Carla said. "I have nothing to hide from her."

Barnes scrunched his toes inside his shoes, gripping his socks, marginally aware that it was one of Kerri Wilson's nervous tics.

Franklin said, "You recently told Kerri Wilson, 'I can't believe I did that.' What did you mean?"

The girl's eyes widened. Franklin stared at her with flat satisfaction. The machine provided these choice moments, like the aftermath of a street magician's performance when some idiot bystander pulls an ace of spades from his own ass.

Carla regained a measure of poise. "I missed the bus yesterday," she said, "so I got a ride."

"You took a ride from a stranger?" Beatrice Montgomery said. She looked at her daughter with overacted horror.

"Like you give a shit," Carla said.

Beatrice's hand moved off her daughter's knee. It came halfway up into a slapping motion and stopped. She used it to brush stringy bangs away from her eyes, smiling nervously at the detectives.

"Unlike some people," Carla said, again rolling her eyes toward her mother, "Kerri's parents were super protective of us. She was supposed to look out for me, and me for her. I missed the bus yesterday because I was"—she glanced at her mother—"making out with a boy. I knew Kerri liked him. I shouldn't have done it."

"What boy?" Franklin said.

Barnes said, "Jimmy Dykes."

Carla's eyes shifted to Barnes. Dumbstruck.

Franklin smirked. "What about the ride?"

Carla stayed stuck on Barnes.

Franklin snapped his fingers in the air.

Carla blinked. "Um . . . I started running home, hoping I could get to the bus stop before Kerri's mom got worried. She likes to see us coming down the street together, you know? Kind of like a buddy system. The bus goes all through a bunch of other subs before it comes to ours on the way back. I figured I could make it if I hurried."

"So what happened?" Franklin said.

"Some guy pulled over and offered me a ride, so I took it."

"What color was his car?" Barnes said.

"Blue."

"What make and model?"

"Huh?"

"What kind of car?"

The girl dropped her head. "Ford." She glanced sidelong at her mother. "Focus."

"Jesus Christ," Beatrice said. "You are so freakin' grounded."

Barnes said, "Can you describe the man who picked you up?"

Carla looked down at her hands. One of her feet rolled nervously around.

"Tell them," Beatrice said. An air of satisfaction descended on the woman. She folded her arms and smiled, sipped from her cup. She threw one leg over the other, suddenly prim and proper, the adult child claiming victory over the real one.

Carla said, "I'm not supposed to take rides from him."

"From who?" Franklin said.

"My dad."

"Last night," Barnes said, "Kerri signaled you with her flashlight from her bedroom window. Is that something you two typically do?"

Carla nodded. "If I'm awake and I see her light, I flash back."

"You saw her light last night?"

Carla nodded again. "I signaled back a few times, but . . ."

"But she never replied," Barnes said. "Did you see anything or anyone? Outside the home or in Kerri's window?"

"No."

"Did you hear anything?"

Carla hesitated a moment. Her eyes welled with tears. She said, "I heard Kerri scream."

8

"If they saw something," Franklin said, "they would have called already."

They were sitting in the car, parked in front of the house with the cedar tree in the backyard, half a block down from the Montgomerys'. They sipped at coffees gone cold. Barnes had knocked on the door to no answer. He tucked one of his business cards into the doorway crack—"Please call me" written on the back.

"You want the school or the dad?" Barnes said.

Franklin shrugged. His slightest movement rocked the vehicle like a Ferris-wheel car. "What's the point of following up with the dad? Gave his daughter a ride. Big deal."

"You know how this goes," Barnes said. "He was in the area. He might have seen something. A mem—"

"A memory pull might reveal our guy standing on a street corner, hours before the incident, watching kids get off a school bus?"

Barnes turned up his palms.

"Christ," Franklin said.

"School or the dad?"

"Dad's outside of the machine," Franklin said. "School's inside. Your territory."

Barnes pulled out and started toward Kenbrook Elementary, taking a left at the first stop sign.

"Buddy system," Franklin said. He snickered. "Man, we had that when I was a kid."

"For field trips?"

"Shit. Field trips? Nah, man, you needed a buddy system just to walk down my block."

"It was a war zone where I grew up," Barnes said, slipping into his patented Franklin impression. "Fallujah's got nothing on Caulfield Ave. Drugs everywhere, cracked-out mothers walking with a baby in shitty diapers, searching for that hit, maybe their Maury Po."

"Eat a dick, white trash," Franklin said. He steamed for a moment, and then said, "There was one dude who lorded over it all. Tyrell Diggs. Drug supplier for everyone within a mile or two. He used to sit on the porch, house at the corner, just across from the bus stop. Me and my friend Marvin used to see him when we'd get off the bus, and he'd say, 'Get over here, you little lawn jockeys.' We'd run like hell. But every day he'd say the same thing, 'Get over here, you little lawn jockeys,' and it was like . . . man, it was like he was showing me where I'd end up if I didn't do something."

"Well, you did something," Barnes said. "You should be proud of yourself and your accomplishments."

"Didn't I already tell you to eat a dick?"

Barnes snorted.

"All I did was get older," Franklin said. He stared off through the windshield, unfocused. "Growth spurt, and suddenly Tyrell Diggs is saying, 'Damn, you one big jockey now. Why don't you let that crank-box monkey come over here and collect something dope?'"

"Crank-box monkey?"

"That's what Marvin looked like to Tyrell, standing next to me. One of those organ-grinder monkeys. As if being compared to a lawn jockey wasn't bad enough. He never grew much past five feet, never cared much for school. Next thing you know I'm getting scholarship offers, and he's my crank-box monkey. My buddy. The kid who used to watch my back and I'd watch his. He's dead now."

"Sorry to hear that."

"Day I left for college, Marvin went right up to that porch where Tyrell Diggs sat for all them years, telling us little lawn jockeys to come over, and he took what Tyrell was offering. He took it, tried to get some crackhead to buy it, and got killed with a homemade blade. Came home for Christmas break and he was gone. Know who was still there, though?"

"Tyrell Diggs."

"Give the man a ribbon."

Barnes looked at his partner, one eyebrow raised. "You do something about it?"

Franklin squinted at Barnes for a moment before looking off. "Here it is, man," he said. "There's always gonna be a Tyrell Diggs, understand? There's always gonna be a cracked-out, toothless mother walking her naked baby down the street. Always gonna be a gun in somebody's face, a glass pipe on somebody's lip. And there will always be a bloodsucker, like Diggs, sitting on the porch of a jacked-up house full of baseheads and murderers, talking about 'Get over here, you little lawn jockeys.' You can pick 'em off like ducks in a shooting gallery, watch 'em fall, but the barker just resets the game and they pop right back up."

"Then you gotta take out the barker."

Franklin shook his head. "No can do, brother."

"Why not?"

"The barker is God."

They drove in silence for a moment. Barnes pulled into the parking lot at Kenbrook Elementary School, threw the vehicle into park.

"Carla said we had the day off." Kerri Wilson's voice from within.

"Shhh."

They got out of the car. Franklin came around and moved the driver's seat all the way back before getting in. He unlocked the steering wheel and moved it up, then closed the door and drove off.

There was a security guard at the front entrance to the school. When Barnes was in elementary school, there'd been no security guards, just fifth graders wearing orange sashes. Safeties. Mostly they'd been kids with a sense of purpose beyond their years. They'd stop you from running, keep you on the sidewalks, write you up if you used a bad word. The word *safety* had a new meaning these days. The security guard wore a dark uniform not so different from a police officer's. His radio was attached to his shoulder near his neck. There was a stitched badge on the sleeve, something generic. He seemed a surprisingly tough customer to be standing at the door of an elementary school.

As Barnes approached, the officer said, "State your business."

Barnes showed his badge. "Looking to speak with the principal, some of the staff."

The security guard looked past Barnes, looked left, right, and then pushed open the door. "They're in the gym. Take the first right, keep your eyes to the left. You can't miss it."

Barnes nodded as he went through the door. Before it shut he caught it and turned back to the guard. "You know the custodial staff here?"

The guard nodded.

"Knew Dale Wilson?"

"Seemed a decent man," the guard said. "Can't say we hit the bar together, though."

"Thanks."

The door clacked as it closed. Barnes started down the hallway. He found the scents of construction paper and paste, pencil shavings. The place seemed tiny from an adult perspective. The halls were lined not with lockers but with coat hooks and wooden benches, all empty. The floor tiles gleamed. There were bulletin boards with announcements, one loaded up with pictures from Our spring field trip, another with antibullying information.

Barnes smirked. There had been no antibullying campaigns when he and Ricky were kids. No need for them—bullies just got bullied back. Barnes himself had taken down Freddie Cohen, a fifth-grade bully who'd taken to picking on third-grade Ricky.

The altercation with Cohen bloomed in his mind. Freddie had been a big, roly-poly kid, and Barnes had said, "Just being fat don't make you tough" before he knocked the kid down on the kickball diamond. It might have been the only time he ever found the witty comment before it was too late to use it. He'd had fewer words for Freddie Cohen at their ten-year high school reunion. The man had recently come into some money, bought a few Piggly Wiggly grocery stores in the suburbs of New Orleans, and moved down there to operate them. He acted like a big shot throughout the evening, buying round after round for all his old classmates, all the while sweating through his button-down shirt. Barnes had slipped out the back door before giving into the temptation to knock the guy on his ass again.

Now he followed the sound of a muffled voice until he came to the gym. He peered through one of the rectangular glass panes on the double door. The glass was crisscrossed with wire in a diamond pattern. Shatter-resistant. Inside the gym there was a man, likely the principal, standing before a bunch of adults seated on the bleachers. He wore a light-gray suit and had a plastered-down comb-over. Thick glasses. Early fifties, maybe late forties. Barnes pushed through the door, and the man stopped talking, turned to him.

Barnes showed his badge to the principal, showed it to the staff on the bleachers. Many nodded; some turned to one another and exchanged looks. Otherwise the gym was now as quiet as a Monday-morning chapel.

"Excuse me a moment," the principal said, holding up a finger to his staff.

As the principal approached, Barnes checked his notes. Mr. Eric Nichol. He flipped the book closed and pocketed it.

"Would you like to speak in private, Detective, uh . . . ?" He stuck out his hand to shake.

"Barnes."

The principal took Barnes's hand into both of this own, gripped it like a rope he'd found while plummeting. "I'm Mr. Nichol, the principal here at Kenbrook."

Barnes turned until Nichol was between him and the staff. He spoke in a low voice. "I'll need to speak to your custodial staff, plus one of your teachers." He looked over the principal's shoulder to find the teacher from Dale Wilson's dream among the staff. He found her pretty face in the crowd. Wilson's heart fluttered in Barnes's chest.

"Mrs. Macintyre?" Nichol's head tilted down, and he looked at Barnes over top his glasses. "Kerri's teacher."

"Oh, God no." Kerri Wilson.

"Shhh."

"No," Barnes said. He flicked his eyes to the teacher again. "Brunette. Blue top, gray skirt."

Principal Nichol looked, then turned back to Barnes. In a low voice, he said, "Ms. Taylor?"

"Don't single her out," Barnes said. "I'd like to speak with her in private. Can that be arranged?"

"But she's not my teacher."

"Shhh."

"I can have her called to my office."

Barnes tapped his pen on his knuckles. "Call the custodial staff down, plus a few teachers, including both Macintyre and Taylor."

Nichol nodded. He turned to the seated staff. "I'll be just a few minutes with the detective. He'd like to speak with some of you in private, so please don't leave until you're dismissed."

9

Principal Eric Nichol sat in the pocket of his U-shaped desk. There was a wall of shelves behind him—mostly filled with binders and textbooks—and a bulletin board on the left-hand side. No cork could be seen beneath the overlapping thumbtacked paperwork. On the right there was a motivational poster. It showed a mountaintop framed in black, and underneath that, ASPIRE. Barnes had already grilled the principal about what he knew, which was virtually nothing. Dale Wilson had been a fine, dependable custodian, his daughter an exemplary student. Oh, there had been some trouble with Kerri being bullied due to the fact that her dad was on staff, but Kerri was a tough little girl. She'd handled it well.

Nichol had gone silent then. His eyes became unfocused. Barnes had seen it before—the moment of clarity that hits someone who had been close to a murder victim, the fresh realization that the victim would never come back. It often came on the heels of the first time they used *was* instead of *is*.

"Call them down now, please," Barnes said.

Nichol snapped out of his trance. He pulled his desktop microphone over to him and pressed the button. It gave a shot of feedback before he spoke into it. "Would the custodial staff as well as Mrs. Macintyre, Mr. Fredrickson, Mrs. Jones, Ms. Taylor, and Mr. Ellison please come down to the principal's office?"

Barnes said, "I assume there's a basement or a boiler room?"

Nichol nodded. "Basement."

"After we're done here, I'd like to see it. Meantime, I'd like to speak with each of the people you've called alone."

"That's no problem," Nichol said. He settled into his chair.

"Mr. Nichol," Barnes said, "that means you."

Nichol smiled. He got up and left the office.

Barnes perched on the edge of Nichol's desk, one leg up, one foot on the ground. He reveled in the novelty of being on this side of things in a principal's office. He'd spent his share of time in the office as a boy, most notably for loading his science-class rocket up with a pack of thunder-bombs. Ricky's idea. They'd exploded beautifully against the blue sky. The kids had oohed and aahed while Mr. Cunningham pinch-gripped Barnes's earlobe and dragged him away.

Through the glass he saw the staff members queuing up in the outer office along the secretary's desk. Ms. Taylor was there. Butterflies in Barnes's stomach.

Nichol sent in the first of four janitors. Barnes grilled the man lightly, specifically asking whether he had any kind of business dealings with Dale Wilson, anything they were cooking up? No.

"Had Wilson ever mentioned any clowns or anything regarding clowns?"

"Huh? No."

It was the same with the rest of the custodial staff.

Mrs. Macintyre was a mess. Her cheeks were awash with tears, her eyes bloodshot. She had a plastic crayon box with *Kerri* printed on a tag stuck to the top. "These were hers." She held out the box with a shaky hand. The crayons inside rattled.

"Get it together, sister." Andrea Wilson's voice.

"Shhh."

Barnes took the box. The woman bawled until he let her go.

The other teachers were appropriately saddened by what had happened. More than that, they were shocked and scared. Barnes's presence brought them the same finality it had brought Mr. Nichol. He grilled them as he did the custodial staff, but it was all just for show, a way to safeguard Ms. Taylor from being ground through the gossip mill. Nichol sent her in last.

Jessica Taylor sat down before Barnes and drew a lock of hair behind her right ear. Barnes's heart rate spiked. Dale Wilson had lusted after this woman with the intensity of a schoolboy crush. Being in her presence had frightened Wilson and turned him mute, just as it was now turning Barnes. He fought to push words from his mouth. "You're new to the district, Ms. Taylor?"

"Yes. Last year I was subbing in Redford. This is my first full-time position. I'm very happy to be here. And please, call me Jessica."

Barnes nodded. "Must have been tough, subbing?"

"The money is okay, especially when you can get a long-term."

He guessed she was in her late twenties. Her face was round and pretty, and she had a small scar nearly hidden in her right eyebrow. Her eyes were large, blue, and expressive, easily her best feature. There was an honesty to her, like she'd tried on a few lies here and there, found they didn't fit, and scratched the concept of dishonesty altogether. "A long-term?"

"Some teachers know they're going to be out for a month or two, maybe pregnancy or some other medical leave, so they seek a long-term sub."

"I see. You knew Kerri Wilson?"

"Only in passing. She was in a different grade, different room."

"And her father?"

"Custodian, right?"

"Yes."

"I guess I saw him in the halls," she said. "Seemed like an okay guy."

"Did he ever approach you or say anything to you?"

"Not that I can recall," Jessica said.

"Nothing about him made you suspicious?"

Jessica cocked her head. Her eyes widened. "He's not a suspect, is he? I mean, he didn't . . . ?"

Barnes shook his head. "Did he ever make you feel uncomfortable?"

Jessica dipped her head and blushed. Barnes could tell she was used to men leering at her the way Wilson had, conjuring fantasies. The girlie magazines of Barnes's youth didn't feature all those naked librarians and teachers for no reason.

She said, "He was married, right?"

"Yes."

"So what's a harmless crush?"

Dale Wilson's cheeks grew hot on Barnes's face. Garbled phonetics echoed in Barnes's mind. "Nothing ever happened between you two?"

"No."

"Can you think of anything out of the ordinary regarding Dale or Kerri recently? Anything that seemed off with either of them?"

She looked off for a moment, then shook her head.

"Does the word *calavera* mean anything to you?"

She shrugged.

"Okay, then," Barnes said. He stood up from the edge of the desk.

"Wait a minute," Jessica said. "Calavera. That's Spanish, right?"

"Yes."

"Dale Wilson knew Spanish."

"How do you know?"

"I guess I'm only assuming he did. Yesterday I was on my way to class after lunch. He was coming out of one of the janitors' closets and something fell from his pocket. An index card. I picked it up and handed it back to him. I wouldn't have read what was on it, but the lettering was so big it was impossible not to see."

"Written in black marker?"

"Yes."

"What did it say?"

"*Demasiado tarde.* Translated into English, it means 'too late.'"

Barnes's adrenaline surged. "Excuse me? Say that again."

"'Too late'?"

"You're sure that's what it means?"

"I'm pretty sure, yeah."

"Did he say anything about it?"

"No. He just thanked me."

"Anything else?"

She shook her head.

Barnes handed her his business card. "If you remember anything else, call me. Anything at all."

"Okay," she said. She took the card and read it, smiling and tilting her head. The lock of hair she'd tucked behind her ear fell loose. She turned and left the principal's office, leaving only her scent behind. Barnes closed his eyes and breathed in and out until Principal Nichol came back in.

"The basement?" Barnes said.

"Follow me," Nichol said. He pulled out a key ring.

They went down the hall toward the back of the building. The index card could be the first break they'd had since Calavera had begun three years ago. What had Dale Wilson gotten himself involved in? Better yet, whom had he gotten involved with? The card might lead the way. Barnes gripped his phone, ready to call Franklin, but he wanted the hard evidence first.

Nichol led him to an unmarked door. He opened it and held the door for Barnes to walk through. The basement. The secret underbelly of the school. For the kids it held the tortures of spiders and snakes and the souls of evil teachers past. They might be disappointed to find it was an ordinary basement—a couple of boilers in one corner, black iron, white PVC, and copper pipes overhead, plus various pressure knobs and gauges. They came to a section of lockers, six of them in army green, set against a cinder-block wall. Each one was padlocked.

"I assume you'd like me to open Wilson's locker?"

"Yes, sir."

Nichol nodded. He began flipping through the keys on his ring. Barnes recalled his father once telling him the most important guy in the building isn't the guy with all the keys, but the guy with no keys. When young John had asked why, Dad replied, "Because all the doors are opened for him."

"Damn," Nichol said. "I'm not sure it's on this set."

Barnes wandered while Nichol tried the keys. He peeked around a nearby corner. There were two white ceramic washbasins with stainless-steel mirrors over them. Barnes sniffed to find the mildew scent of Wilson's dream. He went to the first basin.

No.

He went to the second.

Yes.

Dale Wilson's dream came back to him with arresting clarity. Wilson had been looking at his own face in the mirror, only he imagined it painted like a clown. He had been speaking to himself, chastising himself for never having achieved more with his life than becoming a janitor. His dream had been a vision of what he felt others saw when they looked at him.

Barnes recalled the way he'd smiled at his own face in the mirror that morning, his bald head with bloody bits of toilet paper. The despair he'd felt, the futility. Dale Wilson felt that same despair, that same futility. The man's consciousness rose into Barnes's mind and revealed what he'd been cooking up: he was going to sell his own suicide to a machine dealer with the highest bid. Suicides were rare and munkies paid a lot for them. A way to catch a guaranteed glimpse of hell. As guaranteed as it gets, anyway, without punching your own ticket. Wilson planned to have the machine dealer wire the money to his wife's bank account before pulling the trigger.

Barnes heard the *ch-chunk* of a padlock being opened.

The locker was sparsely filled. Wilson's coveralls were hung on a hook. There was a battered brass watch on the shelf above, steel-toed boots at the locker's bottom. Barnes tugged on a latex glove. He reached into the left-hand pocket of Wilson's coveralls. Nothing. He reached into the right. There. He gripped the edge of the index card and pulled it out. It was dry, but water damaged. The ends were curled up, and the lines on it were blurred, as was the writing—Demasiado Tarde. Barnes slid the card into a Ziploc bag and sealed it. Only then did he take off his glove.

10

"What's it mean?" Captain Darrow said. He was sitting behind his desk at the police station, staring down at the now–fingerprint-dusted index card. Barnes and Franklin sat before him. The office wasn't a big glass-walled place like in the movies. The captain's chair wasn't high-backed or black leather but Office Depot blue felt. The corners of his desk were cracked and flaked away. Particleboard peeked out from beneath plastic veneer. Everything was standard issue and plenty worn.

"Too late," Barnes said.

Captain Darrow looked up. He eyeballed Barnes and then Franklin. "What'd you find on the Montgomery girl's father?"

"Dead end," Franklin said. He consulted his notepad. "Welfare junkie on restraining order to stay away from the kid and the mom. Could hardly keep his eyes open when I was talking to him. We can put him on the machine, suck out what he's got, but you know how it'll go."

"What's the deal with letting Holston in the tech lab?" Barnes said.

Darrow frowned. "It was bound to happen. After all the human-rights maniacs and the protests at the beginning, and now with all the munkies stalking the streets like zombies, to have gotten this far with the machine is a miracle in its own right. After Watkins I'm surprised it took this long for Holston to come sniffing around for a story."

"So why give him direct access?"

"Because someone's going to get it eventually. Would you rather have him get his stories from munkies? They'd shut us down faster than you could spit. You're going to give him an interview, too."

"Screw that."

Darrow held up the bagged index card. "Was it damp in that basement or what?"

"Not particularly," Barnes said. "The card may have been left out in the rain, maybe dropped in a toilet."

"Dropped in a toilet?"

Barnes shrugged. "Dude's a janitor."

A uniformed officer came into the office. He handed a manila envelope to Captain Darrow and then left. Darrow opened the folder, glanced at the contents, closed it. "Two sets of prints on the card."

"Hot damn!" Franklin sat up.

"Let's keep our pants on," Barnes said. "The teacher said she picked up the card and handed it back to Wilson."

"Get her in here," Darrow said. "Gotta rule her out."

Barnes stood.

"Wait a second," Darrow said. "You look like dog shit, Barnes. Why don't you let Franklin bring in the teacher, go get some rest?"

"I'm fine."

"That's the same thing Watkins said."

It was Franklin who'd spoken. Barnes gritted his teeth. He refused to look at his partner. "Come on, Cap," he said. "You know I won't go Watkins on you. Trust me."

Darrow squinted at Barnes. "Pick up the teacher, bring her in here, get her printed, and then go get some rest. You come in here looking like shit tomorrow and I'm taking your badge."

"Let me see that card," Franklin said.

Darrow Frisbee-tossed the bagged index card toward Franklin. The big man looked it over as he stood up.

"What's on your mind?" Darrow said.

"Don't know," Franklin said. "I'll go back to the Wilsons'."

"For what?"

"*Too late*. It's the same as the refrigerator magnets."

"Yeah, and?" Darrow said.

"And I got a curious mind, Cap," Franklin said. He winked. "That's why you pay me the big bucks."

Evening descended as Barnes and Franklin walked across the precinct parking lot toward their cars. Rain began to fall, straight down, big drops. The overhead street lamps blinked to life. Barnes pulled up his collar and said, "Nothing like throwing your partner under the bus, br—"

He was going to say *bro*, but the word was cut off when Franklin yanked him off his feet by the lapels, slammed him into a nearby SUV. "I'll throw you through a wall if I have to, *bro*." They were nose to nose. Barnes's feet weren't touching the ground. "You don't know what Watkins went through. I won't stand by and watch it again."

Barnes's head stung from when it impacted the SUV's side window. His clavicle throbbed, his spine ached. Franklin's former partner, Tom Watkins, was currently in the loony bin, his mind supposedly scrambled by the machine. Barnes looked into Franklin's eyes and saw a grown man with rain on his face, trying to help his new partner, trying to prevent the same mistakes Watkins had made, maybe trying to stop Barnes from losing his mind.

"Fuck you," Barnes said.

Franklin threw him down on the concrete and stood over him. Barnes looked up, shielding his eyes from the rain. Franklin was made a silhouette by the glow from the street lamp above and behind him. He had the impossible proportions of a comic-book villain.

"I had a chance, you know?" Franklin said. "I had a chance to stop Watkins before he hurt anyone." He squatted down, close to Barnes. "He was my partner. You understand that. I trusted him with my life, and he trusted me with his, but when I looked into his eyes the day he shot Dawson, you know what I saw?"

"Enlighten me."

"Someone else."

Barnes looked off. "I'm not Watkins."

Franklin turned and began to walk away. Over his shoulder he said, "Neither was he."

11

Barnes pulled up to Jessica Taylor's three-story brownstone in Brush Park. Row housing was rare in Detroit, and he sat for a minute while the rain drummed the car's roof, thinking he'd been somehow transported to Boston or Pittsburgh. He'd been to Pittsburgh once, had road-tripped and spent the weekend there with some friends his senior year. He'd met an older woman at a bar and tried to pick her up, despite the fact she reeked of cigarettes and a half gallon of perfume. With a smoke-ravaged voice she told him he was sweet, but she was looking for a man with hair on his nuts.

Three of the street lamps on Jessica Taylor's block were working, which was three more than most Detroit city blocks. Brush Park was near the center of the city where you could hear the home-run cheers from Comerica Park or look up and see the skyscrapers. Here you were relatively safe. Walk a half mile outside of downtown and the broken street lamps would be the least of your worries. Barnes pushed through the iron gates and approached the brownstone. He found the buzzer that read TAYLOR and pressed it.

No response.

He pressed it again.

After thirty seconds, he stepped back down the steps and looked up through the rain. An elderly woman was leaning out a window on the second floor, sipping coffee under an umbrella.

"She ain't here," the woman said.

Barnes cocked his head.

"You're looking for Ms. Taylor, right?"

"How did you know that?"

"She told me about them people that were killed. I saw your badge. Two plus two and all that."

"Do you know where she might have gone?"

"She teaches at the Tubman on Thursday nights. Seven thirty to nine. Computer stuff."

"Over there on Temple?"

"That's the one."

"Thanks."

◆ ◆ ◆

Barnes entered the Harriet Tubman Center via the wide staircase that led up to the building's glass front doors. He passed beneath a security camera as he crossed the threshold and shook off the rain. The building was empty and quiet. He checked a schedule on the wall to find GETTING STARTED W/MICROSOFT OFFICE, THU @ 7:30 P.M., RM 202.

He took the stairs to the second floor.

The door to Room 202 was halfway open. Light spilled out of the room and cut hard against the hallway floor. Barnes could hear Jessica Taylor speaking, "Okay, so now that we're in the function field, I want you to type in an equals sign, then 'sum,' that's S-U-M, then a left parenthesis, then 'A1,' colon, 'A4,' right parenthesis."

There were several people in the class but a few empty seats. Barnes snuck into the back of the room and took a seat at a desk with an ancient desktop tower of an off-white color that screamed nineties. Jessica saw him and raised her eyebrows in question, but Barnes shook his head to wave her off: *It can wait.*

She nodded and kept to her lesson, though he could swear she was blushing now. She moved back and forth across the front of the room, where a spreadsheet was projected against an old black chalkboard, to bend over and talk with various students as they struggled with the technology. He felt sick about the way she walked, the way she paid attention to her students' questions, the shape of her body as she turned, bent, and gestured. He told himself that Dale Wilson's desire was fierce.

Ricky would like her.

The thought had come suddenly and painfully. As he sometimes did, Barnes imagined an adult Ricky—or Rick, he guessed, but not Richard—living in a modest apartment in a New York or Chicago neighborhood. He'd know the best thing to order at the nearby diner, he'd call the local bartenders by name, and he'd work out in a boxing club in the basement of the fire department where he worked. His pals would call him Bomber or Turbo—a nickname he'd earned in some secret way, never to be shared with those who weren't there—and playfully clap his back when he turned red with embarrassment. When Barnes and Jessica came from Detroit to visit, Ricky would welcome them into his little apartment, recently picked up but not exactly clean, with a big smile and hugs for them both. Later, when the two brothers had a moment alone, he'd say, "Johnny, she's a keeper."

Jessica Taylor dismissed her class early. The students filed out, some grumbling, some giving Barnes and his badge on its chain a sidelong glance as they went. He smiled and nodded at them, waited at the back while Jessica waited at the front until the room was empty. She put on her jacket and picked up her bag, came over to him. He stood to greet her.

"To what do I owe the pleasure?" she said.

"Turns out I gotta haul you in."

Her eyebrows rose, as did her color.

"Just for fingerprinting," he said, hands up.

"Jesus, man," she said. She slapped him on the chest. "You scared the hell out of me."

Barnes laughed. "Guilty conscience?"

She threw her hands on her hips and glared at him.

"Attitude like that, might have to run a background check."

"You might not like what you find."

"Wait a second. Are you El Chapo?"

"Maybe." She went ahead of him and clicked off the classroom light, walked through the door and into the hallway.

"You must drive a sweet ride, then," Barnes said. "All that drug money."

"Repossessed," she said. "I'm rockin' the SMART bus these days."

"How the mighty have fallen."

Outside, in the street, Barnes held the car door for her. She thanked him and got in. As he rounded the back of the car, he saw a munky-hook standing at the dark mouth of an alleyway, her breath vapor dissipating in the cold air. She wore a furry vest, tight shorts, and black leggings. Her body was for sale, but for your money all you'd get was a trip on the machine—one of her previous experiences. Her memory inventory would be wide. *Want to bang her with a dick bigger than yours? Want to be black? White? A woman?*

The munky-hook called out, "Go for it, sweetie!"

Barnes blushed. His heart fell into his shoes. His legs went rubbery as he made his way to the driver-side door and got in. Had Jessica heard the hook's comment? He couldn't tell. She was looking straight ahead, not giving anything away.

He started the car, put it in drive, and pulled up to the first stop sign. "It'll be quick," he said. "We just need your prints to rule out the second set on the index card, assuming the first set is Wilson's."

She nodded, kept her eyes forward. Tight lips.

He turned down Plum Street.

They were a few minutes from the station now. His nerves were shot. He checked himself in the rearview mirror, mostly to keep Dale Wilson's gaze from her face, her legs. Captain Darrow was right; he did look like dog shit. Felt like it, too. He needed a drink.

Jessica remained pine-board stiff in the passenger seat, hands piled one over the other on her lap. She must have heard the munky-hook's comment, must have noticed him staring at her in the classroom.

They pulled up to the station and found a parking spot. By then the air inside the vehicle was as thick as peanut butter. He turned off the ignition. They sat in silence while raindrops spread out and connected with one another on the windshield.

"Look," Barnes said, "I'm sorry about what that—"

Jessica got out of the car. She turned around and stood inside the passenger-side door, holding it open. She leaned in and said, "I have just one question, Detective Barnes."

"What's that?"

She smirked. "You gonna go for it, sweetie?"

She laughed and slammed the car door, ran across the parking lot through the rain. Barnes sat in the car, watching her in the rearview mirror as she made her way toward the precinct door. Once she was under the awning, she stopped and turned around, hands on her hips just like in the classroom. Remnants of laughter were still on her face.

Ricky would love her.

The rain had gotten worse. It battered the roof of Barnes's car, the street, the sidewalks. He and Jessica were back at her brownstone, parked in the street. She was cleaning the ink from her fingers and thumbs with the wipes they'd provided her at the station. "I can't believe they still use ink," she said. "I thought there'd be some kind of scanner." She balled up the wipes and stuffed them into her bag. She looked out toward her building and sighed. "You wanna go get a coffee or something?"

Barnes clicked his tongue. "Um, well . . ."

"Come on," she said, turning to him. "I'm not a witness, am I? I know there's some rule about fraternizing with witnesses." Her hair was wet, her smile mischievous.

Barnes's stomach lurched as Dale Wilson's sex dream took over his mind. He felt her phantom touch, smelled her soapy scent, felt her hips pressing against his own.

"You won't get in trouble, will you?"

Dale Wilson shook Barnes's head.

"Good." She faced forward in her seat. "There's a twenty-four-hour place just up the street. They do apple pie with a slice of American cheese melted on it. You're buying."

Barnes stared, blinked.

She turned to him again. "Step on it, Vic Mackey."

12

They got a booth along the near wall of the busy diner. The din was filled with voices and laughter, silverware clinking against plates, glasses singing with ice. The rain outside battered the plate glass windows.

"Vic Mackey?" Barnes said. He rubbed a hand over his bald head.

"You never watched *The Shield*?"

"Sure, but . . ."

"I thought Vic was sexy."

"You're damn right he was."

That wonderful smile came to her face, the one that made him hurt.

The waitress brought their coffee. She said, "Your pies are in the salamander, out in a jiff," and drifted away.

They sat in silence. Jessica seemed comfortable in it. She seemed to enjoy teasing out his thoughts by saying nothing. It was the same technique the police used in the interrogation room.

Barnes said, "I wonder why they call it a salamander?"

"The word *salamander*," Jessica said, "in classical Greek, translates to 'fire animal.'"

"First Spanish, now Greek—what's your encore?"

"Would you believe break dancing?"

"Nope."

"Yeah, not so much."

Barnes was weary. A drunken morning and virtually no sleep had left him running on fumes. Still, he would choose no other place to be.

Thoughts of Calavera and the machine were momentarily buried. He felt like a man taking in huge gulps of clean air after nearly drowning.

"Listen," Jessica said. "I want you to tell me something you've never told anyone before."

"You mean like confession?"

"Not necessarily. It can be anything, so long as you've never said it before. Here. I'll go first." She looked at him seriously. "Your ears are amazing."

Barnes chuckled.

"Your turn," she said.

"Your ears are amazing, too."

"Un-uh. It has to be completely original."

"Okay," he said. He matched her serious stare. "I don't like Doritos."

"You communist!"

"Your turn," Barnes said.

"No. Hold on. You don't like Doritos? Is it blue you don't like or red?"

"Either."

"Go back to your homeland, Comrade." She shook her head. "Ben Franklin is turning in his grave. You're going to be attacked by bald eagles later. Don't expect me to help."

He smirked. "Your turn."

"I think the Grand Canyon is boring."

"And I'm the communist?"

"You know they have a book you can buy at the gift shop there, and it's just a list of people who have died at the Grand Canyon."

"Come on."

"It's something like a thousand people. I nearly made the list myself."

"You considered jumping?"

"Yep, from boredom. The Badlands are worse, though. It's like, 'Hey, scorching-hot alien landscape. Want to hang out?' Nope. Your turn."

The pies came before Barnes could play again. Each was covered with an orange-yellow curtain of cheese, broiled to a blackened and crispy top. Jessica clapped her hands lightly before her face. "Yay."

"Damn, that looks good." Chunk Philips.

"You'll never get whipped cream again," Jessica said.

Barnes tried a bite. "Wow."

"See?"

They finished their pies and sipped coffee. The caffeine had little effect on Barnes. His eyelids were heavy. He blinked and shook his head.

"I've kept you out too late," she said.

"Not at all." His shoulders sagged. He yawned. "It's just this case."

"It's the PA Man, isn't it?"

The PA Man. Pickax Man. It was the media term for Calavera, something Jeremiah Holston had coined. They'd successfully managed to keep the killer's poems and mask description away from Holston and the rest of the press, but his killing method had been leaked. "Yeah," Barnes said, "it's him."

"I thought he came and went with the moon. Didn't he strike just a few days ago?"

"Don't believe what you read, particularly from the *Flame*. He's killed on back-to-back nights, sometimes with weeks in between, and once he took six months off."

"So there's no pattern?"

"There's a pattern," Barnes said. His speech felt slow and forced. His eyes were down to slits. He saw her face through eyelashes. "It's just a question of finding it."

"You're exhausted. We should get you home."

The sound of her voice opened his eyes. He was unaware that they'd closed. "I'm not very good company right now. I . . ." His eyes were closing again.

13

Barnes woke up on a couch. He checked his watch: 11:30 a.m. He sprang to his feet and banged his knee on a coffee table he didn't own. He was in an apartment, not his home. The air smelled of freshly cut flowers and brewed tea. He looked around to find hardwood floors, IKEA furniture, a small kitchen. His shoes were set together under the kitchen table, his jacket and holster over the back of a chair. He went over to find a note on the counter.

Dear John,

Ha! Just kidding. This is not that kind of note. I'd still be there if I didn't have to work. Anyway, I didn't mean to bore you to sleep! There's coffee in the cupboard if you feel like it. The door will lock itself when you leave, so no worries.

Jessica

P.S. Nothing happened, but don't kid yourself— you wish it had!

Barnes smiled. He slipped on his shoes, holster, and jacket. He surveyed the apartment again, found which door led to the bathroom and which led to the bedroom. He peeked inside at her bed. A queen mattress. He was tempted to go in and explore, but the thought of invading her privacy sent a wave of nausea through him. He was glad for it. He left the apartment and started down the interior steps of her building. The rest had served him well. He felt vital, like a man chiseled from marble. The only issue was his growling stomach. He checked his phone. Five new messages. He sifted through them as he walked, deleting the hang-ups and telemarketer voice mails.

He came to a voice mail from Captain Darrow. *"I said get some rest, not take a day off."*

Franklin left a voice mail, too. *"Where you at? If you're pissed about yesterday, get over it. Turns out Wilson got online and looked up a Spanish-to-English translator. He put in* demasado, demasido, *whatever, and translated it. I'm at the station. I've got something else, too. Get in here."*

Barnes reached the outer apartment door to find it was raining again. He walked happily across the street to his car, unconcerned with the cold drops on his shoulders and head. He hopped into the vehicle and banged his head on the door frame, his knee on the steering wheel. Jessica must have driven them home from the diner last night. Jesus, he'd gone down hard. Surely she hadn't actually carried him; he must've been functional enough for her to lead him around. He reset the seat, the steering wheel, and adjusted the mirrors, warmed by the idea of her driving his car. He started the car, threw on the wipers, and was about to pull out when his phone chirped. A text message from an unknown number:

So I met this cute guy last night. I'm hoping he might ask me out . . .

Barnes smiled. He typed a reply. I hear he's not just cute, but handsome. Vic Mackey handsome, even.

He threw his phone on the passenger seat and drove. He made it two blocks before he checked his phone for her reply.

Nothing.

He stopped at a coffee shop and went inside, intentionally leaving his phone in the car so he wouldn't check it a hundred times while standing in line. He got an extra-large coffee and an old-fashioned doughnut, which he wolfed down before arriving back at the vehicle. As he unlocked the door, he peeked at the phone through the rain-streaked glass.

No reply.

He got in, picked up the phone, and opened it. Maybe the network was down?

Nope.

"Relax." A mother's voice.

"Shhh."

He drove to the station. Before he could get out of his car, the passenger door opened. Jeremiah Holston stuck his head in.

"What do you want, Holston?"

"My interview."

"Why don't you pull some munky off the street? He'll give you as much as I can."

"Unreliable source," Holston said. "Even the *Flame* has standards. Besides, most munkies aren't getting themselves killed every time they go on the machine."

Barnes sighed. He nodded at the passenger seat, letting Holston know he could hop in. Holston adjusted the seat as far back as it would go, then tilted it back to pimp level. He got in. The car filled up with his hamburger scent.

"You got five minutes."

"It's going to take longer than that."

"Then you'll get multiple sessions. Clock's ticking."

Holston flipped open his notepad. "When you're using the machine, are you aware of yourself?"

"Come on, this is common knowledge, man."

"Mileage varies a little, right? Call it establishing a foundation about *your* experience. Are you absolutely, one hundred percent the victim, or are you still somewhat aware that you're you?"

Barnes sipped his coffee. "If we're talking percentages, I'm ninety-five percent them, five percent me . . . but I can fight for more if I have to. A mind-over-matter sort of thing."

"Don't use percentages in court." The attorney. *"They'll pin you down with them."*

"That falls in line with what most munkies say," Holston said while scribbling on his notepad.

"What can I tell you that they can't?"

Holston folded his notepad closed. "Off the record?"

"Whatever."

"The main difference between them and you is you don't *want* to hook into the machine."

"Yes, he does." The crack addict's voice.

"I've interviewed a thousand munkies," Holston continued, "and I could interview a thousand more, but they all say the same thing. They can't get enough."

"I can. I do."

"And that's what makes you a story." Holston reopened his notepad.

"Let's get something straight," Barnes said. He turned toward the reporter. "I don't like you. Now, when most people say they don't like someone, they mean that they hate them. That's not what I mean. I simply mean that I don't prefer you or your company. It doesn't mean I'll be dishonest with you. You want to know about the machine? Ask your questions. I'll answer them honestly until I start hating you. If that happens, you'll know."

Holston said, "Does it hurt?"

"Yes."

"How long do the effects linger?"

"Sometimes a few hours, sometimes a day or two. It depends on how long I'm with them. That's common, right?"

"Yeah, but . . ."

"But what? I get it. I'm only a story if I'm special. Well, I'm not a story, then. The machine's the machine, for a munky or for me. The only difference is I'm not hooked."

"There's another difference," Holston said. He held Barnes's gaze. "You're forced to *die* as someone else, and it's your job. You can't say no. Some sickos might want to experience a suicide, but only convicted murderers are forced to experience being murdered. The jury's still out on the lasting effects of that."

"I'm not forced," Barnes said. "It's my choice."

"Is it?"

"Time's up."

The rain had slowed to a drizzle. The precinct seemed clean and foreign to the well-rested Barnes as he approached it. He thought of Rip Van Winkle coming down from the mountains. He smelled disinfectant as he moved through the front doors. Two munkies were slouched on a bench near the door—a man and a woman, both sporting sagging Mohawks and bloody knuckles and knees. They were handcuffed to each other and again to the bench, soaked from the rain. There'd be a black-market machine back at their home, maybe an empty bottle of serum, the trigger for whatever crime they'd tried to commit in their sleep-deprived state. Most likely a robbery gone wrong. As Barnes passed, the woman lazily reached out to him but missed. Her hand fell back into her lap. Her bloodshot eyes slowly blinked. Her lips were crusty with dead skin.

Franklin was at his desk.

Barnes said, "What do you have?"

"Well, I'll be humped," Franklin said. He leaned back in his chair and threw his big hands behind his head. "You look just like a summer day."

"Eat a dick," Barnes said, though he couldn't suppress his smile. He plopped down in his own chair and leaned back to match Franklin's eye level.

"You musta got laid or something," Franklin said.

"What. Do. You. Have?"

"Mmm-hmm."

Barnes went deadpan.

Franklin sat upright. "You get my voice mail?"

"Yep."

"Then you know Wilson translated the words."

"Yep."

"The website he visited before that was a cemetery. Turns out he's a widower. Andrea was his second wife. He married his high school sweetheart after they found out she had cancer. Sentimental thing and all that. Marriage lasted six months before she died."

"Jesus."

"I checked Wilson's phone records. Found out he called the cemetery, too. Didn't get through to anyone, though. Might have left them a voice mail. I'm thinking he must have visited recently or was planning to."

"First wife buried there?"

"Sure is. Want to know who else is buried there?"

"Do I?"

"You do."

"Shoot, then."

"All of them."

Barnes sat up in his chair, cocked his head. "All of who?"

"All of Calavera's vics have at least one relative buried there. A grandma, a sibling, whatever. I called over there this morning"—he checked his notepad—"talked with a Mrs. Bruckheimer. Had her run down the list. Found all eight."

"We've got twelve victims, not eight."

"Count families as one. Eight crime scenes."

"Which cemetery?"

"Parkview Memorial."

The clean, rested feeling was replaced with dread. Ricky was buried at Parkview Memorial.

14

It'd been over ten years since Barnes had been to his brother's grave. He'd last gone to see him when he was twenty-two, precisely ten years to the day after Ricky died. Barnes hadn't mustered the courage to go back since. On the twenty-year anniversary last month, he'd been too caught up in the Calavera case.

"What's up?" Franklin said. They were driving to the cemetery, Franklin behind the wheel. He smirked. "You see dead people?"

Barnes assumed Franklin didn't know his story. Save for his parents and maybe Captain Darrow, no one did. *I'm responsible for my younger brother's death* wasn't exactly polite party conversation. Truth told, it wasn't any kind of conversation for Detective John Barnes. "I just don't like cemeteries."

"Who does?" The waitress.

"Shhh."

They pulled up to the cemetery gate, which was an impressive archway of stone and hanging iron lanterns. The gravel drive forked after they passed under the archway. Franklin stayed on the right-hand path.

A dozen different voices sounded off in Barnes's head—shouting, whispering, crying. Their words twisted around one another like brambles in his mind. *"Why?" "No." "Please." "What?" "Don't." "Shouldn't have." "Understand?"*

"Shhh. Shhh. Shhh."

Barnes wished for bourbon. His hands shook. He stuffed them into his armpits beneath his jacket.

Franklin stopped the car where the road forked again. To the left was the memorial center and crematorium. Through past experience Barnes knew the building also served as the cemetery office and a place to receive visitors. Beyond the memorial center there was a second, larger building. Maybe a storage facility for the grave-digging backhoes, lawn equipment, and groundskeeper's tools. The grounds were well manicured. All the recently fallen leaves were gone. After the medieval gate, the cemetery was a surprisingly bright and vibrant place. The message was clear—anything dead here is belowground, not above.

"So what's this guy doing, just picking random names off headstones?" Franklin said.

"No way it's coincidence," Barnes said.

"Worse odds than Lotto."

Barnes nodded.

Franklin looked out the window toward the memorial center. "He's preaching, you know that?"

"The poems tell us that, yeah."

"No. Not the poems. I mean, they're part of it, sure, but those are for us. He's preaching with what he's doing."

"What makes you say that?"

"Something Watkins said before he went off. 'I can see him now,' he said. 'I understand his work.' I thought he'd figured out some clue. So, despite the look in his eyes, I trusted his judgment. I followed him into that safe house, feeling like something was up but telling myself my boy was just having a bad day."

"Dawson?"

Franklin nodded.

Barnes recalled the incident. Tom Watkins, Franklin's previous partner, had been the secondary detective on the case before Barnes was brought in. He'd been the one on the machine, the one suffering its punishment. On the day he *went Watkins*, he and Franklin were going back to talk with one Gerald Dawson—the only victim to have survived an encounter with Calavera—to see whether he recalled anything new, or so Watkins had led Franklin to believe.

Dawson's showdown with Calavera hadn't been a cakewalk; he'd taken a pickax through the chest, just above the heart and straight through his back without clipping a vital organ. He'd been double-lucky—the blade had busted the back off the wooden chair to which he was strapped. His bindings came off as the chair collapsed. Suddenly Dawson found himself running down the street, screaming for help with a pickax sticking out of him. Calavera hadn't bothered to chase, nor had he left a poem at the scene.

When Watkins and Franklin came to see Dawson that day, he was fully recovered though still under police protection in a nondescript safe house in Ferndale. Watkins walked into the living room where Dawson was sitting, drew down with a .45 Magnum loaded with hollow points, and turned Dawson's head into a canoe before Franklin and the uniforms tackled him. There were still some brown stains on the lampshade and drywall behind the couch in that safe house.

Watkins was currently held at Bracken Psychiatric Institute for the Criminally Insane. Word had it he was loopy and incoherent. In any case, his actions created an opening in Homicide, and Barnes had already applied to get out of Vice.

"My theory?" Franklin said. "He thought he was finishing Calavera's work. It wasn't the poems that had gotten to him or the sight of dead bodies. It was the work. The deed. Whatever this mad dog is trying to say with this thing he's doing, the message got through to Watkins. Through the machine."

"The machine is the best tool for this job," Barnes said. "We wouldn't be sitting here right now if I hadn't questioned Jessica Taylor, and I wouldn't have been onto her if Dale Wilson hadn't dreamed about her. Deny that?"

"We wouldn't have checked Wilson's locker at the school? Wouldn't have found the index card? Hell, even without the card, we wouldn't have gone through the last website pages Wilson visited? I was doing that shit by rote."

Barnes exhaled. "Let's just do this."

"An hour ago you looked good," Franklin said. "Now you're back to looking like dog shit. Sneak-drinking?"

"No."

"Sure about that?" He patted Barnes's chest for a flask.

Barnes stared out the window.

Franklin shook his head. He drove down the lane toward the memorial center. They parked and got out. As they approached the doors, a woman came out of the building. She was mid to late fifties, dressed in a beige skirt suit. Her hair and glasses were secretarial. She turned to lock the door behind her, spoke over her shoulder. "Sorry, fellas," she said. "You need to make an appointment."

"Detroit Homicide," Franklin said.

They showed their badges.

"Oh," the woman said. She turned fully toward them. "You're the detective I talked to this morning?"

Franklin nodded. He pointed at himself with his pen. "Lieutenant Detective Franklin." He pointed the pen at Barnes. "Detective Barnes. You're Sharon Bruckheimer?"

"Yes."

"That's B-R-U-C-K . . ."

Barnes looked out across the sprawling cemetery. The grounds were hilly and the place was much larger than it first appeared. The headstones were neat and orderly. They brought to mind the homes on Kensington Street. Cookie-cutter. Here the only differences were the colors of the flowers left in the little brass tubes at each of the graves. Some had no flowers at all. Barnes's heart rate doubled when he noted a massive red cedar near the back fence.

"So what's this all about?" Sharon Bruckheimer said.

"We're investigating a multiple homicide, ma'am," Franklin said. "One of the victims was Dale Wilson. As I explained on the phone, on the night Wilson died, he called your number. His former wife is buried here."

"As I told you earlier, no messages were left."

"We thought we might investigate the grounds," Franklin said.

"It was the Pickax Man, wasn't it?"

"That's confidential, ma'am," Franklin said.

Sharon Bruckheimer frowned. "Well, I'm running late. There's a guidebook in that box over there." She pointed at a mailbox back at the fork in the road. "If you need to find a particular grave, it will help you."

"Might you have seen anyone around, checking out multiple graves here in the last few days?"

"I'm usually just in and out," she said, "and we tend to offer privacy to the people who come here. Oftentimes they're in a fragile state, as you can imagine."

Franklin nodded.

"Is there anything else?"

"No, ma'am," Franklin said, handing her a card, "but please call if you think of anything else."

She snatched the card and started toward the back of the building where there was a small employee parking lot. Two cars. One was a sedan precisely the same color as Sharon Bruckheimer's suit, the other an older-model pickup truck. Looked like a maintenance vehicle.

"One more question, ma'am," Barnes said.

She stopped, looked back.

"Are there any other employees on the premises right now?"

"One of the groundskeepers might be here," she said. She looked back at the truck. "Antonio." She put a hand above her eyes and looked out over the cemetery. "Could be he's out back or in the shed. Feel free to look for him."

"Antonio got a last name?"

"Reyes."

The detectives exchanged a glance. "Is he legal?" Franklin said.

"As legal as you are," she said.

"Does he speak English?"

She seesawed her hand and shrugged.

The detectives stayed put while Sharon Bruckheimer got into the beige sedan. She started her car and pulled out of the parking lot. Franklin waved as she went and then turned to Barnes. "Reyes?"

"Yeah," Barnes said. "Plus there's that cedar tree out back." He pointed. "It'll have the same leaves as the one I found on the Wilsons' back patio. But here's the problem: Calavera speaks fluent English. I've heard him plenty of times on the machine. And he writes those elaborate poems. I'm not sure a guy who speaks"—he seesawed his hand like Sharon Bruckheimer did—"so-so English can be our guy."

"Let's go find out," Franklin said. "Which way?"

Barnes knew the way to his brother's grave. The boy was buried in the Land of Cherubs, a section reserved for children ten years or younger. Ricky had barely made the cut. If they stayed to the right, and then took the next right when the gravel road forked again, they'd eventually wind their way to it. The idea of seeing his brother's headstone sent a frightening pain through Barnes's body. "Let's go this way," he said, pointing the other way. "Check the shed first."

They opened the shed's service door. Inside were backhoes and lawn mowers, various tools of the trade, and a half dozen pickaxes against the far wall. Franklin called into the depths of the shed. "Antonio?"

No reply.

They exited the shed and took the left-hand path up the cemetery grounds. Barnes reached into his interior jacket pocket to find his Batman coin purse. He palmed it and kept it hidden from Franklin's sight. He squeezed it to open the mouth, touched the quarters inside, closed it again. Over and over. He'd done the same thing ten years ago when he visited, and ten years before that at his brother's funeral. His parents, the police, and a therapist told him Ricky's death wasn't his fault. They told him it could have happened to anyone.

They crested the first hill. Barnes pointed. "There."

In the distance there was a man working next to a dark-green golf cart. He wore light-gray coveralls, work gloves, and a black baseball cap pulled low over his eyes. His back was to them, and he was raking a pile of wet leaves toward two large garbage cans strapped to the back of the cart. The cart was parked in an area of old-growth trees and high, bulky headstones. The area was at the base of a hill that rose toward the back of the cemetery and was dotted with hillside crypts. The detectives moved off the gravel and onto the grass. They came silently along the road.

The hair on Barnes's neck stood up. He dismissed the feeling, thinking it had something to do with being in this place with his brother. *Catching Calavera won't be this easy.* His hand pumped the coin purse.

They came within seventy yards of the man and stopped. Barnes heard the swishing of his leaf rake echoing off the headstones around them.

Franklin called out, "Antonio?"

The man stopped raking. His head moved slightly toward them, but his body didn't turn.

Barnes and Franklin exchanged a glance.

Barnes put the coin purse away, put his hand on his Glock.

"Detroit Homicide," Franklin said. They stepped closer to the man, slowly. "We're here to ask you a few questions."

"I'll be right over."

Barnes stiffened at the sound of the man's voice. There wasn't a hint of accent, no struggle with word command. "It's him," he said sotto voce. He drew his gun. Franklin did the same. "Why don't you just stay right there? We'll come to you."

Calavera still hadn't turned to look at them. He ignored Barnes's command and walked toward the golf cart, which was pointing directly away from their position.

"Hold it right there," Franklin bellowed.

Calavera slid the leaf rake, handle first, into a garbage can and hopped into the golf cart on the driver's side. Barnes and Franklin separated. They moved in opposite directions to cover the cart from two sides. Between the headstones, they were like bishops running diagonally on a chessboard. Barnes caught flashes of the golf cart as the graves alternately blocked and opened sightlines.

"Hands up, now!" Franklin said.

Calavera put his hands high above his head, but they were hidden by the cart's convex roof. Barnes thought he saw something metallic in Calavera's right hand as it went up. "Drop your weapon!"

"Is that you, Barnes?" Calavera said. He was still facing the opposite direction but turned his head slightly toward Barnes's voice. "Well, hey, ten-three, good buddy."

Multiple surges of fear washed over Barnes—residual moments of the deaths he'd suffered. He felt a punch to his chest, a break in his clavicle, a pop of his spine.

"Drop the gun!" Franklin said. He dropped to a knee behind a headstone at twenty yards from the golf cart. Barnes was rounding the cart from behind, a distance of thirty yards. He still couldn't see the man's face.

Calavera fired at Franklin. A bullet pinged off stone.

"Son of a bitch," Franklin said. He ducked down and ripped off three aimless shots, gun hand over the top of his cover.

Calavera slid to the ground beyond the cart.

Barnes ran sideways to cut off an escape route. He called to Franklin. "You all right?"

"I'm fine!"

Barnes charged the cart, gun up. No one there. Only a hat and gloves. He stayed low as he scanned the area, couldn't see shit with all the headstones. He moved up one row. Heard distant movement. Saw nothing.

There—a flash of gray two rows down. He fired. Missed.

Franklin fired. Missed.

Calavera fired back.

The detectives moved up and up, securing each row as they went.

There, a sugar skull above a headstone. He was already at the back of the cemetery, up against a cyclone fence covered with ivy. The mask's dead eyes were fixed on Barnes. He fired and missed. The mask dropped out of sight.

"He's at the back," Barnes called out. "Near the fence."

Franklin charged ahead, staying low. He ducked behind the entrance to a family crypt set into the hillside. RUTHERFORD was carved into the marble above the door—a brown wooden rectangle with iron brackets and bolts. Franklin leaned against it, handgun ready.

"I'll cover you," Franklin said. "Come up." He stepped around the side of the crypt and lit up the hillside with bullets. They pinged off the headstones, sending white-and-gray puffs into the air.

Barnes charged up and past the crypt, took shelter behind a headstone. He scanned the hillside and the back fence, eyes just over the top of the granite like an alligator in a river. A gate was now open, a swinging door of ivy.

"See him?" Franklin said.

"He's gone out the back gate," Barnes said. "Cover me." He moved up three rows, expecting to hear his partner's covering gunfire. Instead he heard shattering glass. He took cover. "What the hell, man?"

Silence.

Barnes looked back down the hill. Saw only rows of headstones and the grassy rooftops of the hillside crypts, each one with a stained-glass skylight. He moved down a row, peeked cautiously around a granite stone. His heart seized when he saw the diamond-shaped skylight above the Rutherford crypt was now a dark hole that dropped down into the chamber.

Barnes ran down the hill. He put his back up against the wall of the crypt, steadied himself, and turned the corner, gun aimed.

The crypt door was open.

"Franklin?"

The only reply was a wet gurgle. In the distance Barnes heard an engine turn over and then start. Tires squealed on pavement. He pushed the door fully open. William Franklin was lying facedown on the crypt floor with a bowie knife stuck in his back.

15

"Don't die, you bastard," Barnes said. He'd called in a *ten-double-zero—officer down* and was applying pressure to the wound with a compress he'd torn from his shirt and wrapped around the base of the knife. Franklin's blood was bright red. Lung blood. The shirt material was too thin, and the blood bubbled up between Barnes's fingers and over the backs of his hands.

"Pull the knife out." The crack addict.

"No. You're supposed to leave it in." The mother.

"Shhh."

"Son of a bitch," Franklin said. He spat a glob of red across the crypt floor. "He pulled that door open. I was leaning on it. Fell right in."

"Don't talk," Barnes said.

"Listen," Franklin said. "Don't let him get to you. Go see Watkins."

"Watkins?"

"Stay off that machine. Stay out of my head."

Distant sirens wailed.

"Quiet," Barnes said. "They're coming. You're going to get through this. I won't need the machine because you're going to tell me exactly what you saw."

Franklin's eyes lost focus. His pupils dilated. He whispered something unintelligible.

"Shut up!" Barnes said. The sirens were close now. The ambulance lights spilled through the open door and ran across the crypt walls. Franklin was still whispering. Barnes leaned in close.

"Barker just gonna pop another one up," Franklin said. "It don't matter."

"If it don't matter, then what have you been doing all these years, huh?" Barnes said. "Why get a degree in criminal justice? Why walk a beat? Why make detective? You're full of shit, you know that?"

"Fuck you, Barnes," Franklin said. He closed his eyes. "Fuck you."

Warden was first through the crypt door, the machine in tow. Martinez stayed outside, as there was little room to maneuver inside the crypt.

"Get that thing out of here," Barnes said.

Warden said, "We need to do this while—"

Barnes turned on him. "I said get that goddamn thing out of here."

"You're interfering with an investigation," Warden said. He held battery-operated clippers and was coming down toward Franklin's head with them. "Step out of the way."

Barnes held the bloody compress in his left hand, used his right to loose his Glock and place the barrel against Warden's forehead.

Warden stopped cold. His beady eyes widened.

"Jesus Christ," Captain Darrow said. He stood, arms folded, at the mouth of the crypt. "Get that thing out of here, Warden."

Warden backed the machine out of the crypt. Barnes released the compress and followed.

The paramedics stormed in.

Barnes wiped his hands clean while an ambulance hauled Franklin away. He was still alive, still breathing when the paramedics loaded him into the ambulance.

"I'm gonna overlook that little stunt you just pulled," Darrow said, looking off.

"Like hell you will!" Warden said. He was fuming, the red-dot indent of Barnes's gun barrel visible on his forehead.

"Can it, Warden," Darrow said. "Get your ass to the hospital and follow up with Franklin. Now!"

Warden stomped off.

"Don't put him on the machine," Barnes said. "He'll live. Besides, we'll get what we need from Bruckheimer."

"It's not your call," Darrow said.

Barnes sighed. "I moved ahead too quickly. I left him behind."

"Put it in your report," Darrow said. "Right now we need to go after Reyes. There's an APB on his truck and his plate. We got his home address from the cemetery's employee records. SWAT's gearing up."

Barnes rode in the passenger seat, head against the glass, while Darrow drove. He picked dried blood from beneath his fingernails. His cell phone buzzed. A text message from Jessica.

Maybe Detective Mackey will come by my place tonight around dinnertime, see what I've got cooking?

Barnes didn't reply. He slid the phone back into his pocket, turned his head away from Captain Darrow, and watched the asphalt speed by, the white line on the side of the road. It was like the car was a rolled-up dollar bill inhaling cocaine at an absurd speed. He imagined the car veering off and colliding with a concrete barrier, imagined the impact, his body crashing through the glass and landing outside, busted up like a rag doll. Some housewife might stop her car and get out, come running. She'd throw her hands to her cheeks and say, *Oh my God, oh my God.* And someone else might say, *Somebody call for help,* even though they have a phone in their hand. Later, someone might put a roadside memorial there, on the very spot, and for a few months people would say, *That's where that policeman died.* But soon they'd forget what happened, and they'd wonder what those wilted flowers and that wreath were about. The memorial would eventually be removed, or maybe it would just fall over, and Barnes's blood and bones and teeth would decay and become dust and pebbles on the side of the road. Hundreds and millions of people would drive by, just talking or listening to the latest pop sensation on their radios.

It was the very thing Ricky had feared, even as a young boy. Irrelevance. Maybe he'd had a sense he wouldn't live long. He'd always asked, "What if I was gone? What would you do?"

Barnes had always made a joke of it. "I'd eat your dessert and sell your GI Joes to Candy Harper."

Ricky would hug his knees to his chest and stare off. "Would you really eat my dessert?"

"Hell yeah."

"What if Mom stopped making dessert? I mean, because I was dead and all."

"What if I body-slammed you on a bed of thumbtacks?"

A smirk. "You can try."

Reyes's apartment was on the first floor of a twenty-story apartment building. The superintendent shook his head when they described Reyes.

"Sounds vaguely familiar," he said. "I've only been the super here a few years, though. He pays his rent, fellas. That's all I can say."

The SWAT team was collected outside the apartment door. The super tiptoed down the hall with his master key. He tried it, but the lock wouldn't turn. He whispered, "Must have changed the locks."

The SWAT commander signaled for the compact battering ram. Two uniforms brought it up. They slammed the door open, and SWAT stormed the apartment while Barnes and Darrow waited in the hallway.

A moment later the SWAT commander came out, shaking his head. "No one lives here, boys."

Barnes went inside. The apartment seemed set up for a new renter. The walls were painted stark white and were seemingly untouched. No furniture. No bed. No silverware in the drawers. An empty canvas.

"What about his mail?" Barnes said. "His paychecks from the cemetery? They have to go somewhere." He went back down the hall to the building's foyer. There were several mailboxes along the wall—the flat, aluminum kind with a slot for sliding in letters. One of them was stuffed to the point where no more junk mail could fit inside. It had several official notices stuck to it, letting the occupant know they could pick up their undelivered mail at the post office.

Barnes approached the box. He lifted a folded-over letter to read the name. REYES.

"Don't touch it," Darrow said. He turned to a nearby officer. "Have it dusted."

Barnes went back to the empty apartment.

Kendra MacKenzie felt the emptiness of the room like suffocation. It reminded her of the room in which she'd spent so many years as an invalid. *"I want out of here."*

"Shhh."

Barnes stood in the living room while the crime scene techs buzzed here and there, printing what they could, tweezing strands of hair from the sinks, scooping dust bunnies from the corners of the closets. Captain Darrow stood watch, arms folded, scowling. The apartment felt more like a tomb than the Rutherford crypt. It was a whitewash devoid of life, warmth, or anything remotely human. It might as well have been outer space or a sensory-deprivation chamber. The walls could be padded.

"Excuse me, Detective?"

Barnes turned to the voice. It was the building superintendent. He stood behind the yellow-and-black tape loosely hanging at waist height across the doorway. "Yes?"

"I remembered something about Mr. Reyes. Something I didn't think of before."

"What is it?" Darrow said.

The super moved his eyes to the captain. "He had his name changed a while back. We had to do paperwork to get everything straightened out. Did it all over the phone. He sent me his new documents in the mail."

"Do you remember his old name?"

The super shook his head.

"Do you have the paperwork?"

"It's not kept here, but the building owners might have it."

"Who are they?"

"I work for a company. Rock Hill Management. Based in Florida."

Barnes closed his eyes, gripped the bridge of his nose.

"Thanks," Darrow said.

The super left.

"I'll have Flaherty follow it up," Darrow said.

"Flaherty? You kidding me?" Chunk Philips's voice.

Darrow stared at Barnes, unblinking.

It took a moment for Barnes to realize Chunk Philips's voice had escaped his mouth without his consent. The thought had moved too fast, had taken control, if only momentarily. Barnes felt a new weight on him, something clawing at him, pulling him down by the arms and shoulders. It felt like he was standing knee-deep in the ocean, holding a Ping-Pong paddle and hoping to beat back the waves.

He stepped toward the apartment's sliding glass door, which led to a tiny concrete-slab patio that ended a few feet short of the parking lot. He pulled the handle to slide the door open but found it wouldn't budge; a wooden dowel rod was laid on the tracks. Barnes smirked. He picked the rod up off the tracks, opened the door, and took the rod outside with him. He stood on the slab and looked over a parking lot filled with sedans, pickups, and cruisers while turning the dowel in his hand. He stopped turning it when his fingers brushed something against the side. He peeled away a USB drive taped to the wood. On the drive, written in black Magic Marker, was BARNES.

16

Barnes parked in the alley behind Ziti's Sub and Grub in Corktown. He killed the engine and rubbed his hands over his face. The alley stank of grease and rotted onions. The dumpster against the cinder-block wall, which separated the alley from a barren field, had seen cleaner days, maybe during the Carter administration. Barnes tucked his badge and holster beneath the passenger seat. He got out of the car and walked past the dumpster, looked over the wall through curled, rusty barbwire. The field beyond had once been a crime scene. A teenage boy, Andy Kemp, had been kidnapped and killed, his body concealed in an abandoned house that was once out there among the weeds and chattering insects.

Kemp had started out as an Amber Alert, shifted to a missing person, and ended as a homicide. The case had lingered in the news for weeks after the body was found, not just for obvious reasons but also for the fact that the boy was discovered with $10,000 in his pocket. That brought national attention—reporters from bigger cities.

Years later the boy's murder was still unsolved, the money never explained. It'd been Barnes's first case as a detective, though only as an assistant lent to Homicide from Vice as part of rotation training. His primary job was to observe, take notes, and keep quiet while Franklin and Watkins did their thing. Secondarily, he was to follow up with the boy's extended family members and friends to get an idea of what the kid was like.

Turned out Andy Kemp was a bad seed. Parents and teachers spoke highly of him, said he loved the arts, excelled at writing, and even talked of becoming a police officer someday, but a few cousins and the kids at school told tales of trouble. Some bore witness to animal abuse and pyromania. One cousin showed a scar Andy had given her. She'd lied to her parents about it, scared of her cousin's retaliation. She was one of many who felt Andy Kemp got what he deserved in that abandoned house.

The machine was in its early stages back then; only a few precincts in Michigan had one, though the black market was burgeoning nationwide. They'd used it on what was left of Andy Kemp, hoping to glean something of his killer's identity. Watkins had been the one to get hooked in. He'd reported that the boy's memory pull was a dud. Considering the state of the body, there was no wonder.

Several years ago a gang of local parents had burned down the abandoned house in some misguided protest. Something about it being a place for evildoers to lure children, as though there weren't dozens of similarly abandoned homes nearby. They stood around the blaze with picket signs and grim faces, speaking to reporters about how Andy Kemp was the victim of a system gone wrong and how his murderer was a product of corrupted government. There was a black crater there now, where the building had burned down, where the boy had rotted. No plan to rebuild.

Apart from a handful of the boy's friends and cousins, Barnes was one of the few people who knew Andy Kemp was no one's victim but a bully and likely a burgeoning sociopath. The cousin with the scar had told him Andy was good at hiding. "He knew how to act," she said, "for parents and teachers and stuff. But most of the time it was like he wasn't there. Like, he'd have this blank look on his face all the time, like he was one of those chocolate Easter bunnies. Empty."

A munky appeared at the alley mouth. He was fidgeting in a Pistons jersey worn over stained jean shorts and loose-fitting high-tops. His head was shaved completely bald; suction-cup marks stood out on his temples. "Hey man, hey," he said, "you got a fifty spot? I'll pay you back. I need a tank of gas."

"A tank of gas?"

The main pointed aimlessly. "My family's right around the corner, waiting on me."

"Where are you headed?"

He blinked and found focus. "Huh?"

"You and your family," Barnes said. "Where are you headed?"

"Oh yeah, yeah, yeah," the man said. "We're going down to Ohio. Pick up some fireworks for the Fourth."

"It's September," Barnes said.

"Next year, man, next year. Ha, ha, ha."

"I don't have any money for you."

The man shook his head violently. "No, no, no. I gotta get back to Marie." He crossed his arms over his chest, gripped himself as though he were freezing. He blinked and shivered. "Who are you?" His voice had become like that of a woman.

"Go home. Get some sleep."

"Eat me, buddy, huh?" the woman said. "You prick. Don't tell me what to do." She gripped her crotch and jostled it obscenely.

"Don't forget your family."

The man's face dropped. "My family? What you talkin' now?"

"Around the corner."

"Boy, you on something. You're the one who needs to *go home and get some sleep*." She sauntered away, hips swishing, elbow cocked to support an imaginary purse strap, palm up.

Barnes went to the back of the sub shop. He knocked on a gray steel door, waited a moment, saw a blink of shadow behind the peephole. He waved. Locks clicked and clacked. The door swung open. A tattooed man with a buzz cut stood in the doorway, his arms folded over his chest. He wore a black T-shirt, army-green shorts, and combat boots. He side-nodded, letting Barnes know he could enter.

Barnes stepped inside. He looked past the boxes and canned supplies to see into the kitchen. The shop hustled and bustled. Orders were shouted, knives banged against cutting boards, soup vats steamed. The scents were mouthwatering. To his immediate left there was an old stairwell—steep, thin, damp. He stepped down into the darkness.

The first room at the bottom of the staircase was akin to a root cellar. Boxes of iceberg lettuce, bags of onions, crates of tomatoes. At the far end there was an industrial-size refrigerator. Barnes went to the fridge, stepped around and behind it, moved along the back wall. The space was hardly big enough for him to squeeze through. He came to a steel door and knocked on it. There was no peephole, but a mail slot cut into the door at eye height. The slot opened. A pair of familiar eyes met Barnes's own.

"Mr. Hyde!" the man behind the door said. "What's shakin'?"

Barnes produced a fifty-dollar bill and held it up to the slot.

"Well, then," the man said, "come on in."

The door opened and Barnes entered the room. The man who'd let him in stepped aside, showed him the way forward with an outstretched arm. Barnes didn't know the man's name, had never asked and never would. He'd dubbed him *Raphael*, due to the two katana knives he always wore, which resembled the weapons of the Teenage Mutant Ninja Turtle of the same name. The blades were crisscrossed and tucked into his jeans below a plain white T-shirt, the shirt bunched up behind the handles. He wasn't bald and his temples weren't shaved. Barnes assumed he followed the old drug dealer's code: *Don't get high off your own supply.*

Along the far wall there were three machines and three hospital beds. One of the beds was currently occupied. A woman. She was hooked in, up on her knees and elbows and looking back with her eyes open but seeing only what was being pumped into her skull. She thrust back repeatedly against whoever was there in her mind. Her eyes fluttered in ecstasy. She gnashed at the bit between her teeth.

Barnes looked at Raphael.

Raphael popped his eyebrows and said, "Keisha Clarke."

The woman was tapped into the Hollywood starlet, now disgraced. She'd dated a litany of leading men in her time, and had been threatening to sell her memories for years. Barnes said, "She finally cashed in?"

"Sure did. Her time with Brad Cousins has been selling like . . . you know what, what the hell is a hotcake?"

Barnes shrugged, handed Raphael his money.

"So what's it going to be then, Mr. Hyde?" Raphael said. He slipped the fifty into his back pocket. "Pinball Pete's? Marvin's Marvelous?"

"Putt 'n Games."

"Ah, yes," Raphael said, "the old standby. Get comfy, will ya?" He patted the nearest hospital bed and began typing on the nearby machine's keyboard.

Barnes removed his jacket, rolled up his sleeve. He sat down on the bed, the Batman coin purse concealed in his left hand.

"Got you a clean one," Raphael said, handing Barnes a bit with only a few teeth marks. "Did I ever tell you the one about the barber and the shaving ball?"

"Only every time I come in here," Barnes said.

"It's a good one, though, ain't it?"

"It is," Barnes said. He lay down on the bed, giving his arm to Raphael. The man tied on a rubber strap and inserted the needle, slick as a nurse. He applied the suction cups to Barnes's temples. Barnes put in his bit and closed his eyes.

Edith MacKenzie thought of the rubber tie-downs that'd held her in place in that chair in her living room. *"I don't like this."*

"Shhh."

"Here we go," Raphael said.

The serum moved through Barnes, cooled him. He heard the click of the machine, the hiss.

"Take me out to the ball game," Raphael sang, his voice whispery, dreamlike. "Take me out with the crowd . . ."

Barnes smiled. Through the bit he sang, "Buy me some peanuts and Cracker J—" The machine's surge arched his body. The Vitruvian Man test pattern appeared. "Prepare for transmission."

Barnes smelled the plastic of new arcade-game cabinets, like the interiors of new cars. The man who'd sold this particular memory, Eli, had a photographic mind—an extremely sellable talent in this black market. While sitting on the machine and being recorded, he'd been able to recall an entire youthful afternoon at the arcade. Inside Putt 'n Games it was warm. The sounds of the arcade games layered upon one another with bleeps and lasers and explosions. The casual ear could pick out Pac-Man and Donkey Kong, maybe Galaga. The trained ear, however, could tell right away whether someone was playing Karnov, Arkanoid, or Gauntlet, even though Gauntlet was all the way in the back corner. Barnes's ear was tuned in for the pro-wrestling game Mania Challenge. He'd have to wait to play.

Young Eli started with Tecmo Bowl. The football game was against a wall and tucked between the skee-balls and drop-claws. The sound was broken. He played while stealing embarrassed glimpses at the bikini poster halfway hidden behind one of the drop-claw machines. It was an ad for the movie *Ski School 2*.

Bored with football but with his hormones raging, Eli moved over to Rampage. At the console he took control of Lizzie, the giant lizard, while his friend Marky took Ralph, the giant wolf. They dropped in their quarters and set out to destroy Peoria, Illinois. Another kid came by and almost made it a three-man game by taking over George, the giant gorilla, but he chose to play Contra instead, which was situated right next to Rampage. There were thunderous crashes, screams, whizzing bullets. Eli and Marky crushed buildings and saved distressed damsels. Marky forced Ralph to punch a neon sign and get electrocuted, which in turn made the boy giggle. He laughed even harder when he made Ralph eat a soldier carrying a flamethrower to give the giant wolf heartburn, making him spit flames. Eli made Lizzie knock helicopters from the sky and pulverize towers.

A few more games and the boys quit. They wandered over to the food counter where they ate pizza off greasy paper plates. Barnes tasted the gummy cheese, the bland pepperoni. Eli's fountain Coke was watery but good and cold.

Once Eli was down to his last quarter, he went to Mania Challenge. As the boy approached the game, Barnes's heart began to pound. It'd taken him years on the machine to find the game, and then to find Eli, the man with the vivid memory. As a boy Eli had mastered Mania Challenge. He could take on all comers, and the computer didn't stand a chance, even at the highest levels. He played for an hour while Barnes sat in placid fascination. He'd memorized all Eli's moves but still reveled in every punch, every kick, every flying leap from the top rope. The referee counted "one, two, three" over and over again as Eli defeated all who stood in his path. And then, very abruptly, the boy just walked away from the cabinet.

Darkness and silence.

"End of transmission."

The Vitruvian Man test pattern.

Please Stand By.

Barnes opened his eyes to find Raphael sitting back in a rolling chair, smiling at him. "There's Dr. Jekyll."

The room was empty now. The woman who'd played the part of Keisha Clarke was gone, but the scent of her virtual encounter hung in the air. Barnes fished in his pockets to find another fifty-dollar bill and the USB drive he'd collected from Reyes's empty apartment. He held them out for Raphael to take.

"What's this?" Raphael said. He took the money and the drive.

Barnes shrugged and lay back, the bit still in his mouth. He closed his eyes to the sound of Raphael inserting the USB drive into the machine. Heard the turning dials, the clacking keys. Raphael said, "Looks like just one file on here. It's named Napoleon and Squealer, all one word."

Barnes nodded and closed his eyes.

"Here it comes," Raphael said.

A click and a hiss. The Vitruvian Man. "Prepare for transmission."

Barnes's body arched.

Antonio Reyes sat in a lawn chair in his empty apartment. The sliding-glass door was closed, drapes pulled across it. The only light source was a single lamp on the floor. The carpet was covered in clear, thick plastic, and lying in the center of the room there were two men, facedown. Each wore a dark leather jacket and black pants. With their faces turned away, they were nearly indistinguishable from each other.

Barnes looked down to find his hands screwing a silencer into the end of a handgun. Slowly, methodically, his fingers turned the silencer down into the barrel. Barnes's vision was limited by two holes. His face was hot and sweaty. Something on it. A mask.

"Umph."

Reyes looked up. One of the men was moving now, squirming like a worm. His strange hands—more like hooves, really—were bound behind the back. His ankles were bound as well.

Reyes stood up. He went over to the man and helped him into a kneeling position from behind. The man said something, but only a muffled sound came out. There was duct tape wrapped several times around his head, over his mouth.

The other man stirred. Reyes helped him into a kneeling position as well. He stood behind the two men while they struggled with their restraints and screamed muffled threats from their taped mouths. From behind, it seemed their heads were improperly shaped. Their ears were huge and all wrong; their shoulders were sloping and strange.

Reyes walked around in front of them, the handgun trembling in his hands. Barnes felt confused by what he saw. The two men were not men at all, but pigs. This was no Hollywood makeup job, no CGI. The things before him were pigs dressed and loosely shaped like men. Their eyes were beady and black, their snouts wet and searching, their ears pink and wide.

Their muffled sounds were squeals.

Reyes placed his silenced handgun against the first pig's forehead. He said, "Squealer," and pulled the trigger. The sound was like a punched pillow. The pig's body rocked back and then fell forward as Reyes stepped out of the way. It slumped down and the blood began to seep onto the plastic.

The other was screaming now. Its black eyes were wide and moving crazily. Its body quaked. It closed its eyes when Barnes placed the gun against its forehead. Its squeal was still muffled beneath the tape, but a single, repeated word could be made out. "Please."

Reyes said, "Napoleon," and pulled the trigger. Whump. The pig's body fell straight back over its cracking knees.

Reyes stood still, listening to the sound of blood pooling out over plastic. In his mind's eye there was a girl. Twelve years old, maybe thirteen. She was dark-skinned and pretty, plucking petals from a daisy beneath an apple tree. A tightening pain gripped Barnes's chest. His skin tingled. Endorphins rushed his mind. Reyes's love for this girl was overwhelming.

Reyes blinked. The scene in his mind turned to horror. The girl was no longer beneath a tree, but tied spread-eagle to a twin bed, her naked body slashed apart, her faced carved into a sugar-skull mask.

Darkness and silence.

"End of transmission."

The Vitruvian Man test pattern.

Please Stand By.

17

Barnes walked through a set of automatic doors at Sinai Grace Hospital, a half-empty pint of Jim Beam in his jacket pocket. The hallway floor had been recently buffed. It reflected the overhead fluorescent lights like squiggly equals signs chasing one another around. He entered Franklin's single-bed room to find Warden, Martinez, and a doctor crowded inside. Warden and Martinez monitored the machine's progress. The doctor stood at the foot of the bed, holding a chart and scowling at the technicians. The machine's suction cups were attached to Franklin's fresh bald spots, the needle in his arm. His big body was tensed from the flow. The heart monitor blipped slowly. An accordion-like machine seemed to be breathing for him.

"Take that thing off him," Barnes said. His breath tasted boozy coming out.

"Captain's orders," Warden said without looking up. "You know that."

"Take it off!" Barnes's hand came halfway to the butt of his handgun.

Warden turned to match Barnes's gaze.

"Who is this?" the doctor said to Warden.

Warden gave no reply. He kept his eyes on Barnes.

"If you're not necessary to the operation of his device," the doctor said, "then please leave."

Barnes wouldn't release Warden's stare.

"I said *get out*," the doctor said.

"You know it's not what he wanted," Barnes said.

"Don't tell me what I know," Warden said.

"You're making a mistake."

"Am I, munky? Or is it drunky these days?"

"Oh, hell no." The crack addict.

"Shhh."

Barnes left the room. He sat down outside, eyes fixed on Warden through the plate glass. The doctor left and a nurse went in. She maneuvered around the technicians to tend to Franklin's life-preserving instruments, unable to conceal her annoyance at the police presence.

Barnes drank from his pint.

Martinez came out of the room. She took the seat next to Barnes and sighed.

"What are you sighing about?" Barnes said.

No response.

Barnes turned to her. She looked tired, and she looked Mexican. "You celebrate the Day of the Dead?"

"Gimme a break," Martinez said.

"Maybe you know this Reyes, huh?"

"Hey, asshole, I was born in this country, just like you."

"You didn't answer my first question." Barnes faced forward, took a pull.

"I don't celebrate the Day of the Dead." She paused for a moment. "But my parents do. At least, they used to."

"I've researched it," Barnes said. "Read a hundred books, a thousand web pages. *A celebration and remembrance of those who have passed.* Tell me something I don't know."

Martinez shrugged. "My parents were illegal immigrants. They crossed over in California, where they had my brother and I. We stayed maybe ten years, and then came up to Michigan for the farming seasons. While we were still in California, they used to take us down to the border on the second of November, which was as close as we could get to the graves of our loved ones. We'd bring coffee and tequila, and my mother would make sugar skulls. Dad would spill the drinks out onto the ground."

"I said tell me something I *don't* know."

Martinez shifted in her chair. "My mother cried for days afterward. She thought it was shameful that she couldn't actually visit her mother's and father's graves. Now we don't even go to the border anymore. Can't afford the trip. Instead they just put up an altar, and we celebrate Christmas and pass out Halloween candy, just like you."

"Calavera mentioned an altar. I've read about them, but tell me, from a personal standpoint, what's the significance?"

"Basically it's what you've read. A memorial. Framed photos, colored candles and sugar skulls, tamales and tequila and sweetbreads, whatever else the dead preferred in life. It's not supposed to be sad but joyful."

"Don't be sad. Be joyful." A killer's voice.

"Shhh."

"Your parents," Barnes said. "Did they ever lose their accents?"

Martinez laughed. "You kidding? To this day they hardly know two words of English."

The nurse came out of Franklin's room. "Detective Barnes, you're wasting your time here. Please go. Sober up. Come back tomorrow."

"He's my partner," Barnes said.

"And he's *my* patient," the nurse said. She was a hardened warrior of the ICU, used to dealing with emotional family members, drunks, angry outbursts. Barnes could make no argument she wasn't ready to knock down. He studied her name tag. JUDY. He stood and held out a card for her to take. For a moment she stared at the bottle sticking out of his pocket. Eventually she took the card.

"Please call me with any news."

John Barnes grew up in a trailer park called Flamingo Farms. The park was nestled deep in the trees of Whitehall Forest. There was no sign at the road, only a gravel two-track that you'd probably miss if you weren't looking for it. As boys, Johnny and Ricky didn't know they were poor. They lived in a forest, for Pete's sake. All those suckers on the other side of Calvary Junction lived in subdivisions where the lawns were mowed diagonally and the neighbors shook fists at kids who ran across them. Those kids took vacations to the kind of place Johnny and Ricky lived year-round. They could keep their jet skis and campers; Johnny and Ricky Barnes had their imaginations, their rivers, their trees. They played in them every day, and each night, around five thirty, Mom would lean out the side of their trailer and clang a triangle dinner bell, just like in some old TV show. The boys came flying back home like boomerangs.

Barnes wondered whether Jessica had grown up having dinner at five thirty, too. He hoped so, because it was five thirty and he found himself on the steps of her apartment, a finger above the doorbell next to her name. The umbrella woman on the second floor had smiled when he came up the sidewalk. He pressed the doorbell. He had stopped at a convenience store and guzzled a coffee in the parking lot, then packed his mouth full of those painful mints that came in a tin. He had checked his eyes in the mirror, too, but decided they were beyond repair.

Jessica's voice came through the speaker, only it was some kind of impersonation. Sounded like Julia Child. "Who is it?"

Barnes smiled. "Detective Mackey."

She held the impersonation. "What seems to be the trouble, Officer?"

"I received a call from this address," Barnes said. "Housewife in distress. Needs assistance."

"Well," she said, "in that case—" She coughed, laughed, dropped the impersonation. "My God, I can't do that for long. Come on up."

A buzzer sounded. The door latch clicked. Barnes pushed through and headed up the stairs. When he arrived on her floor, he found her peeking at him through her cracked-open apartment door. He could see just one eye, big and blue, and the scar on her eyebrow. A section of her smile was there, too. Her lipstick was red, her teeth a brilliant white. She opened the door fully as he approached. She was wearing an apron hand-printed in flour, and beneath that a dark-green blouse and blue jeans. Her skin glowed softly, backdropped by the light from inside her apartment. Her shape was accented by the middle tie of the apron.

"She's amazing." A lesbian's voice.

Jessica was so slight, Barnes wondered how she'd gotten him up the stairs and to her couch last night without him remembering it. It felt strange that a woman he barely knew had taken care of him like that.

She backed away from the door to let Barnes through. Her smile was playful and somehow familiar.

He said, "Hi."

She came close, looked up into his eyes, put a hand on his cheek. The sensation of her touch spilled down him, made his shoulder and chest muscles tingle. "Hi."

They stood there for a moment, unmoving, like bronze statues in a park. Alice in Chains was playing softly in the background, one of their lighter albums, *Jar of Flies*. The song was "Rotten Apple." Barnes felt both at home and uneasy in Jessica's presence. He said, "We barely know each other." It wasn't a word of warning, but of wonder.

Jessica's eyes brightened. "I know!" She laughed and spun away from him toward her small kitchen. He peeled off his jacket and holster, threw them over the back of a chair. Her apartment smelled of marinara sauce. He looked at the couch where he'd spent the night. Last night? It didn't seem possible. Surely a week had passed since then.

Jessica sighed as she stirred a wooden spoon in a saucepan, concentrating on the task.

"You okay?" Barnes said.

She stopped stirring and looked up. "I'm sorry I come on so strongly."

"No need to be sorry."

"No," she said, "it's important for me to say. My mom used to tell me I"—she threw up air quotes, one hand still holding the sauce-coated spoon—"'move too fast.' She said I create high expectations only to find disappointment, and that I should learn to take things more slowly."

Barnes fiddled with a pepper grinder on the countertop. "Sounds like good advice."

She watched him for a moment, pursing her lips. "I don't mind being hurt. What I mind is dishonesty. When I met you, I felt something. I'm acting on that feeling. Should I not?"

He shrugged. "I'm a guy."

"What's that supposed to mean?"

"Define *feeling*."

She smirked. "Okay, let's try this. Do you *feel* like eating steak?"

"Sure."

"Then you're effed; we're having spaghetti." She poured the sauce over a ceramic bowl of steaming noodles. "I know it's messy, and probably a terrible choice for a third date, but what the hell."

"This is a third date?"

"Yep. That's the rule these days. You don't sleep with a man until the third date, right?"

Barnes stood there pulling a dumbstruck face, hung on a hook like a skeleton in a science class.

Jessica laughed.

The table was set for two. Nothing fancy, but there was care in the placement. Blue-collar class. She twirled her spaghetti on a fork and took to eating with passion and joy. She crunched into homemade bruschetta and seemed to genuinely savor the taste. It was a wonderful thing to watch. For Barnes, the individual spices and textures came alive for him like they never had before. They drank a bottle of Pinot Noir that tasted better than its price tag. He was careful not to overdo it, knowing, after the pint of bourbon, too much more alcohol in his system and he'd be sloppy.

When dinner was over, Barnes went straight for cliché and helped her with the dishes, picking up the drying towel. She playfully plopped soap bubbles onto his nose and then said, "Oh my God, look at me. I'm like a desperate cougar on the Lifetime channel."

"Is that the channel with all the feelings?"

"You're gonna get it," she said, threatening him with the wooden spoon she was washing.

He took it from her and dried it.

Jessica took a long drink from her wineglass and then grabbed Barnes's wrist. He threw his drying towel over his shoulder as she pulled him across the room toward the couch. She guided him to it and set him down, stood above him, leaning in with both hands on his shoulders. She smelled like wildflowers and dish soap. She lowered her head. Her lips came to his ear. "I like you, Detective Barnes."

He shuddered, pulled an intake of breath. He felt something fall away inside, like a door knocked off its hinges and collapsing backward into his chest. A light shined in on the darkness and dust that was there. His body filled up with its warmth. Dale Wilson wanted to tell Jessica Taylor he loved her, but Barnes felt it was silly to say. His own love for her was not the love of a man and his wife of thirty years, not the love found in some movie where it takes two hours of pain and hilarity for Harry and Sally to admit it, but the simple love of a moment. This moment. The understanding of its gift. It was love in the only sense John Barnes understood it. His life was defined by a few blinding moments with long periods of darkness in between. This moment here, with her, could end right now, and it would still be one of the most brilliant pieces of his existence. He loved her for that gift and needed nothing more.

She backed away and sat down across from him on an armchair. She crossed her legs and smiled, took another sip from her glass. "Tell me more about Detroit homicide detective John Barnes."

Barnes shrugged. "What's there to say?"

"Anything," she said, gesturing with her wineglass. "Everything. Like, what's your favorite color?"

He glanced at her blouse. "Green."

"Favorite movie?"

"Memento."

"Oh my God." She sat forward. "That's the only movie I've ever watched where I immediately started it over and watched it again. It was totally insane. Favorite band?"

"Whatever's on WCSX."

"Any brothers or sisters?"

Barnes looked down, examined the floor, the tops of his shoes. He took a sip of wine.

"Eee . . . bad question?"

"No," he said, still looking down. "I have—*had*—one brother." He looked back up at her.

"I'm sorry," she said. "I don't mean to pry."

"It's okay. It's been a long time."

"He passed?"

He nodded.

"I'm sorry."

"Twenty years ago, last month. We buried him at Parkview Memorial. It's crazy; I was just out there today, following a lead."

"Did you visit him?"

"No."

She held his gaze for a moment, and then said, "Did you want to?"

Barnes took a beat. "I don't know."

Jessica sat back. She seemed to read him, like there were words all over his body. She set down her glass and stood. "Let's go."

"Where?"

"To Parkview Memorial."

"What? No."

"Bullshit. We're going."

Barnes checked his watch: 8:30 p.m. "It'll be closed by now."

"So?" She went to the kitchen, began rummaging around in the drawers. After a moment she found what she was seeking. Out of a drawer came a Ziploc sandwich bag.

Barnes went to her. "What are you doing?"

"Just give me a second."

Jessica went to the cupboard and found a blue canister of Morton salt. She poured about a quarter cup into the sandwich bag, then zipped it up. She pocketed it.

"What's that for?"

"You'll see," she said. She put her arm inside of his and pulled him out of the apartment. They walked together down the stairs.

The cemetery was, as expected, closed. Visiting hours had ended at 8:00 p.m. Barnes drove around to the employee parking lot he'd noted earlier that day. They got out and walked toward the fence. It looked easy enough to hop and gain entry. Barnes scanned the area, saw no cause for concern; the security camera on the nearby fence post was a fake. He offered to help Jessica over, but she shoved him aside and scaled the fence like she'd done it a thousand times.

Maybe she had.

Barnes followed her in.

His feet went cold when they touched the ground on the other side. The sensation sent a chill up through him, brought back the same pain from earlier that day. He backed up against the fence, shook his head.

"I got you," Jessica said, returning her arm to his. She pulled him close and walked him down the gravel path. They stopped at the first fork in the road. Barnes clicked on his flashlight and shined it up and over toward the distant Rutherford crypt. It was closed off by crime scene tape. Barnes recalled the smell of Franklin's blood, felt it on his hands. He swallowed hard and wished for a drink. Jessica pulled him along. They took a right at the fork, and then another right at the next. Soon they were in the Land of Cherubs.

Barnes stopped walking. "You don't understand." He heard Ricky's voice in his ears, *"Come on, Johnny,"* followed by a sound like gunshot. He heard stained glass shattering, then Franklin's voice, wet and weak, *"Barker just gonna pop another one up."*

"I do understand," Jessica said. She turned to face him, put a hand on either side of his face. "You're wounded, John. I can see it in you. You're haunted."

"I don't see how this will help."

"It will." She grabbed his wrist and pulled him forward, but he didn't move.

"It didn't help before."

She stared at him, still clutching his wrist. He could feel she was a little shaky, maybe a little scared. "Trust me," she said, and tugged again at his wrist.

Barnes let her drag him along. Eventually he took the lead and walked with his head down. He hadn't come to his brother's grave in more than ten years, but he weaved his way through the headstones as though following a beaten path.

RICHARD MATTHEW BARNES

My candle burns at both ends,
It will not last the night.
But ah, my foes, and oh, my friends,
It gives a lovely light.

Barnes and Jessica stood before the grave. The light from his flashlight revealed the words chiseled into the stone. She gripped his hand to the point of pain. There were no flowers in Ricky's brass tube. A pang of guilt struck Barnes over it. His brother's remains had spent ten years alone. A decade of indifference. The coin purse in his jacket pocket seemed to pump on its own, countering the rhythm of his heart.

Jessica released his hand and produced the bag of salt she had prepared. She opened it.

If she throws salt on his grave, Barnes thought, *I can't love her. I can't let her curse my brother.*

Jessica handed Barnes the salt. "Throw some over your left shoulder."

Barnes sighed. He'd seen the same move in a hundred cooking shows. He'd seen his mom do it. It was a stupid trick, something to do with warding off bad luck. "That's it?"

"Do you know what it means?" Jessica said.

Technically, he didn't.

"When you throw salt over your left shoulder," she said, "you're throwing it in the face of the demon standing there."

He looked down at the salt, hefted it.

"I know it seems silly," she said, "but all rituals are. They exist to force us to take action. In your case, to physically respond to what's haunting you."

Barnes tucked his flashlight into his armpit and pinched some of the salt. He threw it over his shoulder, heard it shower against the grass and the backs of the nearby headstones. He stood for a moment, waiting for something to change, some feeling of absolution.

"How do you feel?"

He shrugged. The light from his flashlight shifted with the movement. It came to rest on the flowerless brass tube at Ricky's grave. From the corner of his eye, Barnes saw something there, a bit of white cresting the rim of the tube, which was corroded green and brown. He closed the salt bag and pocketed it, gripped his flashlight and moved closer, knelt before it. There was a triangle of paper sticking out from the brass. He pinched it between his fingers and pulled it out. It was an index card, damp from the recent rain. Written on it, in big black letters, was DEMASIADO TARDE.

18 ✓

Barnes stalked down the gravel drive, still in the Land of Cherubs, Jessica on his heels. It had started raining again. He had pocketed the index card and was moving his flashlight across the rows of headstones, spotlighting their brass tubes, which were now reflecting raindrops like jewels in the metal. Most of the tubes contained flowers, either freshly cut or only beginning to sag; nothing was wilted or brown.

He found an empty tube. They went to it. He put his finger inside. No index card.

He searched again and found another empty tube. Again no card.

"The Day of the Dead," Barnes said, ranging his flashlight beam in search of another empty tube, "is for remembering our loved ones lost, for celebrating their lives. If he's bent on this concept—" He stopped walking. "Oh, shit."

"What?"

"This is Calavera's pattern."

"Calavera?"

"The Pickax Man," he said while digging in his pocket for his phone. "*Demasiado tarde.* Too late." He produced the phone and dialed Captain Darrow. The phone rang twice before the call was connected.

"Captain Eugene Darrow's phone."

It was Darrow's wife, Molly. She oftentimes picked up Darrow's cell phone when he was off duty and indisposed. She and Barnes had met at a precinct barbecue after he'd commented on her excellent taco salad. Since then they'd met a few different times, and he always felt a bit like her son. He envisioned her now in the elderly couple's small kitchen, wearing one of Darrow's old Detroit Police T-shirts, something boiling on the stove. "Hi, Molly. It's Barnes. Can you get him?"

"He's in the shower. I'll take you to him." There were sounds of movement on her end of the line. "How are you, Johnny?"

"I'm good," Barnes said. He looked at Jessica, rolled his eyes toward the phone against his ear.

"I mean, with what happened to Billy."

"I'm okay."

Over the phone Barnes heard a door creak open followed by the sound of rushing water. "Eugene!" Molly yelled so loudly Barnes pulled the phone away from his ear. "It's Johnny."

There was a fumbled exchanged before Darrow came on the line. "Whaddya got, Barnes?"

"He's been watching their graves," Barnes said. "At Parkview."

"I'm not following."

Barnes opened his mouth to speak but found he was incapable. His body shook and he fell to his knees as Dale Wilson's broken memories, from so much damage to his head, finally came together like random gears finding one another inside his mind.

Jessica came to his side. "Are you okay?"

Barnes held up a palm. Dale recalled the letter he'd received from the cemetery, asking whether he'd like to pay for special maintenance on his first wife's grave. The service included scrubbing the stone of stains and buildup, weekly flowers, and plucking the weeds. Remarried by then, Wilson had torn the letter in half and tossed it in the trash.

"Ten years after she died." Dale Wilson's voice from within.

"Got the same one. Ten years after." The crack addict.

"Me, too." Edith MacKenzie.

"Yep." Chunk Philips.

"Ten years after." The attorney.

"Me, too." The mother.

"Ten years," Barnes said into the phone. He spoke his next words as the realizations hit him. "He's been working here thirteen years. The murders started three years ago." He spotted another empty tube, went to it, found no card. He checked the date of death. "Only a few years old."

"Detective," Darrow said, "you better start making sense, or you'll find yourself in mandated rehab."

"He's killing people who don't visit their loved ones' graves. Ten years. After that, it's too late."

Darrow was silent for a moment. The only sound was that of his abandoned shower. Barnes imagined him with one foot in the tub, one out, water dripping on Molly's bathroom mat. "He can't be there around the clock," Darrow said. "How does he know who doesn't visit?"

"No flowers," Barnes said. "No upkeep."

"Look into it," Darrow said. He disconnected the call.

Barnes looked at Jessica, who was kneeling with him.

She said, "You're on his list."

◆ ◆ ◆

They pulled up to Jessica's apartment building. The rain spilled down over the passenger-side window in wavy sheets. The working street lamps looked like sparklers in the spray. Barnes turned to tell her good night, but Jessica leaned in and kissed him. He pulled her close by the back of her arm. Moved his hand to her back, felt the softness of her side, her ribs, the strap of her bra.

She pulled back and said, "You're coming up."

After that there were few words, inside Barnes's head or out. She walked Barnes up to her apartment, unlocked the door, let him in, and threw her keys aside. She pulled him over to the couch, pushed him down, and stood above as she had before, her hips level with his face. She dropped to her knees on the couch and straddled him. She placed one hand on either side of his head, pulled him up, and looked down into his eyes. Her cascading hair caressed and tickled his cheeks, his shaved head. "This really is our third date, you know?"

"You're counting the principal's office?"

She nodded.

He placed his hands on her back. She closed her eyes to his touch, tilted her head back. Her eyelids fluttered. He moved his hands up and over her chest, then back down again. She bit her bottom lip, then surged forward for another kiss. Barnes stood up with her in his arms. She wrapped her legs around him and dropped her head to his shoulder and kissed his neck as he carried her into the bedroom.

Barnes slept and dreamed of Ricky. His brother's face wasn't as clear to him as it once had been. Spots of the vision were missing—his hair, his neck, his ears—like someone had been slowly erasing his face at the edges. He was at Calvary Junction in his dream, watching the train go by—*click-clack, click-clack*. The back wheel on his BMX spun. He found the scents of steel and smoke. The certainty of what he'd heard behind him—Ricky's cry, suddenly silenced—echoed in his ears and seeped into his mind like water through a basement's walls.

Click-clack, click-clack.

The scene shifted. Now Barnes was Calavera's eighth victim, Roberta Jensen. Roberta waited tables at Johnny's Coney Island on Five Mile. She walked home from work to her apartment in grease-stained clothes and on exhausted legs, wanting only a hot bath, a gin and tonic, and the season finale of *Dexter* on her DVR. She cringed and sucked through her teeth as she slid into the scalding water up to her neck, closed her eyes, and reached for her icy drink. There was cool air from the window above the tub. She'd opened it a crack for contrast against the water's heat. A sound popped her eyes open. Had it come from the next room? She turned to look through the doorway, heard that window slide open behind her.

Click-clack, click-clack.

Now Barnes was Amanda Jones, Calavera's sixth. Her memory began with the sound of a flushing toilet while she washed her hands in the sink. She walked out of the bathroom, stepped onto the carpet in her hallway, and felt it warm and wet beneath her feet. Confused, she flicked on the hallway light and looked down. It was then she felt a jolt against her back. She found herself on the floor with a strange hunk of iron poking out of her chest.

Click-clack, click-clack.

Now Barnes was Jeffrey Dunham, a local defense attorney and Calavera's ninth victim. His home alarm system had not awakened him on the night he died. Hearing sounds in his kitchen, he ran down the stairs in a silk robe, wielding a baseball bat, ready for the wrong man. Dunham had been envisioning a man in a courtroom, someone he'd been unable to successfully defend. In his memory the man wore a suit that didn't fit right, and his Sunday-school hair fought hard against the gel keeping it in place. The man smirked at Dunham as the jury foreman read the guilty verdict, and after the case was over the man vowed to make the attorney *pay for his ineptitude*. Dunham charged down the stairs, expecting to frighten the man off but wet himself at the sight of a different man altogether—a man in a sugar-skull mask, standing casually in his kitchen.

Click-clack.

Barnes was back at Calvary Junction. The train had passed, and a zombie version of Andy Kemp—the murdered teenage boy who scarred his cousin and scared his classmates—stood on the other side of the tracks with the forest behind him. His decayed body was outlined in red from the morning light. There was a $10,000 bulge in his pants pocket. He was standing over Ricky's smashed bike.

Barnes woke up. He sat up in bed, naked. He turned and put his feet on the floor, reached for a bourbon bottle on the nightstand but found nothing there. He remembered where he was, dropped his head into his hands. His ribs ached from where Roberta Jensen had taken the pickax, his shoulder and neck from Jeffrey Dunham's blows, his back from Amanda Jones's. Something about the dreams nagged at him. A whisper of familiarity more than the usual remnants, something he was missing. He rolled the visions around in his head, trying to get a feel for what it was.

Jessica stirred beside him. "You okay?" Her voice was sleepy. She put a hand on his back.

"Yeah."

"John, you're sweating."

She called me John. Not Barnes, not Vic Mackey. John.

"I'm okay," he said. Through his fingers he stared at the glowing red numbers on the alarm clock on her nightstand. Only ten thirty? He would have guessed it was well past midnight.

She sat up and scooted over to him, wrapped her arms around him from behind, laid a cheek against his back. Her eyelashes tickled him when she blinked. "What is it?"

"I was dreaming of my brother."

Jessica pulled herself closer, gripped her naked body tightly against his. "Tell me."

Barnes lifted his head out of his hands. He looked out through the bedroom door into Jessica's darkened apartment. He could make out the shape of the couch, a chair, a lamp. The city lights threw a yellow hue on them all. These things looked like beings to him, like watchers in the dark. He said, "Ricky loved video games. We both did. I guess it was the time when we grew up, you know? We had the forest nearby, and truth told we spent a lot of our time out there in the trees, making forts, fighting, and exploring, but we had an Atari from when we were young, and a Nintendo once we could afford it. We played those home machines until they wore out, but most of all we loved the real-deal arcade."

"I bet," Jessica said.

"We lived on the other side of Middlebelt," Barnes said, "just a couple miles from Vacationland, the local arcade, but this was a time when arcade games were big, so you could find cabinets just about anywhere. There were two at the gas station near our house. One was Ms. Pac-Man, which was cool, but the other was a game called Mania Challenge, and it was . . . my God, I must be boring you."

"You are *not* boring me," Jessica said. Barnes felt her jaw moving against his back when she spoke. She clutched him tighter than before. He could feel her chest heaving with her breaths.

"It was the sequel to a wrestling game we loved called Mat Mania, which might have been the greatest arcade game in history, but it was only one-player. Strange that they would make a wrestling game only one-player, but they realized their mistake and created Mania Challenge soon after. It was two-player. Ricky and I couldn't have been more excited. We used to collect ten-cent Faygo bottles, you know? And we'd bike up to that gas station every time we had at least five, return them for two quarters, and wrestle each other on Mania Challenge. The characters were Dynamite Tommy and Hurricane Joe, but to us they were Dynamite Ricky and Hurricane John."

"Hurricane John," Jessica whispered.

"One day we found a coin purse at the edge of the river behind our home. It was a black rubber thing with a Batman logo on it. You could squeeze it and the mouth would open. You know the type?"

She nodded against his back.

"It was sitting there on top of the leaves, like someone had just dropped it. I thought it might even be warm when I picked it up, but it wasn't. I'd be a liar if I said we stuck around, waiting for whoever had lost it to come back. We were kids, and there were six quarters inside the purse. I looked at Ricky, he looked at me, and we ran straight home to get our bikes. When we got there I hopped on mine, but Ricky hesitated. His bike chain was badly rusted. Dad had bought us new chains, and I'd already changed mine.

But I'd refused to help Ricky change his, giving him some line about him needing to grow up and take care of his own things. It's hard to remember his face anymore, but I can still hear his voice so clearly. He said, 'Come on, Johnny, help me.' I said, 'It ain't my fault you didn't change it already,' and I rode off toward the gas station, hardly looking back. I had the coin purse, and God help me, if Ricky didn't show up, I'd play all six quarters myself.

"He came after me, though. Pedaled his heart out trying to catch up. I could hear him coming, pumping like crazy on that rusty chain, breathing hard, and when I crossed over the tracks, just as the barrier arms were coming down, I assumed he was right behind me."

Jessica stayed silent. Barnes watched the alarm clock go from 10:41 to 10:42, and then 10:43. When it turned to 10:44, he continued. "When I heard his chain snap, I didn't know what it was. It was buried in the sound of the train's engine, but it was loud, like a gunshot. I heard him call my name. Just *John*. He always called me Johnny. The train had cut him off. I kicked my brake and skidded, turned back to Calvary Junction and looked for him, but he was gone."

Jessica released him. She drew back and away to her side of the bed. Barnes let his head fall back into his hands, felt hot tears bubbling at the edges of his eyes.

"Come here," she said.

He turned to her, saw her through blurry vision, naked, up on an elbow and lying on her side, holding the blanket up for him to enter. He crawled into her embrace, placed his head beneath her chin. She threw the blanket over him and pulled him close. He spoke into her chest. "Is there a third-date rule about a grown man crying in bed?"

"Usually that happens on the fifth date."

Barnes pulled back from her chest, looked into her eyes. Though it was dark, he was close enough to make out her nose, her cheeks, the dark triangle of hollow at her neck. He'd never felt so willing to die. "I have to go."

◆ ◆ ◆

Barnes walked out to his car. He hopped in and pulled the gearshift into drive. He was about to lift his foot from the brake when he saw a man walking toward him down the sidewalk through the rain, smoking a cigarette. He flicked the butt into the street. It shot sparks where it bounced.

It came to Barnes what had been nagging him about his dream. Baseball-bat-waving lawyer Jeffrey Dunham hadn't expected Calavera. He had expected his client, Damon Beckett. The same Damon Beckett that Barnes had met in the church parking lot the day before.

"It wasn't Beckett that hurt me." Jeffrey Dunham's voice.

"Shhh."

Barnes picked up his radio and depressed the button, brought the microphone to his mouth. "Dispatch, this is Detective John Barnes, badge 5-2-2-5."

"Go ahead, 5225."

"Can you run a check on a name? It's Damon Beckett. I'm guessing B-E-C-K-E-T-T."

"One moment."

The man passed by Barnes's car. Barnes watched him in the rearview mirror. The man stopped, cupped his hand to light another smoke, and turned the next corner. The radio crackled when the dispatcher came back. "There are four Damon Becketts in Detroit and the metro area."

"Gimme their ages."

"Fifty-two, thirteen, twenty-seven, thirty-five."

"Bounce the old guy and the kid. Tell me if either of the other two have a sheet."

"Thirty-five is clean. Twenty-seven has one count misdemeanor, drunk and disorderly; one count misdemeanor, DWI; one count felony, concealed weapon. Sentenced one year, out in eight months."

"That's my guy. Send me the address."

19

Barnes pulled to the curb in front of 2548 Bertrand. The tiny house was a few blocks north of Saint Thomas of Assisi, one block south of a neighborhood bar called Shootz. The house had two darkened windows bisected by a concrete porch barely big enough for the folded lawn chair set against the aluminum siding. The home's aging foundation caused it to lean forward like a shamed man's head. It was what Franklin would call a *vampire hut*—no one ever home at night, nothing but drugged-out addicts or munkies during the day. Barnes could predict the interior—a heavy glass TV, sweating furniture, seismographic grime on the walls, and a machine in the back bedroom. He picked up the radio again, got a hold of dispatch, and asked, "My guy Beckett, does he have a registered vehicle?"

"He never renewed after the DWI. Suspended license."

"Thanks."

Where's a munky gonna walk?

"To the bar, dumb-ass." Chunk Philips.

Barnes pulled into the Shootz parking lot. Three vehicles were nestled alongside the building—a lawn-service truck, a rusted-out sedan, an early-model Ford Bronco. The bar's front door had a porthole window in the center; otherwise, the building was windowless and nondescript. There'd be no college girls standing on the tables and swinging their bras over their heads inside Shootz; if these walls could talk, they'd say, *Go to hell.*

Barnes stepped inside the bar to find the scents of yeast and dirty deep fryers. Tom Waits was on the jukebox. The man's voice sounded like demons and angels were playing tug-of-war with his vocal cords. The barroom was mostly filled with flies and sagging lifers. The bartender stood at the far end by the EMPLOYEES ONLY door, her arms folded over a black Pantera tank top, a knee bent with a foot against the wall. She had disinterested eyes and the hair of a drowned poodle. In another life, and with a subtler approach to makeup, she might have been a looker. Still, she had Damon Beckett's attention. He was sitting at the bar, one elbow propped on the lacquered wood, a full shot glass before him. He had a cool confidence concerning the bartender. Barnes envisioned her sitting on the edge of a yellowed bed, clutching a sheet to her bare chest, random bruises on her arms and thighs, shaking her head and saying, "You're such an asshole, Damon," as he headed out the door.

Barnes plopped down next to Beckett and smiled. The man reeked of cigarette smoke. He'd probably be sucking a butt now if not for the bar ban. Beckett turned to him, did a quick double take, and then smiled back. "Moon must be full tonight."

Barnes nodded. "Brings out the finest people."

"That it does, sir," Beckett said, raising his glass. He downed the whiskey and knocked the glass on the bar top. "What can I do you for?"

"Remains to be seen," Barnes said. He signaled to the bartender. She rolled her eyes and popped off the wall, came over reluctantly, toes dragging with each forward step.

"You a friend of his?"

"Maybe."

"Then *maybe* you can tell him he's not getting another drink until he settles his tab." She crossed her arms and sagged.

Barnes raised an eyebrow to Beckett.

Beckett shrugged.

To the bartender, Barnes said, "What's he into you for?"

She kept her eyes on Beckett. "A hell of a lot more than he's got."

"Honey," Beckett said, smiling supremely, "you have no idea how much I got." He turned to one of the lifers against the back wall of the bar. "Ain't that right, Charlie?"

Charlie, who sat on his wooden chair like it was the Harley-Davidson he could never afford, grunted. His arms, thick right down to the wrists and tattooed to a blurry black and blue, looked like castoffs from a slaughterhouse.

Barnes set three twenties on the bar top. "Will this cover it?"

The bartender looked down at the bills. She smirked and said, "With two shots to spare."

Barnes said, "Make mine a bourbon."

"Two," Beckett said.

She left to pour the shots.

Barnes said, "You threatened Jeffrey Dunham."

"Excuse me?"

"Your lawyer. When he couldn't get you off your concealed-weapon charge, you vowed to make him *pay for his ineptitude*."

Beckett shifted in his chair, suddenly interested in the labeled bottles against the wall behind the bar. His hands moved for the pack of smokes in his T-shirt pocket but stopped short, fell back to the bar. The shots arrived. The bartender set them down easy before wandering back toward her wall. Beckett watched her go. "How the hell did you know that?"

"Call it intuition," Barnes said. He downed his bourbon.

"Nah," Beckett said. "No way anyone could have known that. I—oh." He closed his eyes and nodded. "The machine, right?"

Barnes offered a wink.

"Then you know I didn't kill him."

"Not necessarily," Barnes said, "but let's not go there yet. For now I'm just wondering how much you know about the man that did."

"Pickax guy?"

"Bingo." Jeffrey Dunham.

Beckett shrugged. He drank his shot, clacked the glass down.

"You see," Barnes said, "there's something that's been nagging at me about the night Dunham died."

"I'm sure it ain't his brand of pajamas."

"His security alarm never went off. Someone gave his murderer the code."

"They questioned me about all this already," Beckett said. "Some big black dude."

"And I'm sure Detective Franklin did a bang-up job," Barnes said, "but you were one of dozens Dunham defended, and there was no reason to suspect you had anything against him, other than he couldn't get you off the gun rap. Now I'm digging deeper."

A darkness fell over Beckett. "Is that right?"

Barnes spoke slowly. "That's right." He turned on the swiveled stool and opened his body toward Beckett.

"Excuse me a moment," Beckett said, tapping the smokes in his chest pocket. "I gotta have a smoke."

"Oh, hell no," Barnes said. He placed a hand on Beckett's chest. With his other hand he loosed his Glock and placed it hard against Beckett's ribs, kept it hidden beneath the bar top. In a low voice, he said, "This ain't some TV cop show full of bumbledores who can't keep a suspect. Now ease that pistol out of your belt. Put it on the bar."

Beckett sighed and did as he was told. When his pistol tapped down on the wood, the bartender's eyes widened. Her body went rigid.

Barnes picked up Beckett's pistol and tucked it into his waist. "Now let's go talk. Somewhere quiet."

The two men stood. Beckett started toward the exit, but Barnes shook his head and rerouted him toward the back of the bar.

"Hey, man," Beckett said, smirking, "if you're thinking in terms of bathroom stalls, I don't swing that way. Nothin' against your kind, though."

"Shut up," Barnes said. He prodded Beckett toward the jukebox, stood him before it, gun in the munky's back. "Open it."

"What, the jukebox?"

"Don't mess with me, Damon."

Beckett sighed. He called over his shoulder, "Darlin', you want to help me out here?"

The bartender scowled. She lifted the hinged counter that kept her behind the bar top. She made her way over, pulling out a set of keys. She arrived at the jukebox, placed her foot beneath it, and kicked out a wheel lock. She slid the music machine over, exposing a half-size door behind. She showed Barnes dead eyes.

"Open it," he said.

She inserted her key, turned the lock, pushed the short door open. Barnes forced Beckett to stoop, shoved him into the room. He gestured for the bartender to enter as well. She went in. Barnes followed.

The hidden room was just like the one at Ziti's, only the walls were decorated with beer posters and neon signs. There were two machines along the side wall, two beds. Barnes gripped Beckett's elbow and guided him toward the beds. "Have a seat."

"Chill out, buddy," Beckett said.

Buddy?

The word triggered memories like rolling napalm. Barnes reeled back as the room spun around him. He blinked and shook his head, banged the butt of his palm against his temple. When the motion stopped, he saw Calavera standing in the corner—white mask, body clad in black, pickax in hand.

"Freeze," Barnes said. He stepped toward the killer, gun up. He reached back for his handcuffs.

The sound of a ratcheting shotgun stopped Barnes's movement. Time seemed to slow. Calavera evaporated from the scene. The room returned to reality. Barnes turned to find the bartender had picked up a hacked-off Remington 870 Express. She stood there with it aimed at his chest, a Schlitz sign over her shoulder.

She said, "Damon, run."

Time sped up. Barnes turned to find Beckett had already slipped through the short doorway and was pulling the jukebox over to block the door. Barnes ducked through and shouldered the music machine. It spun away. He fell. He stood. Saw the bar door closing. He charged into the parking lot, saw Beckett turn into the alley beside the bar. He ran to the alley. Beckett was scaling the fence. Barnes brought up his Glock.

Too late. Beckett went over, rattling the diamond-patterned metal. Barnes scampered to a nearby dumpster, leaped up, trampled the plastic top, hopped the fence. He landed, rolled over his head back onto his feet. Now down another alley. A light attached to the side of the building, moths and mosquitoes. At the alley mouth Barnes looked left, right, saw a shadow pass beneath a street lamp.

He chased it.

The sound of breaking glass. A wooden crack. A scream. The lights inside a house flicked on. Barnes ran to the house, up the porch, through the kicked-open front door. His feet crunched shattered glass on the carpet. A woman in the kitchen, dressed in a rainbow muumuu, pointing toward the open back door. The scent of a grilled cheese sandwich on the stove top as he moved through.

The rattling sound of another fence being scaled.

Barnes bolted across the yard, hopped the fence.

Another backyard. Beckett's shadow scampered across the driveway along the house's side. Barnes chased it. He looked left, right, left. There, Beckett passing between two cars on a nearby driveway. Barnes dashed, his knees barking, his lungs tightening. The sound of cracking wood. He came to the side of the house, a two-story brick. The gate to the backyard was kicked in, the yard enclosed by a six-foot privacy fence. No way Beckett had scaled that yet.

Barnes slowed to a stop. He scanned the yard, breathing hard. An aluminum toolshed, a blue kiddie pool with fish silhouettes on the outside, a small apple tree in the back right corner.

"Don't make this difficult, Damon."

"He said he'd kill me," Beckett said. The voice seemed to come from straight ahead. *The kiddie pool? Lying behind it?*

"Who said he'd kill you?"

"I did." Antonio Reyes.

"Shhh."

"The guy," Beckett said. "The pickax guy."

Barnes stepped tentatively toward the kiddie pool. "We'll take you into custody. We'll protect you."

"I'm not going back to jail. All I did was give him the code."

"Shoot him." Jeffrey Dunham.

"That's good, Damon," Barnes said, still stepping toward the pool. The water inside looked dark, putrid. "It's not that big a deal. You were threatened, coerced. We can work with that."

"Screw that," Beckett said. "A four-time offender? Snowball's chance."

The voice seemed to change location. *Behind the shed now?* "Just come on out," Barnes said. "Running won't help."

No reply.

Barnes stepped around the kiddie pool, Glock aimed at the darkness behind it. Nothing. A quick glance behind the apple tree. Nothing. He moved toward the shed, gun at shoulder height. He stepped into the black space between the shed and the fence. A mass of shadow near the ground.

"Just stay put, Damon."

With his gun still trained on the shadow, Barnes pulled out his flashlight and shined it into the darkness.

A pile of tires.

He stepped around the tires to find a gap in the boards of the privacy fence, just wide enough for a skinny bastard like Beckett to slip through.

20

The bartender, Jackie Helms, had been stupid enough to still be at the bar when the police arrived. She had been walked out and tucked into the back of a cruiser, her hands cuffed behind her back. A uniformed officer was about to close the door.

"Let me talk to her for a sec," Barnes said.

The uniform shrugged and walked off, leaving the door open. Barnes leaned into the opening, one arm resting on the door frame, the other on the car's roof. He could see now that behind her layers of makeup she was young. Eighteen, maybe less. "What was all that about?"

No response.

"You love him?" Barnes said.

The girl hung her head.

"Look at me."

She looked up. Tears welled in her eyes. Her chin began to quiver.

"Jesus," Barnes said.

"He'll kill him."

"Who?"

"The axman or whatever."

"He told you that?"

She nodded. Tears rappelled down her face on streaks of mascara.

"What else?"

She turned away.

"I'm trying to protect him," Barnes said.

"Yeah, right."

"So what, Daddy didn't hug you so you shack up with a guy like Beckett? Wind up pulling a shotgun on the cops? Fuck the world and all that?"

"You got me all figured out."

"Look at me."

She didn't.

He snapped his fingers.

She looked at him.

"You're willing to go to jail for Damon Beckett? Cut the shit. Tell me what I need to know."

"He said unless Damon gave him the lawyer's alarm code, he'd kill him. That's all I know."

"How would Beckett have the code?"

She tilted her head to wipe her cheeks on her bare shoulders, left black streaks on them. "Isn't this the part where I should ask for a lawyer?"

"Probably," Barnes said, "but you're increasing the chances that Damon meets his old friend first."

"Damon can protect himself."

Barnes pulled back his jacket, showed her Beckett's gun in his belt. "Sure about that?"

She glanced at the gun and then stared at the hard black plastic of the cop-car passenger seat before her.

"He'll be dead before your lawyer shows," Barnes said.

"Damon was going to stick it to that lawyer."

"How?"

"Break into his house, steal from him."

"How'd he get the code?" Jeffrey Dunham.

"Shhh."

"How'd he get the code?" Barnes said.

137

"He knows a guy at DAT Security. Some computer kid. He gives Damon house codes, Damon steals a few things, fences them, and they split the profits."

"This DAT guy, you know his name?"

"No."

"Know what he looks like?"

"Never met him."

"Did Damon ever mention the Pickax Man by name?"

"Just said he was a Mexican guy."

"Anything else?"

She shrugged.

"Think."

She sat still for a moment, her eyes moving back and forth. "After Damon gave him the code, the axman told him to go visit his mother. Damon was weirded out by it."

"His mother still alive?"

"She's been dead a few years, or so he says."

"How about your mother, Jackie?" Amanda Jones's voice.

Jackie pulled a face. "What happened to your voice?"

"Shhh. Jesus Christ."

"What about my mother?" Jackie said.

Barnes said, "She proud of you?"

21

Martinez was alone in the technical lab, asleep on a stool, facedown in an open textbook. One reading lamp was aimed at her improvised study area; otherwise the lab was dark. Barnes stood in the open doorway and watched her for a moment, innocent in sleep.

When he closed the door behind him, Martinez jerked awake and threw her arms up into a karate position. She blinked at Barnes, registered who he was, and dropped her hands. "Jesus. You scared me."

Barnes flicked on the overhead fluorescent lights. They blinked into life—*tink-tink-tink*—exposing the steel gadgetry, white sheets, and black bindings found on the various tools and instruments in the lab. He took a seat on the hospital bed, took off his jacket and holster, rolled up his sleeve. "Pulling an all-nighter?"

She stretched. "It's quieter here than at home. Got a couple roommates majoring in boys with rock-hard abs."

"You don't like rock-hard abs?"

"Rock-hard abs," she said, pointing to her stomach and then pointing to her temple, "rocks in the head."

"What are you studying?"

Martinez lifted the book to show Barnes the title: *Control Theory* by William Glasser, MD.

"Psychology?"

"Yeah."

"What's it about?"

"It's about how our minds are like filing cabinets with tags on the drawers, and if we learn to file things in the right places, we'll live happier lives."

"How's that supposed to work?"

Martinez stretched and yawned. "Well," she said, "take an overweight person who wants to lose some pounds, right?"

Barnes nodded. "No abs. Just your type."

She smirked. "Now imagine this person has a *happiness* drawer in a filing cabinet inside their head. If you were to open that drawer and rifle through it, you'd find pictures of fried chicken and cheeseburgers, you know?"

"I'll take a double pepperoni with a side of ranch."

Martinez tapped her chin. "Crab rangoons and plum sauce."

"Solid," Barnes said.

"Anyway," Martinez said, "those are the sorts of things an overweight person might have in their *happiness* drawer, while in their *pain* or *sadness* drawers you'll find fruits and veggies and diet foods. The idea is if we learn to control what we keep in our drawers—which is basically what we picture happiness or sadness or things like achievement or remorse to be—we can better control the choices we make."

"Makes sense, but how does one go about moving a cheeseburger from one drawer to the other?"

"Haven't read that far yet."

"Well, you've read your manual on Eddie, I assume?" He patted the machine at his side.

"Yes."

"Then let's get to it."

"It's all old stuff."

"What about Franklin?" Barnes said.

Martinez cocked her head.

"You pulled him, right?"

"Against your wishes. And apparently his."

"Cat's out of the bag, then." He was staring at the machine now. It had no face, no personality, no life, and yet it seemed to stare back at him. *What was it Nietzsche said about the abyss?* "I need to go through them all. See what I might have missed."

"It's *really* going to be an all-nighter, then?"

"You up for it?"

Martinez hopped off her stool, tucked her button-down top into her slacks. She went to the coffee maker on the far side of the room, pulled out the carafe, poured a cup. "You're not supposed to do more than an hour at a time. Regulation."

"That's why I'm glad you're here and not Warden. Gonna need you to look the other way on that. Plus, I'd rather do this without Holston snooping around for his story."

Martinez stared at him, jaw muscles back to their familiar twitching tightness. "I knew I should have taken that internship at Bracken."

"I need this."

"You sound like a munky," Martinez said.

"The *case* needs this," Barnes said.

Martinez sighed. "I'll pull the plug if it becomes too much."

"Deal." Barnes lay back on the bed. He stared up at the same ceiling he'd stared at a hundred times or more. It was a drop ceiling with dingy white tiles. Water damaged. One of the tiles had a rip in the corner, showing the beige fibrous material of which it was composed. Martinez came over to the machine. She turned it on and started attaching the tubes.

"How was he when you left him?" Barnes said.

"Franklin?"

"Yeah."

"His vitals were low. One of his lungs got clipped. It collapsed, but the other was strong enough to see him through the surgery. They were prepping him for more blood." She loaded the serum bottle onto Eddie and latched it in. She attached the suction cups to Barnes's temples, turned a dial, and said, "You ready for the needle?"

"Yes."

She inserted the needle into Barnes's arm. Her touch was gentler than Warden's had ever been. She handed him the bit. "Who's first?"

"Franklin. After that, we'll do them top to bottom."

"He's still alive. He'll be able to tell us himself."

"I know," Barnes said, "but we gotta stop this guy. If there's anything in his memor—"

Martinez stopped him with a gesture. "I get it." She turned a dial and flipped a switch. "We were able to pull a couple days off your partner, but I can start you wherever you want."

"Start me a few minutes before he went down."

Martinez typed on a keyboard and pressed the "Return" key. She turned a dial. Eddie clicked and hissed. "Here he comes."

Barnes chomped his bit. His body buzzed for a second, then arched. The Vitruvian Man test pattern appeared. "Prepare for transmission."

Barnes smelled green grass, heard footsteps crunching gravel. He found himself walking down the drive at Parkview Memorial cemetery. Inside Franklin, Barnes felt more powerful than he could have imagined, like he could crush stones with his fists, like nothing could ever knock him down. Franklin looked to his right, and Barnes saw himself through his partner's eyes. He looked like a shambling corpse. A vision of Franklin's former partner, Tom Watkins, bloomed in Franklin's mind. The two were standing outside the safe house in Ferndale. Watkins said, "We're just gonna talk to him, that's all."

The big man's stream of consciousness tripped over to a new vision. He was laughing with a young boy at his side. *Marvin.* Barnes felt an unbridled happiness in Franklin that he'd almost never seen from the outside. The boys sipped sodas in glass bottles as they walked down the street. Good friends. Blood brothers by way of sliced palms. They turned their heads toward a voice: "Hey, you little lawn jockeys."

"There." Now it was Barnes pointing up the road at the cemetery. Franklin looked to see the man raking wet leaves near a golf cart. *Oh, shit. This could be our guy.* His heart boomed. He moved heavily off the gravel to the grass, saw Barnes do the same on the opposite side. They continued toward the groundskeeper. Franklin called out. "Antonio?"

The man stopped raking. He began to turn toward them but stopped.

"Detroit Homicide," Franklin said. "We're here to ask you a few questions."

"I'll be right over," the man said.

"It's him," Barnes whispered. He drew his gun, called to the groundskeeper. "Why don't you just stay right there? We'll come to you."

Franklin broke into a sweat. He drew his gun. Another vision bloomed in his head. He was standing in front of a man inside a battered house. *Tyrell Diggs.* Barnes smelled sweet smoke in the air, sweat, and piss. Diggs smiled to show a row of golden teeth. "You done with that college bullshit?"

"No," Franklin said. Then he put a handgun up to Diggs's sternum and squeezed the trigger.

The phantom gun bucked in Barnes's hand on the hospital bed, the blast echoed in his ears. He felt Franklin's fear and remorse as he looked down on Diggs, the gun now shaking wildly in his fist. Diggs was grasping at the bullet hole in his chest, rolling back and forth.

"He was my friend," Franklin said.

"He was your bitch!"

Franklin stepped forward and put a foot on Diggs's face, trapping it sideways against the stained carpet beneath, squashing together his cheeks and lips, bulging his dying eyes. "You'll go to hell, Tyrell."

Tyrell's eyes stared off at something unseen. He spoke slowly and with difficulty due to the huge foot on his face. "You can't kill me. I'm Tyrell Di—"

Back in the cemetery, Franklin yelled, "Hold it right there!" He ran to his left, diagonally up and away from the golf cart. Losing breath. "Hands up, now!"

Calavera threw his hands above his head.

Barnes said, "Drop your weapon!"

"Is that you, Barnes?" Calavera said. "Well hey, ten-three, good buddy!"

"Drop the gun!" Franklin said. He could see the man's face. Dark-skinned with a wide, flat nose, black eyebrows, and a wide jaw.

Calavera fired at him.

"Son of a bitch." Franklin ducked down and fired back, three shots. Barnes heard his own voice echoing across the cemetery. "You all right?"

"I'm fine!"

Franklin covered Barnes as he went to the cart, shook his head, and moved up into the headstones beyond. He heard distant footsteps, scrapes of clothing against the headstones.

Barnes ducked and fired.

Franklin rose up, fired at a flash of gray between the headstones, ducked back down.

Calavera fired back.

Franklin moved up through the rows of graves. He stopped when he saw Barnes taking aim and firing.

"He's at the back," Barnes said. "Near the fence."

Franklin charged ahead. He ducked behind the entrance to a family crypt nestled into a hillside, up against a solidly built door. "I'll cover you," he said. "Come up." He stepped around the side of the crypt and riddled the hillside with bullets.

"See him?" Franklin said.

"He's gone out the back gate," Barnes said. "Cover me."

Franklin turned to fire but found his clip empty. He pulled back against the door and reached for a new clip. He heard shattering glass nearby. Overhead?

The door behind him fell open.

Barnes groped in the air above the hospital bed as Franklin toppled over like a domino. His body slammed the concrete floor inside the crypt. He dropped his gun on impact. It skittered and bounced against a wall of cubbyholes, each one with a dusty silver urn inside.

Franklin rolled to his front and reached for the gun but felt a punch against his back. His breath disappeared. He gasped. Barnes felt a wetness inside his own lungs, like how he imagined drowning would feel. Franklin looked up to see Calavera, now masked. *He must have slipped past Barnes, come down from the fence,* Franklin thought.

Calavera placed the hot barrel of his nickel-plated handgun against Franklin's head, leaned in close, and said, "Think you'll be visited?"

Franklin tried to speak but only managed a mouthful of blood. Barnes tasted it, the iron scent filling up his nose and throat.

Calavera removed the handgun from Franklin's head and left.

The crypt floor was cold against Franklin's cheek. He spat blood. His mind shifted over to Marvin, walking next to him on the sidewalk. Franklin had grown big by then, and he looked down at his friend. Marvin was wearing the black vest his mother had given him for his birthday, plus the Cincinnati Reds hat his father had left behind so many years ago. So small, and in that getup, he looked just like a crank-box monkey.

I'll be damned.

"Franklin?"

Franklin's mind snapped back to the crypt. It was Barnes in the doorway.

22

Barnes sat on the hospital bed, recovering from Franklin's memory. Martinez had given him some time, claiming she needed a bathroom break. Before she left, they'd briefly spoken of calling in a sketch artist to take down his description of Reyes, but considering the detailed report given by Sharon Bruckheimer of Parkview Memorial, as well as the late hour, Barnes decided it wasn't necessary.

Martinez came back in. "Saw this on your desk," she said, holding out a manila envelope marked BARNES in Magic Marker.

Barnes opened the envelope. It was a cross-referenced list from the Parkview Memorial—each of Calavera's victims linked to the deceased loved one whose grave they'd ignored, the victim's relationship to the neglected loved one, and the loved one's age when they died.

Martinez said, "Edith MacKenzie is next. Ready?"

"I was tied down by that bastard in my living room." Edith's voice. *"My daughter in the next room, helpless."*

Barnes found Edith's name on the list. Next to it was *Mildred Smith, sister, fifty-five years old.* He set down the list and closed his eyes, just now feeling like he could breathe again, after the psychosomatic loss of Franklin's lung. He dropped back onto the hospital bed and put in his bit.

The power surged. The Vitruvian Man test pattern reappeared, stayed for a moment, and then blinked away.

Barnes once again endured Edith's final moments.

Darkness and silence.

"End of transmission."

The Vitruvian Man test pattern.

Please Stand By.

They moved on to Edith's bedridden daughter, Kendra. He suffered the same fears, the same terrors, the same aches and pains in his body as he had the first time he'd been Kendra, two years ago. He noted, as he had before, that Calavera had used the word *detectives* with her instead of *Watkins* or *Barnes*. The MacKenzies were his first victims. Calavera couldn't know which police officers would be assigned to his case. At the end of her memory, Calavera looked down at the paralyzed Kendra and said, "Hello again. Enjoy your first clue." Then he waved to the police through Kendra's dying eyes. "Ten-three."

Darkness and silence.

"End of transmission."

The Vitruvian Man test pattern.

Please Stand By.

Barnes shook out his hands and his feet, attempting to alleviate some of Edith and Kendra MacKenzie's pain. He breathed steadily. He'd gained nothing new from the MacKenzie memories, at least not directly. From within, Kendra MacKenzie recalled the day her mother told her that her horse, Paddie, had originally been Mildred's. "We inherited it from my goddamn sister."

"Ready for Philips?" Martinez said.

Barnes nodded. Chunk Philips's loved one had been *Verna Philips, mother, sixty-seven years old.*

The Vitruvian Man appeared, disappeared.

Chunk sat in his delivery truck, staring at the back of an oyster bar through the cracked windshield. It was dark outside, 4:00 a.m., though still muggy and hot from a scorching day. Chunk didn't want to exit his truck; there was no AC outside to stem his sweat, which Barnes felt collecting under his sagging male breasts. Chunk sighed. *Man, I gotta get that windshield fixed.* The back door to the restaurant opened, and a slight man poked his head out. *The skinny twerp.* Chunk lifted his chin toward the man, who nodded back and smiled with big teeth. Chunk hopped out of the truck and landed heavily on the pavement.

"Hot enough for ya?" the twerp said.

"Damn right, Jordy," Chunk said. He pulled on his jersey gloves and breathed in the rotten-fish stink in the old Detroit alleyway.

"August in Michigan, right?"

"Soon we'll be under a foot of snow," Chunk said.

"Catch you on the flip side," Jordy said. He slipped back into the restaurant, letting the door click closed behind him.

"Catch you on the flip side," Chunk said in a whiny, mocking tone. He set up his conveyor rail of steel casters, placing one end on the back of his truck, the other on the shelf attached to the back of the restaurant. The shelf was below a window covered over with plastic drapes like you used to see over supermarket coolers, a pass-through window for deliveries. Chunk set a box of flash-frozen salmon fillets on the casters and waited. He stared at the red bricks of the building, followed the grout lines up and over and diagonally with his eyes. He thought the man who laid those bricks must have been a good, solid person doing something meaningful for the world. *And here I am, delivering fish.* A memory bloomed in Chunk's mind. *Mother.* She stood over him in an apron, one hand high on her hip, the other pointing a finger in his face. Bloodred fingernails. Barnes tasted a chocolate-chip cookie, felt its texture in his mouth. Verna Philips said, "You'll never amount to anything, Raymond, if you can't keep your hands out of the cookie jar."

Jordy unlocked and opened the small door on the other side of the plastic drapes. Chunk slung the salmon fillets along the conveyor and through the opening. The casters sang out as they spun—*sheeng!*

Thirty-seven boxes to go.

Chunk loaded another box and slung it—*sheeng!*

Thirty-six.

Sheeng!

Thirty-five.

"Hey, Chunk."

Chunk nearly shat himself. He cringed and turned to face the source of the voice that had crept up so quietly behind him. When he saw the mask, Chunk damn near shat again, but he remained composed. "That's Raymond to you, sir; only my friends call me *Chunk*. Whatcha wearing a mask for?"

Barnes felt a ball of pressure on his belly. Although he'd been Chunk Philips twice before, the blade entering his guts still surprised him. He looked down over Chunk's ample frame, saw the blood spilling out over Calavera's hand. He shuddered when Calavera yanked the blade up toward his chest bone.

A moment later Chunk was being dragged forward by his hair, stumbling deeper into the alley. Barnes's eyes saw alternative views of pavement, bricks, scraps of paper, a manhole cover, and Calavera's shoes through blurry blinks. They were generic black sneakers beneath black pants, as frustratingly nondescript as always. Barnes felt a bang and sharp pain in the crown of his head. He looked up to see Chunk was at a dumpster. The steel corner—where the dump-truck arms entered to lift it up—now had some of his hair on it, some of his skin.

"Climb up in there, piggy," Calavera said.

Barnes shook his head no.

Calavera showed him the pickax. "Get in."

Chunk struggled up and over the wall of the dumpster. He crash-landed on his back. For the first time he reached down to touch his stomach. Barnes's hands felt Chunk's slick insides like water weenies in a pool of oil. *I'm going to die a virgin. One lousy blow job from Becky Hartley.* Barnes felt the phantom pain where Becky Hartley had dragged her teeth along Chunk Philips's dick. He looked up from Chunk's dying body to see Calavera above him, standing in the dumpster with the pickax in hand. He said into Chunk's dimming eyes, "Hey, Watkins, find your next clue. Ten-three, good buddy." Then he reared the pickax back over his head.

Chunk's mind returned to that night with Becky. She was a sweet girl, had aimed to please. After he picked her up, she looked at him adoringly and said she was so happy to be out of the house for once. They'd had dinner at a coney island, had seen a movie, and all the while she'd had nothing interesting to say. The mind of a chipmunk. Maybe he'd been too judgmental? After all, who was he?

After the movie they'd parked a few blocks down from her house. Becky reached over and touched his belly. She left her hand there for a moment, and then drew down toward his pants. She struggled with his zipper. Chunk threw back his car seat to give her room to work. She started out by literally blowing on him, not understanding the concept. It felt unexpectedly nice. The poor girl did her best.

The pickax came down. Chunk Philips died to the sound of Jordy's voice calling down the alley, "Hey, Chunk, where'd you go?"

That's Raymond to you, sir. Only my friends call me Chunk.

Darkness and silence.

"End of transmission."

The Vitruvian Man test pattern.

Please Stand By.

Barnes opened his eyes. He sat up to a lightning-rod migraine. Chunk's memory fog was with him. Barnes stayed still until it began to clear out. His chest felt empty, his face crushed, his body weak from Chunk's blood loss.

"You all right?"

It was Martinez.

Barnes nodded.

"Ready for Chamberlain?"

"Not yet."

Barnes lay back and tried to think. The use of Watkins's name—instead of the generic term, *detectives*—was thought to be a break in the case back when Watkins was the secondary, the man on the machine. The assumption was that Calavera had returned to the scene of the MacKenzie murders and had possibly spoken with Watkins or Franklin, posing as a witness or just a gawking bystander. But the clue had led them nowhere.

I'm going to die a virgin.

"Write this down," Barnes said.

"Go ahead," Martinez said.

"Both Kendra MacKenzie and Raymond Philips were virgins when they died."

"Got it."

"Do you have the poems on hand?"

Martinez said, "Yep, which one do you want?"

"Philips."

Barnes kept his eyes closed. He heard Martinez flipping through the pages of the logbook attached by a chain to the machine. He recalled that Chunk Philips's poem had been written on the inside wall of the dumpster, had been slicked over with fish grease and garbage.

"Here it is," Martinez said. She read it aloud.

> You delivered seafood
> And ate what you wanted,
> You drank from the ocean
> Like a humpback whale;
> But krill was inside you
> As the sky was above,
> A piano-size coffin
> For a piano-size male;
> With a spoon in your flipper
> For scooping pea-size calaveras.

Barnes knew the poem by heart, had read it a thousand times, could have recited it with her. All the poems were pictured in his phone—the photos he took himself, plus those he'd downloaded from the case files prior to his assignment—but he'd needed it from a new source, needed it read aloud to get a new feel for it. A lead was germinating. It was like a deer tick boring into him and giving him Lyme disease. He was hardly aware of the tick but felt the disease's effect.

"What's the list say next to Chamberlain?" Barnes said.

"Robert Morris Chamberlain," Martinez said. "Son, two months old."

"Load him."

The test pattern appeared and faded.

Moe Chamberlain's body hummed. Crack cocaine coursed through him like electric current. Thoughts of collection agencies and arrest warrants and starvation faded away. Visions appeared before his eyes, sounds caressed his buzzing ears.

"Hey, baby, they're playing our song."

It was Donna. She swayed before him in a cartoon dress, which was a far sight better than that ragged T-shirt and jeans she always wore. Those ridiculous high-top sneakers.

She twirled like Beauty.

"I'll be your Beast," Moe said. His voice was low and full of reverberation.

"Come here, you," Donna said. She curled her finger to beckon him.

Moe moved toward her, slick as you please. A confident man's walk. He was cool. She led him through the abandoned house transformed into a dope crib. Axminster on the floors. That hole is a stainless-steel laundry chute. That smear a stroke of paint on canvas—Rembrandt or something. He wasn't a squatter. Nah. He wasn't even a man. He was *the* man.

Donna gripped his hand and pulled him through the hallways, one after another in the beautiful, cavernous house.

Finally, the bedroom.

That filthy mattress on the floor is a waterbed. That bald bulb on the cracked lamp is a collection of candles. That drooping drywall tape from the ceiling? Silk drapes.

"Girl," Moe said, "you about to get it."

She giggled.

Moe lay down on the bed and patted the place where he expected her to lie. It was then he noted his hand was shaking. He brought the hand close to his face. No, it wasn't his hand that shook, but his eyes. They were rocketing madly in their sockets. The whole room shook. Everything he could see.

Donna evaporated. The painted panels returned to dreary, battered drywall. The floor became a mess of scrapes, holes, and drug kits. Moe's eyelids flickered. His head fell to the mattress with a thump.

Footsteps in the room.

Donna?

Moe smiled, kept his shivering eyes shut.

She caressed his feet, tied them together with a silk scarf. His smile widened—they'd played this game before. She drew a finger along his leg as she came to his side and took his wrist.

"Hey, now," Moe said. "Not too tight."

"Quiet, you." She tied his wrists behind his back.

Moe ruminated on the feeling of her touch, on memories of the last time Donna felt so kinky. Christ, it'd been forever.

A third scarf connected his bound wrists to his bound ankles. He was trussed up like a Thanksgiving bird.

Roughly, she tilted him onto his back.

"Careful," Moe said, eyes still closed.

"Shhh." She caressed his head with one hand, pressed down on his chin with the other, forcing his mouth open.

The pressure hurt his jaw, his teeth. How long since Donna died? Gotta be four years now. Moe opened his eyes to find a funnel coming down toward his mouth. He gagged when the narrow end stabbed the back of his throat. Above him there was a man, not Donna, and he was wearing a white mask.

Moe tried to scream but only strangled.

The masked man poured talcum powder into the funnel. No doubt from the same talc Moe used to cut the drugs he shared with friends. He coughed and hacked, but it only opened more space for the talcum to fill his mouth, his throat.

Christ, it filled his lungs.

Water spilled from Moe's eyes, cold on his skin. His body shivered with anxiety. His lungs contracted and stayed that way—taut and small. His wrists and ankles burned against the hemp ropes that bound him.

Moe Chamberlain couldn't breathe. He couldn't cry for help, couldn't scream, couldn't even moan. His drugged-out body was paralyzed in shock and fear.

The man in the mask, who was dressed in all black, showed him the useful end of a pickax. "Want it to end?"

Moe nodded.

The man raised his weapon. Moe thought of that old Right Dig commercial, where some seventies guy in bell-bottoms ignores the idea that he should call the power company before digging in his backyard. He ends up electrocuting himself on a buried line.

Before you dig, call RIGHT DIG.

"Hello, Watkins," the masked man said. "It's a pity you can't figure out my clues. I don't want to do this forever."

The pickax came down.

"Ten-three, good buddy."

Darkness and silence.

"End of transmission."

The Vitruvian Man test pattern.

Please Stand By.

Barnes sat up. He choked on talcum powder and felt the drain of Moe Chamberlain's drug use the same way he'd felt Chunk Philips's blood loss. Like the MacKenzies, he recalled nothing new in Moe's memories, nothing that sparked. He felt delirious. He opened his eyes, looked at Martinez, saw Calavera's sugar-skull mask on her face. It frightened him, but he held himself in check, feeling Chamberlain's fog still on him, the taste of talcum in his mouth. He blinked and the mask faded.

Martinez sat there, concern on her face.

Barnes said, "Chamberlain's poem?"

Martinez flipped forward two pages in the logbook. "It was written beneath the mattress."

"Read it."

> You inhaled the whirlwind
> And wolfed down the earth,
> Your veins were subways
> Your brain the central station;
> But poison was delivered
> Instead of thoughts,
> Like delivering fire
> To a burned-out nation;
> With a glass pipe in your hand
> Clutched by five calaveras.

That deer-tick feeling was still there, the disease growing stronger. Barnes lay back down. "What name is next to Nancy Fulmer?"

"David. Brother. Thirty-one years old."

"Load her up."

23

Barnes felt drunk. His head swam with endorphins. Nancy Fulmer had stayed up late on the last night of her life, reading and drinking wine. The novel was poorly written, but the sex scenes were more stimulating than Janine said they'd be, almost more than Nancy could have imagined.

Almost.

Already she'd stopped once to go get some relief from her vibrator, and now she was back into the pages, searching for more. Barnes shivered with the aftershocks of Nancy's orgasm, still emanating from his genitals, up through his chest and arms, down through his legs. She reached for her wineglass and thought, *Whoa, slow down there, sister.*

Then aloud she said, "Oh, screw it," and drank deeply from her glass.

Her mind drifted from the pages of the book to a woman sitting in an office chair, looking up at her. She had cropped hair and a secret smile. *Janine.* Nancy's heart fluttered inside Barnes's chest. In her memory, Janine handed her the book and said, "I know it's got men in it, but just pretend Christian is me"—she winked—"only with a strap-on." She flicked out a hand and slapped Nancy's behind.

Barnes's cheeks flared with Nancy's embarrassment.

"Stop that," Nancy had said through clenched teeth, but at home on her couch she was smiling at the recollection. She set down her book and began caressing herself, imagining the very scene Janine had described—her lover before her, naked, save for the strap-on, which was all black leather and buckles.

A sound of cracking wood stopped Nancy's hands. Janine vaporized from her mind. The house was suddenly quiet; the air felt tactile, cold against her skin. Nancy stood, grimacing at the floorboards creaking beneath her feet. She padded quietly toward the kitchen. Her legs felt weak. She leaned against the doorjamb to steady herself. She peered around the corner into the kitchen and froze at the sight of the shadowy shape just a couple of steps away—a man, arms above his head, something held there. It knocked hollowly against the cupboard behind him, and then flashed forward, clipping Nancy's cheek as it came down.

Barnes felt a loss of gravity as she fell. He gripped the bars of the hospital bed.

Nancy rolled and scrambled back to her feet, felt cold air against her cheek where a flap of skin had been sliced back. Blood blurred the vision in her left eye, but she could see well enough to find the front door. She ran to it, gripped the handle, and pulled.

It didn't budge.

She fumbled with the dead bolt, got it open.

She found the chain lock.

A hand grabbed her hair from behind, whipped her back into the living room. She crashed against the coffee table, landed on the carpet, looked up at the sugar-skull mask.

Her brother came to mind. A full-grown man standing before her with a gold-leaf Bible clutched in one hand. He was thumping the Bible with an open palm, saying, "Their blood shall be on their own hands."

"He said he'd tell them," she screamed at the masked man. "What else could I do?"

Calavera said, "A guilty conscience, piglet? Whatever for?"

Nancy envisioned her parents, David standing before them. The older couple was sitting on a couch beneath a cross on the wall, Jesus's sunken face staring off to the side, their own faces catatonic with the news of Nancy's sexual orientation delivered to them by their pious son. "You're here because of him," she said, "because of what I did?"

"I'm here for what you didn't do," Calavera said, his tone like he was speaking to a child. "But tell me, anyway. What did you do?"

"I killed him, goddammit!"

Calavera cocked his head. "Isn't that something?" He leaned in closer. "You should check into that, Watkins. We can't do this forever."

"Watkins? Who the fu—"

Calavera drew back the pickax. "Ten-three, good buddy."

Nancy Fulmer's hands covered Barnes's face. His neck cracked from the pickax's impact.

Darkness and silence.

"End of transmission."

The Vitruvian Man test pattern.

Please Stand By.

"Relax."

It was Martinez. He opened his eyes. His extremities felt numb, his cheek cold and damp, his head as heavy as a stone. Calavera had used the flat blade of his pickax to sever Nancy Fulmer's head clean away from her neck. Barnes tried to move his hands, but they wouldn't go. He tried his feet. Nothing.

"Quiet now." Martinez again. "Slowly now. Slowly. You're Detective John Barnes, Homicide Division, Detroit Police."

Barnes blinked back the fog. Sharp pains in his body, a dozen different places, like wounds all over him, every bone broken. His cell phone buzzed against his leg. He willed his hand to reach for it. It slowly responded and, by degrees, came to his pocket. By the time the phone was clutched in his shaky grip, Barnes felt he could sit up. He did so slowly, then swung his legs around to dangle from the hospital bed.

"You're done," Martinez said.

Barnes looked down at the message on his cell phone. It was from Jessica.

Miss you already.

158

Some of his ache abated, the fog receded. He closed the phone and put it away. He opened his jaw to let the bit fall out. "I'm here for what you *didn't* do."

"What's that?" Martinez said.

"That's what he told her. She admitted killing her brother, but he was there for what she *didn't* do. Never made the link before."

"Says here David Fulmer's death was ruled accidental."

Barnes nodded. "It was how I was introduced to this case. I had the David Fulmer file. Open-and-shut. He and his sister had gone ice-climbing at Pictured Rocks. Frayed rope. He fell and that was it. I looked into the sister, but not hard. No reason to."

"You didn't look hard enough." Nancy Fulmer.

"Huh?" Martinez said.

Barnes shook his head. "*I* didn't look hard enough. Watkins came to me and checked what I had. But why follow up when the man's murderer was already dead? Why put his parents through the additional pain of knowing their only daughter killed their only son?"

"Okay," Martinez said, "so what *didn't* she do?"

"She didn't visit her brother's grave. Read her poem."

Martinez read out loud.

> Your love was forbidden
> Considered abomination,
> On the shape of a woman
> Your eyes saw fire;
> But to touch is hot
> A blister of water,
> Bitten and flattened
> The taste of desire;
> With a scar on your hand
> Where you ate calaveras.

"What time is it?" Barnes said.

Martinez checked the wall clock. "Six twenty-two."

"Go get some rest. We'll finish later."

"When?"

"When's Warden coming in?"

"He's on call for the weekend, so you're stuck with me."

"Noon, then."

"I'll be here."

Barnes pulled the needle from his arm. He applied his own cotton ball and Band-Aid while Martinez pulled the tubes from the machine and wound them up. He stood and put on his gun, his jacket.

"Where are you going?" Martinez said.

"To see Watkins."

24

Barnes finished a large coffee and half a pint of bourbon on the half-hour drive to Bracken, Michigan. He pulled into the parking lot at the Bracken Institute and threw the gearshift into park. His body was racked with pain at the elbows, the chest, his head, his neck. A mixture of other people's voices fought for time in his head. They threw one another aside like wrestlers in a battle royal. The alcohol helped slow them down. Taking a cue from Martinez's psych book, he imagined a filing cabinet in his head and a drawer labeled OTHER PEOPLE'S MEMORIES. He imagined himself stuffing the MacKenzies in there, stuffing Chunk Philips, Moe Chamberlain, and Nancy Fulmer. They spilled out over the sides like children's toys.

Before him stood three separate buildings. A green-and-white sign pointed to the pediatric ward on the left, the adult ward on the right, and straight ahead for the commons. Breezeways connected them all. The place wasn't some big and ominous thing, like the infamous Danvers. It looked to Barnes like the elementary school he'd recently visited, only this school was surrounded by two fifteen-foot-high fences sporting razor-wire wigs and watchtower spotlights at each corner.

Barnes got out of his car and walked up to the outer gate. He pressed a buzzer and looked up into a video camera perched there. A rough female voice came through the speaker. "State your business."

Barnes showed his badge to the video camera. "Here to visit an old colleague. Tom Watkins."

A buzzer sounded. The gate's lock clicked. Barnes pushed it open and walked through. Before he reached the second gate, another buzzer sounded and the lock clicked. He pushed through and headed toward the commons building. The gates closed behind him, rattling the fences.

The interior of the commons smelled like body odor. The head nurse, a mahogany woman wrapped in stark white, with a back so wide and straight you could hang a painting from it, led Barnes down a breezeway and through the adult gathering room toward Watkins's quarters. She smelled of perfume and bleach, kept her hands clamped together behind her back as she strode through the maze of patients dressed in dingy white. The walls were painted royal blue, supposedly a soothing color. A scrawny guy with dark eyes sat sullenly on a couch. His left hand was wrapped in gauze. A dot of blood had made its way through to the top layer.

They drew near a closed door with a sign on it.

THERAPY

The mahogany woman walked on, but Barnes stopped and looked in through the rectangular glass pane. It was crisscrossed with wire in the same diamond pattern found on the gym door at the elementary school. Inside there was a man lying on a hospital bed. His hands were manacled to the railings, his head and chest strapped down, a bite-riddled bit in his mouth. There was an IV stand providing the man nourishment as though he were in a coma. In a sense, he was. A machine technician sat to the side on a wooden chair. He read a magazine while the man jerked and shuddered at the experiences being pumped into his head.

The nurse appeared at Barnes's side.

"What did he do?" he asked her.

"Tortured a woman." Her speech was terse, as painful to hear in person as through the gate speaker. "Kept her in his basement."

"How long?"

"Six months."

"No. How long a memory pull?"

"They got two full days from the woman he tortured. He's reliving it all."

A swell of terror passed through Barnes. To be on the machine for two full days was beyond his ability to grasp. He watched as the man bucked hard against his restraints and screamed out for help in a woman's voice.

The nurse said, "Watkins is this way."

Tom Watkins sat quietly in his room. He was attached to a wheelchair by leather straps at the wrists and ankles. He wore a battered robe with a wife-beater tank top, boxer shorts beneath. The tank top was stained from food and something else, maybe drool.

The nurse said, "We had ourselves an incident this morning, didn't we, Tom?"

Watkins looked up at her. There were bags under his unfocused eyes. His jaw hung limply. "I'm so sorry, miss," he said. "So sorry."

The head nurse squinted. "Hmm."

Watkins hung his head.

"What did he do?" Barnes said.

The nurse looked at him, sighed through her nose. "He decided his fork would be better placed in Mr. Hill's hand than in his pancakes." She pointed to a chair and then left.

The chair legs grated the floor as Barnes pulled it out from the wall. He sat down. Watkins lifted his head only high enough to see Barnes, to watch him through the tops of his eyes, the lids fluttering. He was drooling now, answering the question about the tank-top stain.

"How you doing, fella?" Barnes said. He patted Watkins's knee.

A smile spread across Watkins's face. *Full Metal Jacket*, Private Pyle in the bathroom. He started with a chuckle, and then broke into a full-on laughing fit that tested the strength of his straps and engorged the veins on his forearms and neck. Barnes sat patiently through it, mentally fighting back the people emerging from the file drawers in his own mind. He wished he hadn't left his pint in the car.

"You know me," Watkins finally said, bringing his head back down. He licked at the drool hanging from his lower lip.

"I do," Barnes said. "We worked together at the precinct."

"No, no, no," Watkins said, shaking his head. "You know me. You know us."

"I know *us*?"

Watkins again threw back his head. "The machiiiiiiiiiiine!" His cry was like fingernails against a chalkboard. The tendons in his neck stood out like cables. His black fingertips turned white against the arms of his wheelchair. He looked like a man screaming down the highest hill on a roller coaster in hell.

"Yes," Barnes said, gripping the bridge of his nose. "I've been on the machine."

Watkins jerked back to attention. His voice reached up an octave when he said, "What's your angle here, son?"

Barnes blinked. Watkins's tone was like that of a woman. His eyes had changed, too. They were clear and sharp. Barnes said, "Um . . . well, I—"

"Spit it out, ya moron!" Watkins said. His eyes had changed again. Angry, shifty. His voice had dropped back down in tone, but he didn't sound like Watkins—he sounded like . . . Jesus . . . he sounded like Chunk Philips.

"I came to ask you about Calavera."

Watkins pushed back against his wheelchair like he'd been slapped. He cringed and shook his head. The index finger on his right hand started a repeated motion. Straight down, right, and then back up, like a triangle. Down, right, diagonally back up, again and again. He said, "Ten-three, good buddy. Ten-three, good buddy. Ten-three, ten-three, ten-three."

Barnes said, "What about ten-three?"

"Ten-three, ten-three, ten-three. You'll find it. Ten-three, ten-three, ten-three."

"I'll find what?"

Watkins went still, though his finger kept moving. "He wants you to find him," he said. "Do you have the clues? You just have to *see* them. What do you *see*? What did you *eat*?"

"I saw that horrible mask." Kendra MacKenzie.

"Talcum powder." Moe Chamberlain.

Barnes said, "I don't understand."

"Riddle me this. What do you *see*? Riddle me that. What did you *eat*? *Peas*?" He laughed again, shifted, morphed, his finger repeatedly drawing the triangle. It was like watching a Transformer constantly changing but never settling on a shape.

"A riddle?" Barnes said. "You figured it out?"

"Oh yes," Watkins said, "oh yes, oh yes. Not all of it, but I was on my way. He was taking me there. He wants to be found, you know? He wants to be *visited*. He wants you to stop him, just like he wanted me to. But I didn't want to. I believe in his work. The world should know him not as a martyr"—he leaned forward and whispered—"but as a god."

"Is that why you killed Dawson that day in the safe house?"

Watkins's finger stopped making the triangle. He looked at Barnes like he'd just realized he was there. He smiled. "Dawson. The survivor. Thought he could hide. Ha. I know what Dawson did."

"Dawson was never on the machine," Barnes said. "He refused it. And then you came along, and, well, let's just say you made an attachment impossible."

Watkins smiled. "Gee, so sorry about that."

"What did Dawson do?"

Watkins sat still for a moment. The Transformer action was slowing down. It was like smoke reversing back into a chimney. All movement stopped, even the eyes, and then, in a child's voice, Watkins said, "He hurt me." Watkins squirmed, rubbed a cheek against his shoulder.

Barnes said, "Who are you?"

In the same child's voice, Watkins said, "It's me, dummy."

Barnes sank into his chair. His head swam in delirium. It was Ricky. He was sure of it. How did this madman have Ricky inside him? *It doesn't matter. Just leave. Go. Run.* He tried to stand but found he lacked the strength. He dropped his head into his hands. The idea that Ricky was trapped in this man, in this place. He reached for the Glock in his armpit but found the holster empty. He'd left it at the desk, their precautionary enforcement measure.

"Quit crying, ya pussy," Watkins said.

Barnes looked up. "Why did you leave me?"

"I didn't leave you."

"You did. You let that train take you away, and I—"

"I don't know you, shithead."

Barnes blinked. "Who are you?"

"Andy Kemp. Don't call me Andrew. That's for the bitches."

Not Ricky.

Andy Kemp. First he'd been in Barnes's dream, and now he was here, in Watkins. Andy Kemp, the unsolved mystery that Watkins claimed didn't leave a memory to pull, the body too far gone, the connections a mess.

Watkins lied. Kemp's memory pull wasn't a dud.

"Gerald Dawson," Barnes said. "He was the one who hurt you—wasn't he, Andy?"

"Fuck Dawson."

"You're a clever kid," Barnes said. "You got inside Watkins."

Andy winked, smiled.

"You used Watkins to kill Dawson. Revenge from beyond the grave."

Andy shrugged, showed a petted lip, turned up his palms.

"Killing Dawson was a bad thing, kid. It landed Watkins in this place."

"He's happy here." At that, Andy's visage dashed away from Watkins's face like a swipe on an iPad. Watkins's head fell and his eyes came up, back to Private Pyle.

Barnes said, "Andy?"

Watkins said, "Get out of here."

"Calm down, Tom. I want to talk to Andy again."

"Get out of here!" Watkins squirmed and strained against the straps of his chair. It rocked side to side on its wheels.

Barnes leaned in close. "Talk to me, Andy. Tell me how you knew Dawson."

Watkins spat in Barnes's face.

Barnes wiped the spit with his jacket sleeve. He found his legs, stood up, and backed away. Watkins continued to writhe and strain against his restraints. "Get out of here!" The chair fell sideways, and Watkins struggled against the floor, his cheek flat against the green tiles.

The head nurse entered the room with two orderlies, one at either side. The orderlies came in and picked up Watkins, reset his chair. His tormented eyes never left Barnes. "Get out of here!"

The head nurse turned to Barnes. "You might do as the man says."

25

Jeremiah Holston was in the psych ward parking lot, outside of the double gates. He leaned up against Barnes's car with his arms folded over his chest.

"You followed me?" Barnes said. He was waiting for the second gate to buzz and release him. The people in his head whispered curiously among themselves.

Holston smirked. "Took a cab," he said. "Figured you might offer me a ride home; we could finish the interview along the way."

"Must have been an expensive ride."

Holston shrugged.

"And what if I just leave you here?"

"I thought you didn't hate me yet."

"Not yet," Barnes said. The gate buzzed and unlocked. He made his way through and came to the driver's side of his car. "Get in."

Barnes moved the pint of bourbon to the back. Holston got in. They pulled onto the highway and headed south. Barnes said, "This is it. You've got however long it takes us to get back to Detroit. After that, we're done."

"What's crackin' in Bracken?" Holston said.

"Watkins. He was on the machine with Cala—I mean, with the Pickax Man—before I was. I was checking if he might have had different experiences, seen different things."

"And did he?"

"Not really."

"Oh yes, he did." Detective Franklin's voice.

"Shhh."

"Shhh yourself, bastard."

"You were going to say Cala something. Cala what?"

"That's confidential."

"I thought you were going to be honest with me."

"If it doesn't potentially hurt the case, I will. If my answer could bring in false leads or spawn some copycat, no soap."

"Come on, Barnes. Off the record is off the record."

"Bat Boy's record is never off."

Holston scoffed. "So then, how was Watkins?"

"Not good."

"The machine messed him up."

"He was a good man." Detective Franklin.

"It could've messed him up," Barnes said. "Sure."

"How could there be any doubt? He was a decorated detective and a family man. Now he's a murderer, a mental case reduced to mush, and you're giving me *it could've?*"

"Like it or lump it."

"Just give me more than *could've.*"

Barnes nodded. "Detective Watkins was affected by the acts of the criminals he chased. He began to believe some things, and he acted on those beliefs. Was his use of the machine a factor in why he lost his marbles? Possibly. Can I say that with any certainty? No."

"Did he give you any help?"

Barnes thought of Watkins wriggling against the chair, his cheek on the floor, drool on his chest. The man was clearly out of his mind, but the answer to Holston's question was "Yes."

"Something still in him," Holston said. "Something haunting him. The same thing is happening to you, now."

"No."

"Bullshit, Barnes. How long have we known each other? Five years? Ten? I've never seen you such a ghost."

"You think because you've been the guy with a microphone in my face a few times you know me?"

"What don't I know?"

Barnes's mind flashed to Calvary Junction, to Ricky. For the first time his memory of the place, of his brother's death, felt lighter. He didn't feel that instant sense of guilt and remorse.

"Maybe it was the salt." Edith MacKenzie.

"Let's just say," Barnes said, "I'm not just some munky stuck in the machine."

"No one's saying that, Barnes. Jesus Christ, man, can't you see I'm trying to help you? You and any other detective who's been hooked to that machine. You keep dying over and over on that goddamn device. That's how we punish criminals, for God's sake. So how can it be that it's *not* destroying you?"

"We all have a penance to pay."

"So what, you deserve it?"

"Maybe."

"Why?"

Barnes didn't respond.

"You might as well tell me. I'll find out anyway."

Barnes said, "Don't make me start hating you."

Holston shook his head.

"You really want to help me?"

"Of course."

"Then you're going to do me a favor."

26

Barnes dropped Holston off at his newspaper office—a nondescript building in an industrial park full of nondescript buildings. His cell phone rang as the reporter grew smaller in the rearview mirror. Barnes answered it.

"Detective, this is Judy Nolan from Sinai Grace. I'm one of the nurses looking after your partner, Detective Franklin."

"I'm right here. What's up?" Detective Franklin.

"Excuse me?" the nurse said.

"Goddammit, stop it," Barnes said.

"Who are you talking to?" the nurse said.

"I'm sorry," Barnes said. "Just . . . how's he doing?"

"Well, he's awake now," the nurse said. "We believe he's going to pull through. Please don't visit until tomorrow. He needs rest. I only called because I thought you'd like to know his condition has improved."

"Thank you."

"Not until tomorrow, okay? It's what's best for him."

"Not until tomorrow."

Barnes disconnected the call. He pulled to the roadside and stopped the vehicle. He looked at his reflection in the rearview mirror. The man he saw there was a shell, a corpse, a ghost. His eyes were as dark and sunken as those on the mask he chased, his skin as waxy and false. He imagined the sugar skull over his face.

Moe Chamberlain screamed.

Edith MacKenzie cried.

Chunk Philips roared in anger.

Barnes mentally stuffed the victims into their proper drawers. When they came crawling back out, he punched them down with prejudice until all activity stopped.

Martinez was in the tech lab, sitting on the edge of the hospital bed, when Barnes walked in. She was fiddling with the railing on the hospital bed. Officer Flaherty was standing next to her, arms folded over his chest, gum smacking.

"What are you doing here?" Flaherty said.

"I could ask you the same thing," Barnes said. He took off his jacket and started on his holster. He could smell Flaherty's grape gum. "Get out."

"Captain's orders. You're not to get on this machine."

"You're going to stop me?"

"If I have to," Flaherty said. He smiled, kept chewing.

It struck Barnes then that he'd been wrong: Flaherty hadn't been bullied as a kid—he was the bully. Guys like him and Freddie Cohen, the kid that used to bully Ricky. They grew up, got jobs, and stayed bullies. *Just being fat don't make you tough.* Barnes snickered.

"Something funny?" Flaherty said.

"Why you got such a hard-on for me, Flaherty? What did I ever do to you?"

Flaherty shrugged. "I guess I just don't like your face."

"How unoriginal," Barnes said. He made a fist and stepped toward the officer, but before he could swing, Flaherty dropped down like a marionette cut from its strings.

Martinez had blackjacked him with the stainless-steel railing she'd been unscrewing.

"You'll get fired for that," Barnes said.

"I guess so," Martinez said. She hopped down from the bed and picked up Flaherty's feet, nodded for Barnes to help out. Barnes took

Flaherty's front half, scooping him up by the armpits. They carried him to the second hospital bed across the room. They laid Flaherty down and threw a sheet over him. Barnes locked the tech lab door.

"You hear Franklin's all right?" Martinez said.

Barnes nodded. "That nurse warned me about going over there today. Sounded like she'd have my hide."

"You don't look good. How'd it go with Watkins?"

Barnes poured himself a coffee. "He's fine."

She clucked her tongue. "Right."

Barnes smiled.

"You sure you want to do this?" Martinez said. "We didn't get much from the first go-round."

"Something Watkins said is sticking with me. He figured out there was a riddle. Solved some of it."

"Great. What's the answer?"

"Solved *some*, not all. He knew where it was going." Barnes sipped from a Styrofoam cup. "Who's up?"

"Fred Jones."

"Who's his loved one?"

Martinez consulted the logbook. "Jennifer. Stillborn daughter."

"Our daughter." Amanda Jones.

Barnes heard the echo of Amanda Jones's bathroom faucet, felt her bare feet squelching the carpet, felt the stomach drop of her forward fall when the pickax drove her down. He lay back on the bed while Martinez prepped the machine.

A click and a hiss. The bit. The surge. The Vitruvian Man. "Prepare for transmission."

Fred Jones dreamed of flying. Barnes felt as though he'd risen off the hospital bed as Jones soared over the city, looking down at the streets, the cars, the people. He felt the wind rippling against his clothes as he swerved up and down and side to side. He called out happily, "Woo-hoo!"

Fred woke up when his wife shoved him. "You were squealing again."

"I was?"

She got up and padded across the room, out into the hallway. Light came from the bathroom, spilled into the bedroom, and then tapered away when she closed the bathroom door.

"What was that?" Fred Jones said aloud. He'd seen something in the hall. Barnes saw it, too. *An arm?* It'd been sleeved in black and flat against the wall, like someone was hiding there. Fred heard a hiss, something sliding. He threw back the covers and got out of bed. He went to the hallway and turned on the light. No one there. He came down the hall, past the bathroom, and into the guest room. He flicked on the light.

Empty.

A sense of loss struck Barnes. Jones saw a guest bedroom—the double bed, a chest of drawers, and a generic print framed and hung on each wall. He closed his eyes and imagined the room differently, the way he wished it would be—littered with children's things, a twin bed, posters of pink cartoon ponies, "Jennifer" in sticky letters on the wall. He inhaled the imagined scents of Play-Doh and glue, of plastic dolls.

He stepped farther into the guest room, pushing the door more widely open, but it would only go so far. There was something behind it, blocking it. He pushed again, but the door bounced back at him. He shouldered it angrily. It flew wide open as the man in the skull mask stepped out from the space between the door and the wall. Jones fell to his knees and looked up. The man stood above him, clad in all black, leaning on a pickax like it was a horse-head cane. The mask was unemotional, but the eyes deep in the holes were curious, and to Fred Jones, maybe a little sad.

I'm glad you never made it to us, my sweet girl. I'm glad you never suffered like the rest of us trapped in this world.

The pickax came up to the side and down like a pendulum. It pierced Fred Jones's ribs and tracked across to the opposite side, bulging the skin. Barnes fell back into the hallway, felt himself yanked sideways as the weapon was removed. Fred Jones closed his eyes and tried to imagine what heaven might be like for Jennifer, tried to imagine what her face might look like. It felt good to know he'd be with her soon.

A toilet flushed as the pickax chopped through his throat. The watery sound masked the *thock* the ax made on the floor beneath. Jones opened his eyes to see Calavera reaching over to turn out the hallway light.

Darkness and silence.

"End of transmission."

The Vitruvian Man test pattern.

Please Stand By.

Barnes clutched one hand around the pain in his throat, another at the pain in his ribs. He swallowed and it felt like fire.

"You're okay," Martinez said.

Barnes scanned Fred Jones's final moments. He'd found nothing before and hadn't held out much hope for this time around, but . . . the shoes. Jones had seen them. They were black and generic, as always, but along the lowest part of the dark pants there had been something brown.

Mud?

No.

Barnes sat up, spat out the bit, caught it. His throat burned when he said, "The day Fred and Amanda Jones died, what season?"

Martinez checked the logbook. "It was early this March. Wintertime."

"There was a burr."

"Huh?"

"On his pants. A burr. Where did they live?"

"Apartment building downtown," Martinez said. "The Wickerton."

"That's a high-rise," Barnes said. "No yards nearby, no trees. Park's a mile away, but he had a burr on his pants." *A burr on his pants and a cedar leaf stuck to his shoe.* "Write it down and load Amanda."

27

A toilet flushed. Barnes washed his hands in the bathroom sink at Fred and Amanda Jones's apartment. Amanda stepped out of the bathroom and into the hallway, where she felt warm, wet carpet beneath her feet. She flicked on a light and looked down.

What the—

The blow took her wind and knocked her down. The long handle of the pickax banged against the drywall and stopped her from turning over.

The skull mask lowered itself into Amanda Jones's sight line. Calavera said, "Hello, Barnes."

Barnes?

"I'm so disappointed in Detective Watkins," Calavera said. He tugged at the edges of his black gloves, securing them more tightly. "I wanted him to visit me, but he had to go and kill poor Dawson. I hear they're sending the good detective up to Bracken. Gonna study him, no doubt. Gonna put him on the machine. All piggies receive their punishment."

Darkness crept into Amanda Jones's vision, closing like a camera's aperture. Calavera slapped her cheek, brought her to attention. Barnes cringed at the sting. Calavera pointed a gloved index finger into Amanda's face. He said, "You have to read the clues," and he moved his finger in what Barnes thought was the same triangle Tom Watkins made, except that Calavera stopped short.

Not a triangle, but an L shape.

"Ten-three, good buddy."

Darkness and silence.

"End of transmission."

The Vitruvian Man test pattern.

Please Stand By.

Barnes sat up. He cried out from the accumulated pain in his body. Tears burst from his eyes. It was like he'd been hit by one car and run over by the next. He shuddered with the cold of blood loss, struggled to breathe.

"Enough," Martinez said. She stood and pulled the suction cups from Barnes's temples. Yanked the bit from his mouth.

"It's okay," Barnes said. He reached out and gripped Martinez's wrist. He envisioned the L shape Calavera had made with this finger. "I got it. I found it."

Martinez sat back down.

"Ten-three, good buddy," Barnes said. He laughed. It brought him agony. Electrified shards stung him at every joint. "Read the Jones poem."

"Come on," Martinez said. "You said you've got it. What is it?"

"Bear with me," Barnes said. "Read the poem."

> Your child was taken
> Your insides left barren,
> Both man and woman
> Suffered the pain;
> But admit the relief
> You felt when you knew,
> No changing of diapers
> No going insane;
> While you sleep easy and dream
> Not quite three calaveras.

Barnes smiled, nodded his head. He said, "Now the Jensen poem. Only the last line."

Martinez flipped a page and read.

A day for calaveras.

"Now the Dunham poem, only the last line."

That leads to calaveras.

"And the Wilson poem," Barnes said. He had opened up his phone and was looking at the picture he'd taken at the Wilson home.

To dust seven calaveras.

"How many lines in each poem?"

Martinez checked. "Ten."

Barnes made the downward part of an L shape with his index finger. "And what's the third word in the last line of each?" Barnes finished the L shape. "Ten-three. Tenth line, third word. Say those words aloud—see, pea, five, ate, three, for, to, seven."

"See, pea, five, ate, three, for, to, seven."

"What's that sound like to you?"

She shrugged. "Just a bunch of words."

"Say them fast."

"See-pea-five-ate-three-for-to-seven."

"What's that sound like?"

"Like an account number."

"Right," Barnes said. "CP583427."

Martinez wrote the number down. She looked up. "What is it?"

Flaherty stirred from underneath his sheet across the room.

"Go," Barnes said. "Get out of here. Take that number to Darrow and have him run it—plates and serial numbers, account numbers, whatever—see what comes out."

She left the room as Flaherty was peeling back the sheet over his face. Barnes pulled out the needle and applied a cotton ball and Band-Aid. He stood up unsteadily and began removing Eddie's tubes.

"Wha?" Flaherty said. "What happened?"

Barnes stuffed the tubing and the needle into the hazmat box on Eddie's cart. "Slip and fall. You better get some new shoes, buddy."

Flaherty sat up slowly. He touched the back of his head where there was a bloody lump. "I slipped?"

"Sure did," Barnes said. He put on his holster. "Only after you knocked me for a good one."

"You're not supposed to be on that machine," Flaherty said. His eyes were dazed. He cringed and sucked through his teeth as he tapped at the sore on the back of his head.

Bolts of blue lightning shot through Barnes as he put on his jacket. He gritted his teeth as he pushed his hands and arms down through the sleeves. He limped toward the door.

28 ✓

Barnes stood outside Jackie Helms's holding cell in the precinct basement. She was sleeping on a thin mattress, one hand beneath her head, the other tucked between the knees of her stonewashed jeans. Her hair had fallen over her face. The fluorescent lights made her skin look like processed cheese. She might have been passably confident in the darkness of Shootz—running the bar, pouring drinks, smiling, and snickering with the regulars—but in a jail cell she was a scared kid.

Barnes knocked on the bars.

No response.

"Jackie. Wake up."

"I'm not asleep, jerk. I'm just ignoring you."

Barnes crooned, "Nobody knows the trouble I've seen."

Jackie turned over on the bed to face away from him, flipped him off.

"Your lawyer didn't show up yet, huh?"

No response.

"You know, Jackie, you pointed that weapon at *me*."

"So?"

"So, I'm the one who pressed charges."

Her head picked up from the mattress.

"That's right. It means I can just as easily drop the charges and you can go home."

Jackie sat up. She spun on the bed to face him, brushed the hair back away from her eyes. Her cheeks were sunken and smeared with dried mascara. She clasped her hands together. "Please. I have a little pup at home."

"What breed?" Kerri Wilson.

"Boston Terrier."

"Black and white? Cute little bugged-out eyes?"

Jackie nodded, looked quizzically at Barnes. "Your voice keeps cracking. You all right?"

Barnes cleared his throat. "You scratch my back?"

"Mister," Jackie said, "I'll give you a full-on back massage with oils and candles and all that shit if you get me out of here."

"Happy ending?" Chunk Philips.

Jackie rolled her eyes.

Barnes blinked, focused on Jackie. "Here's the deal, first you tell me if you know what this code means: CP583427."

"I don't know. A license plate?"

"No. Think hard. Something Beckett might have mentioned? Maybe something to do with security systems?"

Jackie closed her eyes and bit her lip. After a moment new tears fell from between her closed eyelids. Her chin started quivering.

"Don't start that shit."

She opened her eyes. "I'm sorry. I don't know what it means. Please let me out of here."

"Maybe Beckett knows?"

"Maybe."

"Okay, I need to talk to Beckett. We've had eyes on his place since last night. We know he's not there, and we know he's not at Shootz. You tell me where I might find him, and I'll drop the charges against you. Understand? No snipe-hunt bullshit."

"I don't know," Jackie said. "I don't know him as well as you think. We were just . . . you know, friends with benefits." She wiped snot from her nose and looked off.

"Think, Jackie. The conversations before and after sex."

"Yeah, right."

"He had to have said something."

"All he ever did was get drunk at the bar and sleep it off. Occasionally we'd fuck, and in the morning he'd head off to the church."

"For MA meetings?"

"That was only on Thursdays. He went there all the time."

"For what?"

"I don't know, something about needing sanctuary." She threw up air quotes around *sanctuary*. "Always figured he was bullshitting, just looking for a way to get me out of the house. Figured he just hid around some corner and came back after I left, but one time I stayed all afternoon and he never came back." She crossed her arms. "Ain't shit to eat at his place. I practically starved."

Sanctuary. A tingle washed over Barnes's skin. He knew where Beckett was hiding out. "Thank you, Jackie. I'll get you processed and out of here as soon as possible." He headed down the hall.

From behind, Jackie said, "What the hell's a snipe hunt?"

Barnes stood outside the wooded lot behind Saint Thomas of Assisi. The land was church owned, fenced in, and posted with No Trespassing signs every eight feet—cordial invitations to kids and vagrants. He dropped down and shimmied beneath the fence at a low spot in the ground. The same low spot he and Ricky used so many Sundays ago.

Leaves spun as they fell on a bed of brown needles. The scent of sap in the air. Barnes came to the large oak and found the old hatch, Sanctuary carved into the panels. Ricky would always say *Heave ho!* before they pulled the doors open. Barnes squatted down and pulled open the hatch. The hinges barked with rust as the doors rose up and then banged down on the forest floor. From the dark depths of the tunnel came a scent Barnes recognized all too well.

Death.

Barnes climbed down the three wooden steps to the tunnel's earthen floor. He shined his flashlight the length of the darkness. Damon Beckett's corpse was near the end of the tunnel, up against the wall. He'd no doubt retreated deeper into the darkness when his murderer entered the shaft and found him. Barnes moved along the tunnel toward the body, kicking through a sea of empty liquor bottles and dirty hypodermic needles. He hadn't pegged Beckett as a heroin addict, but neither did he believe Beckett was the only lowlife to hide out in the sanctuary. The stench grew stronger as he drew closer. Barnes kept his light down until he was nearly there, and then he put the beam on the body. Beckett's face was mashed in, and there were two holes in him. One a small point, just above the right shoulder. It'd clipped away the humerus bone and left his arm hanging from skin. The second hole was in his chest—a flat, vertical entry wound through the heart. The pickax had missed his cigarette pack by half an inch. Barnes shined the flashlight up above Beckett's head. There were words written in Magic Marker on the concrete wall that sealed the tunnel off from the church.

BRING THE MACHINE.

Barnes went back to the tunnel opening, climbed out, and called dispatch. He left before the cruisers arrived.

29

"What happened?" Jessica said. She gingerly peeled Barnes's jacket off his shoulders and down. They were standing in her small kitchen.

"Can I use your computer?"

"Tell me what's wrong." She stood before him holding his jacket with two hands, concern on her face.

"Whopper headache."

"Aspirin?"

He shook his head.

She threw his jacket over a chair and went to a cupboard above the stove. She pulled out a bottle, blew off some dust, and showed it to him. Wild Turkey Single Barrel. "Will this help?"

"Yes."

They sat down on her couch, him with her computer on his lap, each of them with a tumbler. Barnes drank his first pour quickly and then poured another. He brought up Google and typed in CP583427. Before he pressed "Enter," he said, "Talk to me."

"About what?"

He pressed the key. "You."

"Not much to tell, I guess."

The search came back with two results. One was a page of Chinese lettering. The other seemed to be a system dump of some meaningless computer language.

"My dad traveled for his job," Jessica said, "which meant he was never around. My mom was overprotective, so when I got around to my rebellious teenage years, I started acting out—drinking, smoking, boys, and every other damn thing."

Barnes tried CP-583427. This time there were hundreds of hits. The top one was for an Omaha hockey league. One of the in-game pictures had been labeled with the same serial code, automatic indexing from a camera. Barnes copied the website's address and pasted it into the body of an e-mail.

"After a while my mom checked out. I pretty much grew up on my own. I only saw my dad on the weekends. It was like they were divorced. He just played it cool until he was gone again. Why rock the boat, you know? We were like roommates. At eighteen, I split."

The next few search hits were pdf files of property tax records in Idaho. Barnes copied their addresses and pasted them into the same e-mail. He said, "Where'd you go?"

"Here and there. California for a while, spent some time on the beach. Lived in Chicago for half a year, New Orleans, Charleston, Boston. I saved some money, and eventually I found my way back here. Seems nuts in hindsight, but there's something about the hell of Detroit that makes a person proud, you know?"

Barnes nodded.

"I did my undergrad and got my teaching cert from Oakland, started out subbing in Redford, got my first job at Kenbrook just this new school year." She smiled. "And then I met a handsome stranger who swept me off my feet."

Barnes had filled up a long e-mail with website addresses for anything that seemed like a lead, mentally noting a variety of matching serial codes for pianos and bar stools and cribs. But the deer-tick feeling never increased at what he found. He smirked at Jessica. "Who is he? I'll kick his ass."

"Oh, he's pretty tough. You might have trouble with that."

Half the fifth of Wild Turkey was gone. Barnes was buzzed. The pain in his body had subsided, but he still felt battered. His eyes burned from the computer screen, from fatigue. He sent himself the e-mail with all the website addresses, felt his cell phone vibrate to let him know it was received, and closed Jessica's laptop.

Jessica put down her tumbler and came over to him, tossed the laptop aside, straddled him, loosened his tie.

The people inside Barnes's head kicked open their drawers. They crawled out full of lust and longing. Chunk Philips quivered with desire, as did the rest of the boys, but Nancy Fulmer shoved them aside and took center stage.

"Finally, the right body."

Their combined feelings brought a new kind of intensity to Barnes—an orgy of eyes and erogenous zones, of broken hearts in need of mending. Jessica's weight was light on him, on them, but still painful to Barnes with all his damage. He smiled through the pain. "I'm as tough as they come."

She kissed him and bit his lower lip.

Nancy Fulmer had an orgasm.

30

Barnes woke up in Jessica's bed. He checked the clock on the night-stand: 5:00 a.m. He slid out from under the covers and found his clothing, his shoes. The people in his head had receded while he slept, though his body was still sore. He moved out into the living room and put on his clothes, his holster, his jacket. He checked his phone for text messages. There was one from dispatch.

Nothing on the number so far. Still searching.

He found a note on the inside of the apartment door, taped where he wouldn't miss it when he left.

Think I love you.

He looked in on her, saw her sleeping peacefully, her hair a mess, her chest slowly expanding and contracting. One foot stuck out from beneath the covers. Damn this job. He could slide back in next to her right now, breathe in her scent, touch her warm skin, pull her close. He could never know another crime, never again be attached to the machine.

"*Stay.*" Amanda Jones.

"*Shhh.*"

He went out to his car and drove to the hospital.

A receptionist told Barnes visiting hours hadn't yet begun. He showed her his badge. She frowned at it but let him pass. Franklin was awake, propped up by the adjustable bed, circles shaved into his temples. There was a plastic mug on the table by his bedside, a translucent bendy straw sticking out of it, drops of water stuck inside. The lights of the machinery around Franklin's bed were red and green and orange. They blipped on and off like faraway stars. Barnes pulled up a chair and sat down.

Franklin said, "Hey."

"How you doin', big fella?"

"Better than you, ya freakin' zombie."

Barnes nodded to the accordion machine pumping over Franklin's head, the one helping him breathe. "I doubt that."

Franklin pursed his lips beneath the oxygen tube that ran to his nose. "I saw his face at the cemetery."

"I know."

Franklin's eyes narrowed to slits. "You've been on the machine."

Barnes nodded.

"As me."

Barnes nodded.

"Thought I was a goner, eh?"

Barnes held his partner's stare for what felt like ten minutes. Finally, he said, "Yes."

"Takes more than a knife in the back to kill Big Billy." He smiled wide.

"I'm glad for that."

"So give me the lowdown. Where we at?"

"You killed him," Barnes said.

"Killed who?"

"Tyrell Diggs. You shot him in the chest."

Franklin blinked, looked down at his hands. He stayed there a moment, and then looked up. "So what, you gonna arrest me?"

"You have the right to remain silent."

"Shee-it," Franklin said, "I waive that mothafuckin' right."

"You're full of shit, you know that?"

"How's that?"

Barnes impersonated Franklin's voice. "Ducks in a shooting gallery. They just pop back up. The barker is God."

"They do. He is."

Barnes sighed. "Someone has to knock the ducks down. Otherwise the bad guys multiply, and eventually they win."

Franklin began a reply but broke into a coughing fit. A nurse rushed in. She used a bowl to catch the coagulated blood he spat out. She helped him with some water.

Once Franklin settled down, the nurse turned to Barnes. "He shouldn't be talking. You shouldn't be here."

"Oh, hell no." Detective Franklin's voice from inside.

Barnes said, "I'll do all the talking from here on out. Promise."

She shook her head disapprovingly and left.

"Like hell you will," Franklin said with a strained voice. His eyes were glassy from the coughing fit. "You listen to me. Tyrell Diggs got what was coming to him. The man was evil. He delivered pain and misery to the people on my block. It was a pleasure to snuff him out, but that don't mean he wasn't just replaced by the next evil bastard to come along."

"So what's the point, then? Why kill him?"

Franklin shrugged. "Hope?"

"Come on."

"I don't know, Barnes. I really don't. I'm sitting here in this hospital bed, stabbed in the back by a dude, they tell me, who's knocking off people because they never took the time to visit their dead relatives. You saying there's a point behind all this?"

"You're the one selling hope."

"Here's what I'm selling—you leave the world a better place than when you entered it. That's all there is. For us it means we take down bad guys. For the dude who owns Lafayette it means serving the best goddamned coney dogs you're ever gonna eat. For some Peace Corps sap it means putting rice in some poor kid's bowl and swatting the flies off him. It doesn't matter what you choose, it only matters what you can make stick."

"Remember Andy Kemp?"

Franklin cocked his head, thought for a moment, and then nodded. "That high school kid. Kidnapped and murdered. Ten thousand in his pocket. Memory pull was empty. Unsolved."

"Not anymore. It was Dawson. Watkins saw it in the machine."

Franklin shook his head.

Barnes looked off. "I never told you about my brother."

"Cap told me. Before you were put on this case."

"Then you know."

"So? That doesn't mean—"

"He was just a kid," Barnes said. "Never did nothing bad to anyone, and I killed him just the same as that train killed him, the same as Tyrell Diggs killed Marvin. Diggs wasn't the one who stuck that homemade blade in Marvin, right? But it was his fault just the same. You understand that."

"You loved your brother. You didn't want him to die."

"I didn't stop it."

"Then forgive yourself, dickhead. Get some closure."

Barnes looked down. Somewhere in the conversation he'd reached into his jacket and pulled out the coin purse. The mouth was opening and closing in his hand, his fingers darting in to touch the quarters. He clenched the purse in his fist. "The only closure I deserve"—he lifted his available hand and made the motion of a lid falling down—"is from inside a casket."

"So that's it, then? Your brother died in an accident, so you should die, too? You should subject yourself to the punishment of that machine until it tears you apart?"

Barnes shook his head. He put the coin purse in his outer jacket pocket, touched the Ziploc bag of salt that was still there. He said, "CP583427."

"What's that?"

"That's the big clue Reyes has been trying to make us see. Some serial number or code. Haven't figured it out yet. Mean anything to you?"

"Not off the top."

Barnes looked out the window. The sun was beginning its ascent. Red rays of light made Barnes squint his eyes. They reflected off a urine bag hanging from the side of Franklin's bed. "They got a tube in your dick?"

"Yeah, it's long as hell. They had to fix two of them together for me."

Both detectives laughed. Their laughter crescendoed until Barnes repeatedly slapped his knee. The Franklin in Barnes's head laughed to beat them both.

Afterward, Barnes's inner Franklin faded back into Barnes's mind. The pain in Barnes's body began to fall away. The real Franklin said, "What are you gonna do now?"

"With you here in the hospital, I've gotta do my own desk work," Barnes said. "I've got a list of websites that came up when I searched for that number. Going to comb through them and see what sticks."

31

Barnes sat in the precinct parking lot. He read the text message on his phone for what felt like the tenth time. It had come from Jessica.

Hello, lover. Why did you leave?

He didn't have an answer for her, wasn't sure he wanted to give one. He had a partner in the hospital and was on a hot case. He assumed she understood that. He pocketed his phone, got out of the car, and headed into the station. He was stopped by Darrow on the way to his desk.

"My office. Now."

Barnes followed Darrow into his office, plopped down in a chair. "Good news about Franklin, eh?"

"I'm taking you off the case."

"What?"

"Beckett is dead. You've run yourself ragged on this thing, and that little stunt you pulled with Flaherty has forced my hand."

Barnes sighed. His cell phone buzzed against his leg. He said, "Cap, no one knows this guy like I do. We've got an APB on his truck, and a BOLO on his description. I'll find something in Beckett, plus this serial number—"

"Which so far has amounted to jack."

"I've got the burr and the cedar leaf. It might not have come from the cemetery. Reyes might live out in the backwoods. Maybe Whitehall." The Flamingo Farms trailer park flashed into Barnes's mind.

He mentally traveled past his old home and down to the river where he and Ricky used to play. Had there been burrs along the way? Burrs at the riverbank?

"Whitehall is huge, Barnes. What do you suggest we do, go out there with some dogs? That'd take months. On a burr and a leaf, are you nuts?"

"A chopper."

"And do what? Send in SWAT on every tent we find? It's public property. We'd be disturbing every outdoor nut from here to Canada."

"Not all of it is public property," Barnes said. "There's private ownership at the edges and along the Rouge River. I grew up out there."

Darrow nodded. "We'll look into the property records."

"We find this guy's real name yet?"

"Still waiting to hear back from the secretary of state. Goddamn morons."

Barnes's cell phone buzzed again. "Hold up a sec," he said, and then checked the phone. Two new text messages from Jessica.

Come on, Barnes, get back here and fuck me.

And then:

You know you want to . . .

Darrow said, "Put that away and pay attention."

Barnes put the phone away.

"You're off the case, and that's final. Don't fight me on it. Just go home, take a few days off. Jesus Christ, lay off the bottle and get some sleep."

"Who's on it?"

"None of your business."

"Bullshit. Who?"

"Flaherty just passed his detective exam."

"Oh, you prick," Barnes said. He stood up.

"Watch that tone," Darrow said.

"You can't put that asshole on my case. That's salt in the wound."

"He's already on it," Darrow said. "Now walk away before I take your badge."

Barnes slammed the door behind him. The windows shook. Everyone looked up from their paperwork.

Barnes went to Flaherty's desk. The asshole wasn't there. He went to the technical lab and peeked through the window. Warden was inside, tending to Flaherty on the bed, hooked up to Eddie. His body jerked in reaction to the punishment. Barnes's cell phone buzzed again. Another text message from Jessica.

Come visit me, Barnes. Come fuck me. Now!

He felt sick. He replied.

Can you please stop?

"Barnes."

He looked up to find Martinez peeking around a hallway corner. She gestured with her head for Barnes to come over, her ponytail swayed with the movement. Barnes pocketed his phone and went over. "Darrow fire you?"

"Flaherty figured out what really went down. Guess that makes him a detective, after all. They had someone watch me while I packed up my stuff, then they walked me out the door. I'm not supposed to be here, but I had to come back and let you know."

"Know what?"

"Antonio Reyes," she said. "He's on the machine. He's got memories in the central system."

"How?"

"Former victim. Secretary of state was taking too long to get back, so Flaherty followed up with Rock Hill Management in Florida. Found out Reyes's former name is Arturo Perez. They ran a background on him. I guess he survived a point-blank shotgun blast to the chest. Nothing short of a miracle."

"I was just in with Darrow. He didn't mention it. Said the secretary of state was dragging their feet."

Martinez shrugged.

Barnes looked back at the technical lab door. Flaherty was attached to Eddie, but a second machine was in there, too. He said, "Wait for me outside," and went to the door.

Warden looked up when Barnes entered the lab. The barrel mark on his forehead had grown into a bruise. Barnes pointed at the second machine. "I need it."

"You're kidding, right?" Warden said. "I'm a second away from reporting you just for being in this room."

Barnes nodded toward Flaherty on the hospital bed. "Who's he hooked into? Beckett?"

"Go away, Barnes."

"I need Reyes. He was once a vic, name of Arturo Perez. I can catch him."

"I don't care—" A wave of realization washed over Warden's face. He blinked a few times. "Did you say Arturo Perez?"

"Yes."

"Zero-zero-zero-zero-nine."

Barnes raised his eyebrows.

"That was his file number. One of the first ever on the machine. Third or fourth that I harvested." He placed a hand on his chest. "He was blown open. No one thought he'd make it. Some drug-runner thing. The Fero brothers, I think."

"Please."

Warden shook his head. "No. Why should I help you? I can just as easily hook Flaherty to Perez and achieve the same result, only I won't lose my job over it."

Barnes closed his eyes. For a moment he stood in darkness, in the silence of the room, above Flaherty's murmurs and shakes. His mind's eye saw his brother's face, receding at the edges, his little smile being chipped away, his eyes fading. He said, "I have nothing to bargain with. I am no more than a drunk and a munky who nearly got his partner killed. I deserve no favors from you or anyone else, and I deserve no forgiveness." He opened his eyes and found Warden. "But I'm asking anyway, because I believe I can catch this guy before he hurts anyone else, and if I believe it, maybe you'll believe it, and maybe you'll help me, and all this won't have been a goddamn waste."

Warden smirked. "You practice that in the mirror?"

"Help me," Barnes said.

Warden looked at the machine. He placed a hand on it, drummed his fingers. "Have it back in a half hour."

32

Barnes wheeled the machine out the side door of the precinct. Martinez was kicking stones at the far end of the parking lot. He signaled for her to come over as he pushed the machine behind a dumpster. He took off his jacket, threw it down on the concrete, and set his handgun and phone in the folds. He rolled back a sleeve and booted aside a discarded coffee cup.

Martinez came around the side of the dumpster. "How's the battery?"

"Good."

"We'll need a Wi-Fi signal to tap into the server."

Barnes checked the signal-strength indicator on the machine. "We're close enough to the building. It should work." He put the suction cups on his own temples and slid down to his butt, back against the dumpster. He looked up at her.

She started prepping the machine.

"Zero-zero-zero-zero-nine," Barnes said. "That's his file number."

Martinez typed and turned dials on the console. She secured the serum, prepped the needle.

Barnes said, "Thank you for this."

"Yeah, well, I hear they're still looking for help at the Bracken Institute."

"I'll give you a good reference."

"Damn right you will." She squatted to insert the needle into his arm.

◆　◆　◆

Arturo Perez stood in Parkview Memorial cemetery. A chilly wind ripped across the landscape and cooled the tears on his face. He looked down at three open graves in a row, each one with an expensive coffin lowered into it, piles of dark-brown earth beside. Stabbed into the rightmost pile was a pickax, its handle at a forty-five-degree angle to the ground.

Perez's mind was short-circuiting. Confusion pierced by painful jolts of light and sound. A chaotic swirl of emotions, physical senses, disjointed visions. Everything he saw squiggled. He looked at the grave on the left—his mother, Maria. A horrifying image of her dead body, bound, gagged, and flayed, ripped across his vision. It sent searing pain through Barnes's left eye. In the middle was the grave of Perez's father, Rodrigo. Another vision came, causing Barnes to blink and cringe— Perez's father, stripped from the waist down and dangling by his neck from a rope in his kitchen, a white tank top stretched above his distended belly, his ankles bound to his wrists so there'd be room for him to hang. His tongue and genitals had gone purple. Barnes pushed back against the dumpster.

On the right was the grave of Perez's younger sister, Margarita. He'd found her bound spread-eagle to her twin bed, almost certainly raped before her throat was cut. The blood had pooled beneath her face, which had been carved with the markings of a sugar-skull mask.

The Feros, Perez thought. They'd promised, should he ever cross them, what they would do to his family—Margarita in particular. They'd kept their promise, down to the final detail of her dead skin mask. "You know," a smirking Randall Fero had said of Arturo Perez's kid sister, "for only thirteen, she's got some great tits."

Perez recalled the contract he'd made with the Fero brothers, a couple of well-known Detroit human and drug traffickers. They were running operations on both the Mexican and Canadian borders. Standing before his family's southeast Michigan burial plot, Perez could feel the Central American heat, the scents and sounds of the cantina inside which his deal with the Feros had been struck. They would smuggle him and his family across the border and provide them with papers in exchange for five years as a drug mule between Detroit and Windsor. In Canada he'd meet with their contact, swallow a dozen balloons of heroin at a time, and bring them back over the Ambassador Bridge.

Arturo had done three good months of running. In that short time he'd shat out nearly a thousand heroin balloons for the Feros. He'd pluck them from the toilet, clean them with a toothbrush and hand soap, and deliver them smelling sweet and on time, every time, until the day he came up one balloon short.

Barnes's eyes went into REM. He shook his head as a painful, jagged memory dragged its way through Perez's mind. He arrived home from a trip to Windsor with his stomach taut. He hugged each of his family members in turn, spending extra time with his arms around his kid sister, reveling in her touch, the feel of her chest against his own. Afterward he headed straight for the bathroom. One balloon was lost in his system, caught up like a stubborn bowel movement. His intestines felt tied in a knot.

After cleaning what he'd managed to pass, he left the house and delivered the goods on time, as usual. He explained to the Feros that he was one balloon short, and promised to deliver the final balloon after it arrived. The Feros laughed. Arturo recalled their smiling faces like demons, their teeth like fangs. They clapped his shoulder and assured him they'd take his delivery once it was ready, recommending he eat some of their mother's *pasta e fagioli* to help things along.

Perez went back home and sat on the toilet. He pushed and pushed until something happened.

Unfortunately, the something that happened was the balloon bursting.

Within seconds he fell off the toilet and was face-flat, his body shuddering on the mosaic floor tile. In the precinct parking lot, Barnes's body trembled from the remembered overdose. His elbows banged the dumpster behind him. His eyes felt like they would pop.

Perez barfed across the tiles before his throat constricted, pushing his tongue out and gagging him. His arms and legs went stiff. He could hear his family in the next room. They were watching VHS reruns of *Seinfeld*. He heard the front door burst open, heard Margarita scream as his vision faded to black.

Arturo fell to his knees before his family's graves. New tears erupted and spilled down. He'd saved most of what the Feros had paid him—envisioning a nice home in a clean suburb for his family—and now half the money was gone, spent on these burial plots, their well-adorned coffins. He screamed at the sky. It was like a megaphone of feedback in Barnes's ears.

Perez looked to his left, out across the cemetery. The land was riddled with headstones and crypts, but there was no one visiting. He scanned left to right across the entire grounds, all the way back to the archway at the front. No one. An ocean of loved ones lost, and no one to be with them, no one to care. His family, here in this unfamiliar land, had been given no funeral. There had been no preacher saying words above them. They only had their son, their brother, who couldn't shit a drug balloon to save their lives, as witness to their interment.

Arturo rose from his knees. He picked up the pickax and used it to begin shoveling dirt onto his mother's grave. The tool wasn't right for the job, but given time it would get it done. He chopped at the dirt, recalling his mother's gratitude for what he'd done for them in working with the Feros. Her tears. The way they'd collected in the wrinkles around her mouth and traveled down to hang from her chin before falling to dampen her clothing. She had thanked him for finding them this new home, this new life.

Arturo was caked in dirt by the time his mother was buried and the earth above her coffin was tamped flat. He threw off his jacket and began burying his father, recalling the man's bloated body hanging from a rope, the strange shape of his bruised genitals.

Barnes was exhausted by the time Perez began burying his sister. His arms hung limply at his sides, his legs were like fallen logs, his hands full of phantom blisters. The tireless Perez furiously chopped the dirt and scooped it onto his sister's coffin. He recalled her smile, her laughter, her love for peanut-butter cups and milk. He watched her chase a butterfly, watched her hold a stiff upper lip over a skinned knee, watched her stand up to Mom and get slapped for her defiance. He recalled how much joy she'd expressed at her new American crush. A boy in her school. For a while it was only *Andrew this, Andrew that.*

The bad memory followed. The day Arturo expressed his love to her. "Of course you love me, Artie," she'd said, her smile dazzling, her eyes bubbling. "You're my brother." She reached up to touch his cheek. He gripped her wrist and pulled her close, kissed her lips.

Margarita screamed.

He let her go.

She ran.

Barnes felt pain in Arturo's chest. An aching wound beneath the skin, the bones. The taste of the young girl's saliva on Arturo's lips.

His family now buried, Arturo Perez walked through the empty cemetery toward the gate. His jacket was in his hand, his starched shirt now torn and tattered, his pants and shoes destroyed.

"Hey!"

Perez stopped, looked back. A thing stood there. He struggled to recall its name. Sharon something. He'd met it yesterday, bringing in his drug-mule money to buy the holes and coffins in which his family would rest, paying extra to expedite their burials. Through his malfunctioning mind he saw Sharon as a pig, frothy-mouthed and standing on hind legs, its trotters splitting wide at the ground to keep it balanced and upright. He blinked and shook his head, but the vision remained.

"You're pretty good with that pickax," Sharon Bruckheimer said, showing sharp teeth and a fat tongue.

Arturo stared.

"You looking for work?"

Arturo shrugged. He felt like the pig might look better bleeding from multiple wounds or yelping in pain. Maybe its head on a spike, vacant eyes.

"Take some time to mourn. Come back when you're ready. I'll find something for you."

Arturo Perez passed under the cemetery archway. He began down the sidewalk. A vehicle pulled up next to him.

"Thought you were dead in that bathroom."

It was Gerald Fero, or at least an animal wearing his face. He was leaning out the passenger side of a black pickup truck, an over-under shotgun pointed at Perez. Behind him, in the driver's seat, was a pig wearing a Randall Fero mask. Perez wondered how they'd both look lying on the ground with holes in them, their legs twitching in death throes.

"Can't believe you survived a burst balloon," the Gerald animal said. "Guess you weren't trying to rip us off, after all."

Behind him, the Randall animal chuckled. "Want your job back?"

Arturo shook his head no.

"Wasn't really a question, idiot," the Randall animal said. "Take the job or my brother pulls the trigger."

Arturo dropped his jacket and spread out his arms. Barnes's knuckles rapped against the dumpster wall. Perez stood there waiting. The Gerald animal shook its head in disbelief. It lifted the gun to its shoulder and fired.

Darkness and silence.

"End of transmission."

The Vitruvian Man test pattern.

Please Stand By.

Barnes popped the suction cups from his own temples. He pulled the needle out of his arm. Martinez was holding his cell phone, reading the screen. Barnes stood to find his legs unsteady, his arms throbbing in pain. The Fero brothers. They'd disappeared nearly a decade ago in what was thought to be a gangland hit. Gone like Jimmy Hoffa. No suspects. Now Barnes knew better. Squealer and Napoleon.

"They've got a new crime scene," Martinez said. "Just came in off dispatch. You know that teacher Dale Wilson had a thing for?"

Barnes's heart fell, his stomach shriveled. He steadied himself with a hand against the dumpster.

"You okay?" Martinez said.

She reached out for him, but he put up a palm to stop her. "Just tell me."

"Cruisers are headed to her place right now," she said. "Something went down. No code yet. Just a nine-one-one called in by a neighbor."

Barnes took his phone from her. He checked the messages. After the dispatch message, there was a new one from Jessica's number.

10-3, good buddy ;)

33

Barnes turned off Plum Street to see red-and-blue gumball lights spinning and spraying the nearby buildings. The street was blocked by cruisers parked at angles. He slammed the brakes, threw it in park, and hopped out of the car. He ran toward Jessica's building.

His legs grew weaker as he approached. He stumbled, fell, got back up. Kept going.

A uniform stopped him at the edge of the scene. He showed his badge and the man let him pass. He moved up the sidewalk toward the brownstone's outer door.

"You did this!"

Barnes stopped and looked up. It was the umbrella woman from the second floor. She was crying, her face twisted in pain.

"You led him here!"

Her accusation cracked him, drained his value into the gutter. He continued forward in desperation.

The brownstone's outer door had been kicked open. It had fallen into the building. The wooden jamb was splintered. There were flower petals on the floor leading up the stairs. Barnes climbed the steps, smashing petals as he went, turning them dark. He heard voices and sounds from above. Men talking. Feet moving. He imagined Warden standing over Jessica's dead body, shaving circles into her temples. He imagined her foot still sticking out from beneath the covers, just as it was when he left.

He came around the corner to find her apartment door open. There were uniformed officers inside, technicians doing fingerprint work, flashbulbs popping and then warming back up with their high-pitched screams.

Barnes stopped at the threshold. How long ago had he left? Three hours? He stepped into the apartment, looked left. The altar. It was stacked on the countertop in Jessica's kitchen, three rows high. Sugar skulls lined the base in a variety of colors. There were candles and flowers, sweets, and tiny bottles of Cuervo Gold. On each of the shelves there were small black picture frames, nine in total.

Barnes examined the pictures, starting at the bottom left. The first held the funeral program for Mildred Smith, the woman who'd given Edith MacKenzie the horse that would cripple her daughter. Mildred was smiling as she looked back over her shoulder in a professional photo session, her hand awkwardly touching her chin. Next came the program for Verna Philips, whose son, she said, would never amount to anything. Her photo looked like it was taken during a backyard barbecue. Chunk was there, at her side, his face round, his eyes buried. After that was the program for Robert Morris Chamberlain, unlucky enough to have been born to two crack addicts. His photo was that of a newborn child wearing patches and wires.

The people in Barnes's head cried out at the sight of their loved ones lost. Barnes gripped the countertop to keep his balance. He glanced at the remaining programs until he came to David Fulmer, a face he recognized. The strangest immortalization of them all. This man had been killed by his own sister, who was then killed by a madman because she never visited his grave. If that wasn't odd enough, the man who killed her had built an altar to him. As the wicked witch might say, *What a world*.

"I'm sorry, David. I'm so sorry." Nancy Fulmer.

Barnes came to the top of the altar. The photo here wasn't from a funeral program, but a cutout from a newspaper article covering the untimely death of young Richard M. Barnes, tragically taken too early. Hit by a train while trying to cross the tracks on his bike. No mention of the chain snapping and trapping him there, helpless.

Barnes walked away from the altar toward the bedroom. His heart pounded as he neared the door. There were voices inside, officers moving, elbows and feet flashing in and out of his vision. A female officer was standing with her back bent over the bed. Jessica was there.

Not dead.

She was sitting up, elbows on her knees, eyes closed and facing the female officer, who was wiping the paint from her face. She'd been painted into a death bride—a skull of white, dark circles around her eyes, teeth painted over her lips, which had been stretched to the point where they cracked and bled. She'd been crying. Her wrists and ankles were ripped and raw where she'd been bound. Her hands shook.

This is what Barnes had brought to her door. This is what it meant to know John and all his friends. To try to love them. A searing pain emerged in Barnes's stomach. It made its way up through his chest and into his head, where it locked on like a vise.

He backed out of the doorway.

34

Barnes arrived at Calvary Junction. He parked his car at the gas station where Mania Challenge had once been, where he and Ricky had played so many games. The station was open. There was one man pumping gas into an SUV. Barnes waited for the man to finish and drive away, leaving the gas station empty save for the old attendant inside, whose head was bent over a magazine.

Barnes got out of the car and dropped his keys on the asphalt, peeled off his jacket, and threw it on the hood of his sedan. He went to the three white crosses at the junction, knelt down before them, and looked for Ricky's name.

There.

Richard M. Barnes. His own handwriting from twenty years ago. Someone had written another name over most of it, but he could see Ricky was still there. Barnes kissed his fingertips and pressed them against his brother's name.

The ground beneath his knees began to shake. The crossing came to life with its bells and lights. The barrier arms came down. Barnes stood. He moved past the near barrier arm and onto the tracks. He stood on the ties and faced the oncoming train. The train grew as it approached, blooming like a thundercloud on the horizon. The cinders at his feet began to hop. He reached toward his jacket pocket for the coin purse, but the jacket wasn't there; he'd taken it off at the car.

Barnes ran from the tracks, ducked the barrier, and sprinted back to the gas station. There was a second car parked next to his own. He grabbed his jacket, reached into the inside pocket. Empty. The train sounded its horn. He checked the left outer pocket. Empty. He checked the right outer pocket. The coin purse was there, next to the bag of salt Jessica had given him at the cemetery. He snatched up the coin purse and started back toward the tracks but found himself tackled to the ground.

Barnes turned over to find Jeremiah Holston getting up, dusting himself off.

Barnes got up to run, but Holston shoved him back down. "Stay down, moron."

Again Barnes tried to run, but Holston grabbed him and threw him against his car, pinned him there with his body weight. Barnes looked over Holston's shoulder. The train barreled through the junction. A big Canadian Pacific, pulling boxcar after boxcar overflowing with black coal. The nearby leaves lifted into the air, the barrier arms rippled in the wind.

Too late.

Barnes screamed. He head-butted Holston, sent him reeling. He ran toward the train and whipped the coin purse at the passing cars. It exploded against the rusty metal, sending quarters flying. He stopped and fell to his knees when he saw the serial numbers painted on the outer walls of the passing cars.

CP-898412 . . . CP-878527 . . . CP-965471.

35

Barnes snatched up his keys from the asphalt. He put on his jacket. Holston was leaning against his own car. He held a wadded tissue over his left eye to stem the dripping blood.

"You're still following me?" Barnes said.

Holston shrugged. "Slow day at the office."

"Why do you care what happens to me?"

Holston sighed and looked off. "I gotta sleep at night."

"You do me that favor?"

Holston nodded. He reached in through the open window of his car and pulled out a folded newspaper, held it out.

Barnes took the paper, stuffed it into his jacket, and got into his car. He peeled out of the parking lot into Calvary Junction, turning onto the tracks. The train was a dot in the distance. He straightened his tires and stomped the gas pedal. The car bounced on the ties. His teeth rattled. His bones ached where they banged one another at the joints. The rearview mirrors were knocked out of alignment. He lost ground on the train, fought to keep the steering wheel straight against the battering from below.

The left back tire blew. The car tilted down and nearly veered off the tracks. Barnes held on. Kept going.

The right front tire blew. The car jerked back into alignment so hard Barnes's head clipped the driver-side window. He pushed forward on the two remaining tires, his vision blurry.

When the left front tire blew, the car snapped to a halt, the two front rims dropping hard between the ties, the back end lifting into the air, almost toppling over the front, before slamming back down.

Barnes staggered out of the vehicle and started running. He was in Whitehall Forest now, out past any depths he'd known before. His lungs burned, his eyes spilled tears against the icy wind. He could smell the pines and the earthy water. The Rouge River was out there, rushing mindlessly over stone and silt with no concern for the human world it sliced through like a wound. The Flamingo Farms trailer park was out there, too, and his old tree fort, maybe inhabited by some other kids now, maybe gone to the animals.

And Calavera was out there. The deer-tick feeling told him so. Arturo Perez confirmed it from within.

Barnes thought, *Where is he?*

"I don't want to die." Arturo Perez.

Barnes caught up to the train, which had slowed and stopped at a railway-yard switching station. He came to the edge of the yard at a jog, breathing hard, swallowing the smell of coal and oil. At the outskirts there were stacks of empty boxcars, a large crane to move them around, and in the distance an old helicopter in an overgrown field.

Barnes moved to the center of the yard. There were men in orange vests about, some doing engine repairs, others checking manifests, others unloading coal from the cars into wheeled carts. There was a squat building there, too, a trailer like those found at construction sites.

Barnes went to the building and pulled open the door. There were two men inside. One was middle-aged. He wore thick glasses and a red-and-black-checkered flannel. He was going over some notes on a yellow pad. The other man was ancient. He wore green suspenders and was seemingly asleep on a battered love seat near the back. His mouth was agape.

The middle-aged man at the notepad looked up. "Can I help you?"

Barnes showed his badge. "I need help with a serial number. Might belong to one of your boxcars."

The man pursed his lips. "Do you have the number?"

Barnes took the pen from the man's hand. He wrote the number down on the pad the man had been using. The man looked at the number and shook his head. "It's a Canadian Pacific number, sure, but we got a lot of boxcars coming through here. To be able to recall one just by number? No chance."

Barnes gripped the bridge of his nose. "Is there a tracking system?"

"Yes," the man said. He stood up and went to a computer monitor on a desk at the center of the trailer. The old man's eyes were now open, his mouth closed, but he hadn't yet stirred.

"I can try to look it up," the first man said, "but the odds of it being anywhere nearby are slim."

"Can you try?"

"Give me the number again."

"CP-583427."

The man typed with only his index fingers, looking up and down from the screen to the keyboard with each stroke. He got it all in and emphatically tapped the "Return" button. After a moment he said, "Out of service."

"What's that mean?"

"These boxcars don't last forever. Once one gets too rusted out or damaged, they get retired, so to speak." He smiled, raised his eyebrows above his glasses.

"What happens to them?"

"Usually recycling."

"What's the chance an out-of-service boxcar wouldn't be recycled?"

"Not good."

"But there *is* a chance."

It was the old man at the back who spoke. He sat up, nodding his head in slow ups and downs. "Used to be we'd sell them off to private owners. Back in my day we used them for fishing or hunting camps."

"Could this boxcar have been sold to a private owner?"

The younger man looked at the computer screen. "It doesn't say anything about that here."

"That computer wouldn't know rabbit shit from pinto beans," the older man said. "Just about any car that starts with a six or below is going to be on *paper* record." He gestured toward a stack of boxes against the back wall of the trailer.

Barnes stepped toward the boxes. There were dozens of them, all marked. He found the one he wanted—CP-57500 TO CP-59500. He pulled the box from the stacks and riffled through the files inside until he found CP-583427. He yanked the file and opened it. There was a record of the boxcar's travels, including dates, times, origins, destinations, and loads. He scanned through the pages until he got to the last entry.

Damaged. Private sale.

"Says here it was damaged and sold."

The old man smirked, nodded.

Barnes flipped to the rear of the file folder and found a receipt. Adrenaline surged when he saw the buyer was named A. Perez. The sale was dated January 17, 2004. "This is the man I'm looking for. Arturo Perez. Does that sound familiar to either of you?"

The younger man shook his head no.

The older man said, "Mexican fella?"

"Yes."

"What does it say beneath the bill of sale there?"

Barnes looked at the receipt again. Beneath the line item for the purchase of the boxcar was another item, written in blue pen. "It says, *Lift, three hundred and fifty dollars.*"

The old man nodded again. "I remember him. Big jaw on that guy, right?"

"That's him."

"The boxcar had only just a dent on one side, but we couldn't manage to pull it out. Costs more than a new car to cut out the panel and weld one back in, so it went down as damaged. The fella you're looking for, he came around looking for one a few weeks beforehand, so we called him up, let him know we had one."

"And *lift?*" Barnes said.

"I delivered it for him. Picked it up with my chopper"—he thumbed toward the trailer window in the direction of the helicopter outside—"dropped it on his property."

"Where?"

"Out there in Whitehall. Bought himself a remote acre or two along the Rouge, if I recall."

"Can you take me there?"

"I might could, but that chopper ain't been running for years now. Just take Eight Mile back to Featherton Road and hang a left. Go about a mile to the river. Once you get there you'll have to hoof it a half mile or so into the woods, straight west. Stick to the riverbank and you'll find it."

"I need a car."

The younger man said, "What's this man done?"

"You've heard of the Pickax Man?"

For a moment they all sat silent, and then the old man tossed a set of keys to Barnes. "My truck's the red F-150 just outside this here trailer. Do me a favor. Go and put a bullet in that bastard."

36

Barnes pulled to the shoulder on Featherton Road. He stepped out of the old man's truck and walked until he was standing on a bridge over the Rouge River. To the east the river banked and angled north through some hardwoods. To the west it was all red cedars. The bushes along the roadside were covered with burrs.

Barnes moved west along the riverbank, stepping carefully over fallen trees, boulders, and cutouts. A quarter mile into the woods he spotted a tarp-covered truck a hundred feet to the north. Likely it was parked at the end of an overgrown two-track. Barnes pulled out his cell phone. He typed a text to Jessica's number.

I'm coming to visit you.

He drew his Glock, held it near his thigh as he continued along the riverbank.

His phone buzzed in reply.

You found my address?

Barnes typed.

CP-583427.

The reply was immediate.

Bravo.

Then another reply.

When should I expect you?

Barnes typed.

Soon.

Barnes climbed over the trunk of a fallen cedar. When he came down on the other side, he caught a glimpse of red in the distance. He ducked down and moved his head slowly, side to side and up and down like a cautious deer, until he found what was he was looking for—a serial number, in white lettering against red paint on the boxcar's side: CP-583427.

The people inside him emerged from their drawers. Their pains returned to his body, their fears and angers to his mind—each one fought for control of his thoughts and movements. His hands shook. It took intense focus to dial Captain Darrow.

Darrow answered. "Where are you?"

"We've got him, Cap," Barnes whispered. "He's out in Whitehall. The serial number was for a Canadian Pacific boxcar."

"He's in your custody?"

"Track this phone's location. Bring the machine." He set the phone down on the cedar trunk, left it connected to the call. He moved toward the boxcar, both hands now on his weapon, the tinny echoes of Darrow's voice coming from the speaker. "Barnes! Do not advance without backup!"

He came to a wide cedar with low, sweeping limbs. It was at the edge of the small clearing where the boxcar had been dropped. He moved beneath the limbs of the tree and up against the trunk, staying covered in the shadow the tree provided.

Chunk Philips felt it was a good place to hide.

Jeffrey Dunham agreed.

Calavera's voice rang out. "I can hear you, Barnes."

Barnes settled his back against the tree. He stole a glance toward the boxcar. On the near side was the door, three-quarters open. The outer latch looked like a complicated affair, but there was one long bar sticking out. Above it, in white paint, was the word *lock* with a down arrow. Dale Wilson thought the boxcar looked like the live animal trap the school used to capture raccoons and badgers.

"You're not here to arrest me, are you?" Calavera said.

"I'm here for your blood," Moe Chamberlain said.

"That's the spirit," Calavera replied.

Barnes chanced another peek at the boxcar. His eyes had adapted to the dark beneath the pine, and he could see into the black beyond the open doorway. Calavera was inside, sitting against the back wall, his knees pulled up, a nickel-plated handgun in his hand. Around him were the dregs of a campground—a kerosene heater, a single electric hot plate with a pot on it, a car battery. Attached to the battery was a small electrical-outlet converter. Barnes followed the wire as it traveled up a nearby table leg and led to a machine—a black-market version, one of the early models. No network connectivity. The only memories it could hold were on USB.

"Will you come visit my grave?" Calavera said.

Amanda Jones replied, *"No."*

Chunk Philips said, *"People don't visit assholes' graves."*

"Piggies visit Jim Morrison's grave all the time."

Fred Jones laughed.

"But maybe you're right, Barnes. Maybe none of the animals will come see me. Maybe you'll have me cremated and dumped in that river there, huh? But at least they'll visit their loved ones again. We break our promises to the dead—don't we, Detective? We let them rot in the ground while we diddle our lives away."

Edith MacKenzie said, *"It's a waste of life to dwell on the dead."*

"That's hilarious coming from you, buddy," Calavera said.

"You leave John out of this," Kendra MacKenzie said.

"Say what?" Calavera said.

Barnes fought Kendra back. He focused to form a thought. "You killed the Fero brothers."

"Oh," Calavera said, "you've been me, have you? Inside the machine? Not very pleasant to be Arturo Perez, is it?"

"We can get you the help you need."

"Aw, Barnesy, don't try to sell me that shit."

"What about your legacy?" Barnes said. He peeked again at the boxcar, saw Calavera tapping the handgun against his own temple.

"It's already cast in stone," Calavera said. "Kill me, and I become legend."

Chunk Philips said, *"That's what you think, asshole!"*

Fred Jones said, *"Oh my God, I get it now!"*

"You get *what* now?" Calavera said.

Barnes began stuffing the others back into their drawers. One by one he punched them down and in, placing his index finger over their lips as he did so. *Let me handle this.* They nodded their heads and settled down, watching from their drawers like patrons at some bizarre drive-in.

Barnes pulled out the newspaper Holston had given him. From behind the tree he made a show of unfolding it, ruffling the pages, and clearing his throat. He began reading aloud. "The Pickax Man is your run-of-the-mill sociopath. He chooses his victims at random, showing no apparent pattern."

"What is that?"

"Today's edition of the *Motown Flame*, hot off the press. Shall I continue?"

"Bullshit."

"In a world where mothers drown their own children, where ritual beheadings are common, and serial killers are treated like rock stars, the Pickax Man is a breath of fresh air: he's just an ordinary madman, killing without reason, intelligence, or flare. He's more like a rabid dog than a man, and I ask you, dear reader, do you care what a rabid dog does? Of course not. You just want him quietly and namelessly put down."

"Bullshit."

Barnes refolded the paper and stuffed it inside itself like a paperboy would. He reached around the tree and flicked it toward the boxcar. It landed just outside the open doorway. Calavera came to the front of the car, reached out, snatched it up, and retreated.

Barnes waited a moment, and then said, "Still ready to die?"

Calavera flicked the paper out of the boxcar with a laugh. It was a giddy little sound that rose to a high pitch before dying down to intermittent chuckles.

Arturo Perez, from within Barnes, said, *Who the hell is that? I never laughed like that in my life.*

A new voice emerged from the boxcar. A young voice. "You dumbasses never tracked down the money."

"What money?" Barnes said.

"The ten thousand dollars, Barnes. Where did it come from?"

Barnes scanned his memories, came up empty.

"Andy Kemp's money, *Detective.*"

Barnes shook his head, confused. His mind's eye saw Andy Kemp's decayed corpse, the rotting skin, the bloated fingers and nostrils. He recalled reaching into the boy's front pocket to retrieve the thick wad of hundred-dollar bills.

"My money, dummy!"

Barnes said, "Andy?"

"Well, duh."

"What are you doing here?" Barnes said. He peeked around the tree to see Calavera's mouth moving to Andy Kemp's voice.

"I've been here all along, shithead. Waiting for you."

"I don't understand."

"Ya know, for a detective you're pure shit at figuring things out." He sighed. "Okay, look . . . Arturo paid me for my memories, understand? His little sister and I had been hanging out before she got whacked. She let me feel her tits a few times, but that was it, the dumb bitch. Hardly knew English. Anyway, her perv older brother had a serious crush on her. And what I had was what he wanted. The sicko paid me—get it? I sat in his loser apartment every night for a week, hooked into his busted-ass machine. It took forever to pull those titty memories from me. Once it was done he handed me the ten grand. Next day he had me killed."

"Why?" Barnes said. "He got what he wanted. He paid you."

"Sure, Perez was just going to let me walk, but then he thought I might come around, asking for more cash. He was right about that. I was going to blackmail him for the rest of his perverted life. That's some gross shit, even by my standards. Of course, it took me a while in his head to figure that out. That heroin balloon really jacked him up, ya know? He sees people as animals and shit. Pigs, mostly. He despises people who don't visit their dead relatives, left them passive-aggressive notes. Made people feel guilty if they ever did decide to show up. And every night when he'd come back to the machine and his little sister's titties, I was waiting for him. Didn't take much for me to gain control. There wasn't much left of his brain, maybe not much to begin with. Once I was in control, I took revenge for what the Feros did to his family."

"Why'd Perez hire Dawson to kill you? Why didn't he kill you himself?"

"I told you. He's a pussy. Didn't want to get his hands dirty. Dawson was a lowlife meth head. Perez paid him a hundred bucks to take me out. Dumb-ass never checked my pockets. He got scared and ran."

"Why did you lead me here?" Barnes said.

"You never solved my murder, Barnes. Not you or Watkins. Couple of dumb-asses. I had to give you *some* clues to keep you coming. How else was I going to show you who murdered me? Besides, I want to be done with this perv and move on."

Barnes shook his head in amazement. "Your teachers said you excelled at writing. They never mentioned poetry."

"Those swirling turds wouldn't know good writing from a hole in their head. Those poems I left were shit. But you needed to believe that dumb-ass Artie wrote them. All that Day of the Dead crap."

"You could have just lived on, Andy. You could have taken Perez's body and made a life for yourself."

"Where's the fun in that? What's the point? So I can end up a mind-less pig like you? I'll pass."

"If I kill Reyes, you'll die."

"I'm already dead, dummy. Now I'm just bored."

Barnes stayed silent. He fought through a riot in his mind. Whispers and shouts, rage and despair. "Why did you let Jessica live?"

Andy offered no reply.

Barnes peeked around the tree. Calavera was there, in the boxcar, shaking his head from side to side. He thumped his temple with the butt of his palm.

Barnes said, "Why?"

Calavera looked up. He blinked rapidly, seemed to register Barnes for the first time. His voice took on a Mexican accent, and the words came out with the struggle of a second language when he said, "I stopped him. I make him stop."

"Please. I don't want to die." Arturo Perez.

"You love her," Antonio Reyes said from the boxcar.

Barnes said, "You're under arrest for the murders of"—the tim-bre of his voice changed to match that of—"Edith MacKenzie . . ." It changed again, this time to "Kendra MacKenzie . . ." and again to

"Raymond Philips . . ." And then "Maurice Chamberlain . . . Fred Jones . . . Amanda Jones . . . Nancy Fulmer . . . Roberta Jensen . . . Jeffrey Dunham . . . Dale Wilson . . . Andrea Wilson . . . Kerri Wilson . . ." Barnes's timbre returned to his own as he added, "And Damon Beckett. You have the right to remain silent. Anything you say can and wi—"

Calavera cut him off with gunfire. Barnes ducked back. Bullets showered the trees beyond his position. Barnes looked up, saw bits of the blue sky through the tree limbs. "I'm coming, little brother." He rolled out and stood, pushed through the low boughs, and started toward the boxcar, gun drawn and aimed.

Calavera scrambled back. He fired from cover, lighting up the car's interior like camera flashes. Barnes took a bullet to the left upper chest. It peeled him back, but he stayed on his feet, kept moving forward.

Calavera shot again.

Barnes's right shoulder exploded in pain. He held his weapon, still aimed, and staggered forward, unwilling to fire. He deserved this death. For Ricky. For all of them. He stumbled toward the open door, just a few feet away now.

Calavera fired again.

Kneecapped, Barnes went down. He crawled up toward the boxcar, ducked around to the outside of the open door and backed up against it. He used his good leg and thrust as hard as he could against the door. It closed halfway on squealing hinges.

Calavera's voice had returned to that of Andy Kemp: "What the hell?"

Barnes thrust again, smiled when he heard Kemp say, "Oh no, no, no. That's not fair!"

Barnes picked up his heel, dug it into the soft soil, and kicked with all his remaining strength. The boxcar door slammed shut. He reached up to the long handle and dragged it down into the locked position.

Kemp's voice was now muffled from inside the boxcar. "You bastard! Open this door. Let me out!" He pounded and kicked. He fired, but the handgun only clicked. Out of bullets.

The forest came alive with the sounds of sirens, soon red-and-blue lights. Barnes sat with his back against the boxcar. Life was leaving his body. Kemp continued to scream and pound and dry-fire his weapon. Barnes tuned him out. He moved the Glock to his left hand.

Cold.

He pocketed his right hand to pull his jacket around his midsection, found Jessica's bag of salt. He pulled it out and looked down at it . . . and then he began to laugh. He opened the bag and dumped some of the salt on his ruined knee. The pain was exquisite, like napalm rolling up through his thigh into his hip. He poured some on to his bleeding shoulder, cried out in horrible pain, kept laughing.

The paramedics made their way through the woods, carrying a stretcher. Warden was behind them with the machine, bumping the wheels over the rough terrain.

Good ol' Warden.

Barnes waited until the paramedics were within range. He aimed his weapon at them and said, "No closer."

The paramedics stopped for a moment, exchanged a glance, shrugged, and kept coming. Barnes closed one eye, took aim, and fired. The bullet tore a hole through the stretcher. The paramedics dropped their ends, ducked, and ran.

Warden wheeled Eddie up to Barnes's side. He began attaching the hoses, the needle.

"Help me," Barnes said, indicating his jacket. He dropped his handgun.

Warden helped Barnes peel off his jacket.

Darkness crowded Barnes's vision. The end was upon him now. He ripped open his shirt, sending buttons flying. The hole in his chest had leaked blood over his belly, his pants. Warden attached the suction cups to his bald temples. He pushed the needle into his arm, turned on the machine. "Stay alive for me." He offered a hospice worker's smile.

Barnes closed his eyes and concentrated, rewound through his memories until he found himself sitting in his parked car at Calvary Junction just three days before. He recalled stumbling drunkenly out of the vehicle, going to the tracks, waiting for the train to destroy him. He mentally walked himself through everything that had happened since then, including all the time he'd spent on the machine. He concentrated on every pain he'd experienced, every torture, every victim, and every brilliant moment with Jessica. He then dwelled on the pain of what he'd brought to her, stayed with the torturing images of her raw wrists and ankles, her cracked and bloody lips, her death mask. He mired himself in the vision, soaked in the gut-wrenching agony of the pain he'd brought her. Then he sat down in the love he felt for her and dwelled in the horrible emptiness of finding such love only to feel it now draining away along with his life. He walked himself right up to this moment, the moment when Warden had hooked him into the machine and smiled that hospice smile.

It was then that Barnes forced faith to enter his mind. For the first time since he was a boy, he allowed the invigorating power of hope to course through him, to lift his spirits, to bring him joy. It felt good to hope. He hoped for Ricky's forgiveness. He hoped for redemption. Perversely, and with a sneer on his face, he hoped that he might live, and that he might see her again.

Then Detective John Barnes poured the rest of Jessica Taylor's salt into the wound above his heart.

37

Darkness and silence.
　"End of transmission."
　The Vitruvian Man test pattern.
　Please Stand By.

38

Andy Kemp woke up screaming. His chest felt like a crater of fire and char. Psychosomatic agony coursed through Antonio Reyes's body to Kemp's shoulder, his knee, his punctured lungs, his severed head, his broken ribs, his caved-in skull, the salt in his wounds. Tears drizzled away from his eyes and dripped from the suction cups attached to his shaven temples. The victims in his head cried out in anger, in hatred for him. They taunted and berated him. He struggled against the manacles at his wrists and ankles in his hospital bed.

"Shhh. Goddammit, shut up!"

Kemp blinked rapidly, but the fog would not recede. The victims stayed with him, as they had each time he'd been on the machine. Longer and longer they stayed. They pounded at his brain like blacksmiths on hot iron. Sparks of pain scattered and burned him. He screamed and wailed.

"Shhh. Quiet now."

The voice seemed familiar.

Kemp closed his eyes and shook his head. He blinked again, found he could see. The blurry room was four royal-blue concrete walls and a steel door with a shatter-resistant window. The woman above him was dressed in all white, like a nurse. Her black hair was tied up behind her head.

"I know you," Kemp said. He checked her name tag. MARTINEZ. "Yes, of course. You worked with Barnes. You helped him."

"You're with us now?" Martinez said.

"Where am I?" Kemp said. "What's happening?"

"You ask that every time," she said, "and every time I tell you you're in the Bracken Institute for the Criminally Insane, and that you've been on the machine for three days as part of your sentence." She slid a needle out of Kemp's left arm. The spot stung, burned. She wrapped up the tubes and dropped them into a hazmat box. She pulled another needle from his right arm and did the same. She plucked the suction cups from his temples.

"You're a nurse now?" Kemp said.

"No," she said. "I administer this machine for the hospital. Took the job after being let go from the police department. I've told you this many times over the years."

The steel door opened, and the big nurse came in. She took away an IV drip and held the door while Martinez began to roll the machine over the threshold. The big nurse said to him, "I'll bring you to your room in a moment."

Sheila Martinez and the big nurse left, letting the door close behind them. Andy Kemp, forever trapped in a body he wanted only to borrow, sobbed openly in the empty room. His excruciating body pain was dwarfed by sorrow and numbed by despair, for his heart was once again filled with guilt, with lost love, and with the damnable misery of John Barnes's unrequited hope.

EPILOGUE

Barnes sat on the wooden steps that led up to his porch, his leather tool belt unbuckled and set at his side. There was a framing hammer in the steel loop, 16d sinker nails in the main pouch, a twenty-five-foot measuring tape buttoned in its place. He sat with his forearms on his knees and a beer held loosely in his right hand, dangling in the space between his legs. It was Friday afternoon, and the foreman had let the crew off early. Barnes had come home to an empty house, pulled the beer from the fridge, and headed out to the porch, letting the cheap screen door bang and rattle as it closed behind him.

He took a swig, set the bottle down, and examined his hands. They were calloused and muscular now, lightly coated with drywall dust and blue snap-line chalk. His silver wedding ring was battered and beautiful. He clapped his hands and rubbed them together, sending dust into the air. He then ran his fingers through a full head of hair. His surgically repaired shoulder ached. There was titanium in there now, beneath the scars. Same with his knee. They both gave him trouble at times.

Barnes placed a hand on the scar above his heart. He pressed down on it like a button. It tickled and stung. He waited for the victims in his head to comment, but they were quiet now. Had been for some time. He smiled and leaned back against the stairs, placing his elbows on the step above and behind him. He kicked out his legs and crossed them at the ankles.

A school bus appeared at the end of his road. The air brakes sounded off as the bus came to a stop at the corner. Jessica was waiting there alongside two other mothers. It was a warm autumn day but growing crisp as evening approached. Jessica wore a sweater and a long skirt.

Richard J. Barnes hopped off the bus with both feet and landed like a paratrooper, Batman backpack firmly attached. He ran a few circles around his mother before taking her hand. They spoke with each other as they headed down the sidewalk toward home.

The boy's face lit up when he saw his dad.

ACKNOWLEDGMENTS

There was never a time in my life when I felt incapable of achieving my dreams. I attribute this to my parents, who made sacrifices on my behalf before I was even born, before I was capable of understanding. I know they did, because I'm doing the same for my own kids—the beautiful, ungrateful little twerps.

Thanks, Mom. Thanks, Dad.

Thanks, twerps.

Thank you to music, bourbon, and Stanley Kubrick. Thank you to whoever invented those huge plastic tubs of cheese balls. Thank you to George Orwell for writing *1984* and making me walk circles around the living room, unsure if I was devastated or delighted, but certain that I needed to pay the gift forward. Thank you to John Steinbeck for *Of Mice and Men*, Peter Hedges for *What's Eating Gilbert Grape*, and Patrick deWitt for *The Sisters Brothers*.

Thank you to Thomas Harris for existing in this world.

Thank you to Jessica Tribble, David Downing, Sarah Shaw, and everyone else at Thomas & Mercer for turning my mad ramblings into coherence.

Thank you to Barbara Poelle for your wit and persistence (after you read this, ask me what I almost wrote here instead).

And thank you to Nichole. Goddamn, you're a great girl.

ABOUT THE AUTHOR

Scott J. Holliday was born and raised in Detroit. In addition to a life-long love of books and reading, he's pursued a range of curiosities and interests, including glassblowing, boxing, and much more. His two previous novels are *Stonefly* and *Normal*, the latter of which earned him recognition in INKUBATE.com's Literary Blockbuster Challenge. He loves to cook and create stories for his wife and two daughters.